SAVING MORGAN

MB PANICHI

Bella
BOOKS

2013

Bella Books, Inc.
P.O. Box 10543
Tallahassee, FL 32302

First Bella Books Edition 2013

Editor: Nene Adams
Cover Designed by: Kiaro Creative

ISBN: 978-1-59493-365-3

About the Author

MB Panichi lives in Richfield, Minnesota with her wife and their two dogs: Dave, a border collie/lab mix who loves to swim, and Maci, a shih tzu with a mind of her own. *Saving Morgan* is MB's first published book. When she isn't holding down her day job as a software developer, MB plays drums in a variety band when gigs come up, and dreams wistfully about her "heavy metal" days.

Dedication

This one is for my mom, Ruby, who gave to me a love of words and books, and for my friend Roy, who was the first to teach me to "show, not tell." I miss you both.

Acknowledgement

This has been a long and wonderful journey, with so many helpers on the way. First, thanks to my wife April for putting up with having a writer in the house, and for her love, support and patience. Love you, Sweet Pea!!! Thanks, next, to all my writer friends and writers' groups for their support, encouragement, and critiques—Jessie, Lori, Mary L., all the Queer Writers and the BABA's—you guys all know who you are, and you're all great!! Special thanks to my GLCS mentors, Pol Robinson and Fran Heckrotte, for their wisdom and insights. Fran was integral in helping me to get my manuscript to the point where I felt comfortable submitting it, and I learned a TON working with her. Thanks, too, to Nene Adams, my fearless editor at Bella, and Karin Kallmaker for taking a chance on me! And, of course, thanks to all my relatives and friends who supported and encouraged me through the whole crazy process. You're all the best!!!

CHAPTER ONE

As the Moon Base dome dimmed to an evening tint, Shaine Wendt picked her way along the crowded main street. She efficiently dodged pedestrians and the occasional delivery trucks and hover-bikes weaving between them.

Wearing a long-sleeved tunic, pocketed cargo pants belted at the ankles, and work boots, she thought she fit in well, but knew her military past remained part of her style and bearing. She had let the top of her regulation-length buzzcut grow out into fire-red spikes, though she kept the sides shaved. She moved with a purposeful, loose-limbed stride, her head up and her shoulders back, no longer bothered by the vague hint of a limp she still carried from the loss of half her right leg to an IED explosion ten years ago.

Shaine remained aloof from the other people on the street, though she automatically assessed and cataloged everything and everyone. She took in the enticing smells of food cooking, sorting out the rich, old Earth ethnic aromas from the bland, predictable odors of preprocessed meals. Occasionally, the thick tang of intoxicants wafted from open doors along with the babble of voices and music.

She paused in front of a bar, attracted by the fluorescent neon curling in flashing detail around the entrance. A slightly less gaudy sign in the front window announced "Rose's Roost." She shoved her hands in her pants pockets and walked through the open doorway.

Pausing just inside, she scrutinized the dimly lit room. Knots of people gathered around tables scattered throughout the low-ceilinged space. A handful of dancers clustered on the matchbox-sized dance floor in the rear. The thumping bass beat rumbled through her chest, even though the music wasn't all that loud. She crossed to the horseshoe-shaped bar just past the entrance and claimed a stool against the wall.

The heavyset bartender with a salt-and-pepper crewcut sauntered over. She swiped a rag across the bar's already shiny surface. "Hey, honey, what can I get ya?"

"Whatever's on tap is fine."

The bartender swung the damp towel over her shoulder and grabbed a mug off the shelf hanging from the ceiling at the center of the bar. She filled the mug one-handed from an auto-dispenser and slid it over to Shaine. "You new, Red? Don't think I've seen you around."

Shaine raised a brow. "Red?"

"Well, ya ain't told me your name." The bartender held out a meaty hand and gave Shaine a blatant, grinning leer. "Rose Hallsey."

Shaine stared pointedly at Rose for a second before giving up a smile. "Shaine Wendt." She clasped the extended hand with a firm grip. "Only been on Base a month. And if you call me Red again, I'll beat you senseless."

Rose laughed. "You got it." She studied Shaine with dark, curious eyes. "You ex-Earth Guard?"

"Yeah, a while back."

"Thought you had that look about ya. I was Fifth Guard Out-System Cavalry. Retired a couple years ago, came up here to take this place over for a friend."

"Cav's a good group. Worked with 'em a couple times. I got a medical discharge out of Special Ops."

Rose's eyebrows rose. "No kidding? You're a tough one."

Shaine shrugged. "Like I said, been a while. Just doing the mechanic thing these days."

"Tab's on the house tonight, then."

Shaine lifted her glass. "Thanks."

"No problem."

Shaine settled against the wall and took a deep swallow of her beer. She had been on Moon Base five weeks, transferring from a job as a covert agent for Mann-Maru Security. So far, working maintenance here was a decent gig. Definitely beat the claustrophobic atmosphere of working in the mining facilities out in the Asteroid Belt or having to deal with the twisted intrigues of corporate security. She sighed while observing the people around her. *I wanted a normal life*, she reminded herself. *Now I have it. So why do I feel like I'm completely at loose ends?*

Loud voices from the entry attracted her attention. A mixed group of men and women walked in, jostling each other and laughing. Several wore loose-fitting, kelly-green jerseys bearing a stylized cartoon of a frothing guard dog with the slogan "Devil Dawgs—We Bite" in a dripping, blood-red font. She recognized the name of the team from the local grav-ball rec league sports reports.

Her gaze flicked over the boisterous and somewhat mismatched crew who appeared focused on the ball player at the center. Slim, diminutive and scruffy-looking, the woman had cropped black hair with bangs flopping unevenly over wide-set eyes. She gave the squat, compactly built man beside her a teasing push.

Laughing, he shoved her back and tousled her hair in what seemed to Shaine like a friendly, almost brotherly gesture. The arms of his jersey were cut off, revealing biceps and forearms covered in tattoos. Black, red and gold tribal patterns curled and twisted in geometric motifs up his arms and the sides of his neck.

The broad-shouldered woman towering at the head of the group waved a hand at the bartender. "Hey, Rose! Can you grab a round for us?" She draped an arm around the shoulders of the slender, black-haired woman in the middle who looked up, revealing a bandage taped over her left eyebrow. Shaine also noticed a dark stain down the front of her jersey. "And a double shot shot for Morgan, here. She kicked serious ass tonight."

Rose returned the wave with a wide smile. "Hi, Ally. You guys win tonight?"

"Yeah. Five to two. Chissley went after Morgan again, but, man, she ripped into him!" Ally laughed as the group crowded around a table close to the bar. The team and their friends slapped Morgan on the back and on the butt, razzing and congratulating her while they settled in.

The tattooed guy shouted, "Rosie, bring a couple extra shots, hey?"

"Pony up the cash, Digger! You still owe me from last week."

"Yeah, yeah." He grinned and laughed.

Shaine sipped her drink while she watched the team's interactions, singling out the star ball player. *Morgan.* Mentally she repeated the name, feeling there was something familiar about the woman, but unable to identify what. *I should know her.* Had she seen Morgan around the maintenance docks?

Morgan's pale, almost translucent complexion identified her as a "spacer"—someone who had lived a lot of years in artificial light—so she wouldn't have been anyone Shaine knew from Earth. Nor did she recognize Morgan from her time working in the Belt.

Shaine finished off her beer and set the glass down, feeling suddenly very alone. She contemplated just heading home. It made no sense to sit here drinking by herself.

"Another?" Rose asked.

Shaine hesitated and finally shrugged. At least she was among people here. She didn't find any attraction in sitting alone in her apartment. "Sure, why not."

Rose poured out another glass and gestured with her chin. "The Dawgs are one of the best grav-ball teams in the rec league," she commented. "You play any ball?"

"Not really. Used to do some pickup games in the Guard, just for kicks. Usually degenerated into zero-g wrestling free-for-alls."

"Well, they're good, that bunch. The little one, Morgan Rahn, she's their primary forward. Tough kid. Fast and accurate. Has a hell of a body slam, too. Seen her smack the snot out of guys three times her size."

Shaine studied Morgan slouching in her seat as her friends carried the conversation. If it weren't for the bandage and the blood, she wouldn't have picked out Morgan for a fighter. *Morgan Rahn.*

A round of laughter went up around the table. Morgan's face lit up with a wicked grin.

Shaine's breath hitched. *Damn. She's hot.* She grabbed for the glass of beer in front of her and downed a sizable swallow. *Put your eyes back in their sockets, dumbass. Finish your drink and leave before you do something stupid, like actually walk over there and talk to her. Morgan Rahn sure as hell wouldn't be interested in a fucked-up ex-commando assassin.* She shook her head and focused elsewhere.

Two women appeared in the bar's entryway. The shorter of the pair hung possessively on her escort's arm. They seemed exceptionally overdressed for the establishment. The description "high-class sophisticated bitches" popped into Shaine's head. She immediately disliked them.

The taller woman's deep auburn hair fell in thick waves past her bare shoulders. She wore a sleek metallic-bronze dress split to mid-thigh and knee-high spike-heeled boots. She paused, scanning the room. Her attention seemed to focus on the group of grav-ball players. Full lips curled into a too-wide smile. She strode toward them, pulling her companion along.

"Aw, fuck. That ain't a good thing," Rose muttered. Shaine noted that Rose's gaze focused on the newcomers.

As the well-dressed twosome approached the grav-ball team and their friends, the ball player whom Rose had called Ally stood up, hands clenched at her sides. "What do you want, Gina?" she growled. "Maybe I should do the world a favor and kick your sorry ass back Earthside."

Gina ignored her and turned a seductive smile on Morgan. "Miss me, baby?" she drawled.

Morgan stared at her with bored, empty eyes. "No."

Gina stepped in and grabbed Morgan's jaw to kiss her roughly. Morgan didn't react to the bruising attack. Gina released her and backed away. "Hmm…" Her mouth twisted into a contemptuous smile. "I guess not. Good thing you're replaceable."

"Fuck off, Gina," Morgan said flatly.

Gina laughed, pulling her companion closer.

Digger stood up, glaring dangerously. When Gina walked away, he dropped a protective hand on Morgan's shoulder.

Shaine found herself standing beside the bar, poised on the balls of her feet, her hands tightly fisted at her sides. She took a long breath, forcing her tensed muscles to relax. Good to know her fighting instincts were still intact, she supposed, even if it wasn't her fight. Or any of her business. It was no longer her job to keep the peace. Besides, Morgan's friends appeared more than ready to defend her honor.

She backed mechanically onto the barstool, unable to tear her gaze from Morgan Rahn. The woman wore a dark, unreadable expression, and her arms were crossed protectively over her chest. No, it wasn't her job to save Morgan Rahn from bitches like that, she thought. But she knew she would have done it in a second if the situation warranted.

As though aware of someone watching her, Morgan glanced up. Wide gray eyes focused on Shaine and their gazes locked.

For an endless second Shaine's existence tunneled into a conduit between them. Heart pounding, she blinked and looked away. She leaned against the bar and pulled in a shaky breath, tightening her fingers around the cool mug. A quick backward glance confirmed Morgan still watching her curiously. A shiver ran down her spine. *Oh, hell, I really, really need to leave.*

CHAPTER TWO

Duffel bag slung over her shoulder, Senior Systems Mechanic Morgan Rahn plodded into the ready room with a sigh. *Another day, another credit.* She glanced around the tightly arranged staging area. Ben and Charri stood in front of their lockers changing into the skintight liners worn under their spacesuits. Digger and Strom hadn't wandered in yet.

She went to her locker on the opposite side of the room and dropped her duffel on the bench while absently tapping her passcode into the keypad.

"Hey, Morg, how was the club last night?"

Morgan glanced behind her to see Charri smiling over her shoulder. Her best friend was a petite woman with kinky blond hair and an exuberant personality. Morgan shrugged. "It wasn't bad—got there late, though, and Ally's girlfriend didn't show. Mitchell told me to tell you hello."

Ben snorted. "He's such a dick."

Charri swatted him. "Don't be mean."

The ready room door hissed open and Digger stomped in. "Fucking blast-brains in security had to go through all my stuff," he growled as he dropped his bag in front of the locker next to Morgan's. "I am so fucking sick of this crap. Damned Inquisition."

"It's supposed to make us feel safer," Morgan commented dryly. "I heard they were hassling Walker and Benny Smithe yesterday because they were filling shifts out in the Belt. Apparently anyone who's worked the Belt is a budding terrorist now, too."

Charri shook her head. "The paranoia around here is getting out of hand."

"And look how much good it's doing," Digger muttered. He stripped off his shirt to reveal the intricate tattoos covering his back. "You see the news last night? Another 'unexplained' mining explosion."

"Unexplained my ass," Ben said. "Somebody's making a lot of money off all this."

Morgan added, "If it was hurting Mann-Maru Industries that bad, the terrorists would've been shut down a long time ago."

Derek Strom, their crew chief, strolled into the ready room carrying the usual stack of handheld computers. "All right, we got orders." He tossed each team member a comp pad and glanced around the room. "Sound off so I know who's doing what."

Digger glanced at his pad. "I'm checking—probably replacing—the valves for the main thruster fuel lines."

"Some topside hull repair," Chari responded. "Nothing major."

Ben scrolled through his list. "Doing hull check with Charri. And a couple of vent seals."

"Morgan?" Strom asked.

"They've got me running replacement control leads to the main thrusters, but the micro-fuser on my suit is still burnt out," she said. "Maintenance said they won't have a replacement for me until the day after tomorrow. Hey, Digg, you wanna trade jobs? Your suit fuser's working."

Digger scowled. "How about switching suits again—I'm shit-all with the fuser. I'd rather work the fuel lines."

"That okay with you, Strom?" Morgan asked.

"Sure, long as the work gets done," Derek said. "Let me know if maintenance doesn't get that fuser fixed on your suit soon, Morgan. Otherwise, I'm going to make the suit switch permanent on the records. This is—what? The third time this shift cycle you guys have switched?" He shook his head, made a note into his comp pad, and added, "I'll be forward. Scanner assembly has a bad connection. Okay, people, let's get this show on the road."

Fifteen minutes later, sealed in their vacuum suits, Morgan and her work crew crowded into the air lock. When the outer door slid open, Strom jumped down first. Boots barely touching the ground, he bounced gracefully toward the massive scaffolding structure a hundred meters away where an intra-planetary cargo ship was docked.

Morgan recognized the ship as a Mann-Maru R330 Heavy Hauler, primarily used to transport processed and unprocessed metals from the mines in the Asteroid Belt back to Moon Base. The body of the R330 resembled a slightly flattened football with the cargo hold in the wide central area. A smaller ovoid at the front held the cockpit. Three thrusters took up the back third of the hauler, inverted cones emerging from the top and lower sides of the ship.

Morgan bounced to the surface behind Strom, kicking in the thruster pack mounted on her back and guiding herself toward the bottom of the ship. She inverted her body midflight, allowing the magnetic soles of her boots to connect to the hull with a solid clunk, then cut the power and pushed the handlebars out of her way.

Standing on the ship's underbelly, she pulled the comp pad from its holster and scrolled through the blueprints to check the location of the hatch she needed to access. Out of the corner of her eye, she saw Digger bounce past her and disappear behind the thruster casings.

Leaving one boot connected to the deck, she dropped to the other knee and leaned over the maintenance hatch. She spun the wheel and snapped open the hatch cover, securing it against the hull. Within moments, she lost herself in replacing the two blown-out connectors, only half-listening to the constant chatter between Charri and Ben, and Digger's occasional expletives.

"What the fuck—"

Morgan glanced in Digger's direction, alerted by the panicked tone of his voice. A bright flare blinded her. Digger screamed. His voice cut off abruptly.

"Digger!" Blinking spots from her vision, she pushed to her feet. Digger's blue-striped suit fell slowly away from the ship toward the dusty ground.

"Strom!" Morgan shouted, "Digger!" She yanked the jet pack's handlebars down and thumbed the controls, launching herself off the ship.

Strom barked, "Digger! Report!"

"Say something, you stupid bastard!" Morgan shouted. Thrusters at full throttle, she whipped between the heavy support girders. As she shot through the scaffolding toward Digger's slowly falling body, he hit the ground and bounced slightly. The suit turned. She saw the right arm of his vac suit was missing below the elbow and the front of the suit blackened.

Strom reached Digger as his body settled onto the gray surface. Feathering the controls on the jet pack to stop himself, he pulled Digger close enough to see his suit's life-control sensors. When Morgan reached them a second later, he snapped, "Morgan, back off!"

"Hey!" she protested, about to rail at Strom until she got a glimpse of Digger's shattered, gore-splattered faceplate. "Oh, God," she breathed, her stomach twisting violently as she spun away. "Please, no, not again." Blinded by stinging tears and desperately trying not to throw up, she hardly noticed when Ben and Charri grabbed her arms, pulling her away from where Strom knelt over Digger's body.

Strom's voice carried harshly across her helmet speakers. "Control, this is crew 435. We've got a code red breach emergency. Send out a boat, code red. Repeat. Send out a code-red recovery boat."

Morgan heard the other's breaths across the com static, but nobody seemed to have anything to say. She kept her eyes averted from Digger's suit and tried to focus on breathing. Jaw clenched, she stared past the sprawl of scaffolding and docked haulers until she spotted flashing red and blue lights. A swarm of emergency vehicles headed in their direction.

Ben muttered, "Here comes the cavalry."

Strom said quietly, "Just do whatever they say."

Morgan swallowed hard. With the recent rise in terrorist activity against Mann-Maru Industries and other corporate conglomerates, security had become increasingly heavy-handed. She watched the approaching vehicles with a growing sense of dread and anger. *Digger is dead. What do they think Security is going to do? Bring him back to fucking life?*

Within moments, emergency skiffs surrounded the area. Security personnel double-timed out of the vehicles. A sharp voice snapped across her helmet com. "Everyone stay calm and cooperate with Security personnel."

At least a dozen guards with drawn laser rifles created a perimeter around her and the others. Three more guards joined their group.

The first guard took Charri by the arm. "Come with me." He started to pull her away.

Charri cried out, "Ben!"

"Hey, what are you doing?" Ben turned toward her.

"Ben!" Charri's voice broke on a sob.

Morgan wrenched out of her guard's grasp, yelling, "She's scared, you idiot, leave her the fuck alone!"

The guard grabbed Morgan again. His voice thundered through her helmet speakers. "Stop it! Shut up! Nobody's hurting anyone."

Morgan felt the blood pounding in her ears. "Fucking bastards," she hissed.

Charri demanded plaintively, "Why are—"

Her voice cut off with an audible click and another cut in. "This is Lieutenant Tommas. Please cooperate with Security personnel. For your own safety, this area must be secured. Noncompliance will not be tolerated."

Morgan glanced at her helmet's heads-up display. "Command channel only" flashed in red. The guard pulled her forward. She forced herself to relax and let him direct her back toward Moon Base.

The recovery skiff approached. Red and blue running lights flashing, the neon yellow skiff slid past to slew to a stop beside

Digger and Strom and a cadre from Security. Morgan blinked back hot tears. The guard yanked her ahead when she half-turned to watch. She glared at him, her anger surging. *Have some respect, asshole, they're gonna take my best friend's body away.*

The guards herded her and the rest of the team to a hatch and into a cramped air lock. They were instructed to keep their suits and helmets sealed even after exiting into a holding area.

Morgan looked around. Ten Security personnel wearing black fatigues lined the wall opposite the air lock. Ben stood behind her, Strom and his escort in front of her and slightly to the right. Charri stood just to her left. Behind the faceplate, Charri's eyes were wide with shock and fear, which pissed her off and made her want to bang heads.

She opened her mouth to say something, then thought about it and clamped her jaw shut. Irritating Security wasn't going to do anyone any good.

An officer sporting captain's stripes stepped forward and spoke into a transceiver clipped to his ear. His deep voice echoed through Morgan's helmet speakers. "I am Captain Ettaak. Each of you will be debriefed separately. Please follow the directions of your escorts." He nodded toward the squad behind him.

Two guards stepped forward. Strom's guard nudged him in their direction.

Strom stumped forward and was led away by the two guards.

A female sergeant whose name badge read "Keffin" led Morgan away. She noticed they were followed by an expressionless young private. Plodding along a glaringly white hallway, she struggled with the weight of the vac suit, annoyed she was forced to wear it sealed in full gravity and atmosphere. Her thighs strained as she struggled not to drag the heavy boots across the floor.

Ahead of her, Strom and his two guards disappeared through an unmarked door.

When Morgan and her escort reached the next door, Sergeant Keffin palmed the sensor on the wall beside it and went aside. The private positioned himself to wait outside the entrance.

Keffin gestured. "In," she ordered.

Morgan lumbered into a dimly lit room.

As the door shut behind her, Keffin said, "You can take the suit off now."

Morgan sighed. *About time.* She unlocked the seals on her gloves, and for a stomach-wrenching moment remembered she wore Digger's suit. Digger had been wearing hers. *Oh, God. If we hadn't switched jobs and suits it would have been me.*

Her whole body shuddered at the realization. Her gloves slipped from suddenly nerveless fingers. She swallowed hard and fumbled with shaking hands to release the collar at her neck. Air flooded over her face when she tugged off the helmet and took a gasping breath. The faded scent of Digger's aftershave clung to the back of her throat. She set the helmet on the floor, then straightened and undid the seal along the right front and shrugged the suit off her shoulders. The empty torso slumped behind her, the collar clanking as it hit the floor. She unplugged the bio-monitor interface from her liner and stepped free. She moved to pick up the suit.

Keffin barked, "Stop. Don't touch it."

Morgan looked up.

"Leave it. It's evidence. We don't want it tampered with."

"Tampered with," Morgan repeated. "Okay." She shook her head. What the hell did they think she was going to do to the suit?

The sergeant stared, apparently daring her to start something. She gestured at the cot against the back wall. "We'll need your suit liner as well. There's a coverall on the bed for you to change into."

For the first time, Morgan really looked around at her surroundings. The room contained a bed, a commode, a small sink, and a table with two chairs. At the end of the bed lay a folded gray jumpsuit, a flat pillow and a thin blanket. She wondered how long they planned to hold her. She walked to the cot and pulled off the form-fitting liner. Cool air raised goosebumps on her exposed skin. When she grabbed the jumpsuit, Keffin cleared her throat.

"Sorry. Need to do a body scan first."

Morgan turned slowly to face the woman. "You're kidding, right?" She didn't care that she was naked, but she knew they could do a body scan through her clothes. *Fucking voyeur.*

Keffin shrugged. "Not my rules."

Morgan rolled her eyes and held her arms out to her sides.

Keffin crossed the room holding a palm-sized scanner. After a couple of sweeps over Morgan's body, she stepped back. "You're clean. Go ahead and get dressed."

Morgan grabbed the coverall and pulled it on.

Keffin watched with an indifferent expression and commented, "Nice body art, Rahn."

Morgan said, "Y'know, if you're going to stand there and leer at me, you could at least come up with a decent line."

Keffin smirked and tapped the transceiver in her ear. "Send evidence recovery in."

Moments later, two men entered the room and silently bagged the vac suit and liner. Morgan shook her head at this new evidence of insanity.

"Make yourself comfortable, Rahn. A debrief team will be with you shortly." Keffin marched out.

Morgan sighed. Did "shortly" mean ten minutes, an hour, or a day? She turned to the cot and dropped down on it, sitting with her back against the wall. Wrapping the thin blanket around herself, she clutched the pillow to her middle. Exhaustion and sadness flowed over her.

Behind her closed eyes, images flashed. Her friend was dead. Gone. She would never hear his voice again, never get to roll her eyes at another of his rude jokes, never get a big sweaty hug after a grav-ball game, and never get to tease him about some woman he was ogling. She curled around the pillow and pulled her knees up to her chest. *Damn it, Digger, what happened? How could you be dead?*

Was it her fault? He'd been wearing her suit. If they hadn't switched, would she have been killed? What could she have missed? She was certain the diagnostics had run clean last night. She pictured her hands moving over the control panel on her suit. Green lights had flickered across the small display. Even the checks for the suit's power tools had come back clean. Everything was good last night. She had no doubts.

Even so, something had caused an explosion big enough to blow off Digger's arm, shatter his helmet, and char the front of his suit. Hell, did the blast even have anything to do with her suit?

Had a component in the thruster assembly blown? She shook her head. Off-line thrusters didn't simply explode, not when the ship was powered down in dry dock. And she knew the ship had been powered down because the control leads she'd worked on had been in standby mode.

What could she have missed? Damn it, they should never have traded suits. She should have convinced Digg to switch jobs instead. She felt she was headed down a dangerous mental road and forced herself to stop the impending wreck. *I've been through this before*, she told herself. *It's not my fault. There's nothing I could have done. Shit happens. People get hurt. People die. It's part of the job. I've known the risks since I was twelve.*

Morgan sucked in a deep breath and fought to control the crush of memories and emotions. Her mom had been killed in space—a harsh, unexpected death. She doubted she would ever come to terms with either the loss or her anger over it.

The hiss of the opening door interrupted her thoughts. She straightened, pushing the pillow off her lap.

A baby-faced, black-uniformed man entered the room. He nodded at her. "Good morning, Ms. Rahn. I'm Investigator Mike Rajekk. I want to ask you a few questions about what happened today."

She eyed him warily and shrugged an acknowledgment without moving from the cot.

He offered a professional smile and sat at the small table, setting down his comp pad. Morgan watched while he tapped on the screen, apparently getting his thoughts together.

"Could you tell me what happened today?" he asked.

She frowned. *I don't know what happened. I just know Digger's dead.* She looked down at her hands, swallowing the grief and shutting out the pain. "Digger was doing thruster maintenance. He yelled, and I looked over and saw a flash, like a small explosion. I heard him scream. Digger's faceplate was cracked, his suit burned, and half his arm was gone."

"Where were you at the time of the explosion?"

"I was on the underside of the ship. Digger was up by the port thrusters."

"You switched vac suits," he said. "Why?"

Morgan's shoulders stiffened. "My fuser is busted. You can check the maintenance logs. I put in for repair a couple days ago. Strom knows about it, too. The fuser on Digg's suit worked. He hated to do fuser work, so we switched." She ran her tongue over dry lips. "We've done it before. It's not a big deal."

Rajekk nodded and asked blandly, "Who was the last of your crew to leave the ready room last night?"

Morgan hesitated, thinking. "It would have been Strom. Digger left first, and I left with Ben and Charri."

"And you didn't go back during the time after you initially left and when you arrived this morning?"

"No."

He made a quick note. "Thank you, Ms. Rahn." He slid the chair back and stood.

"Then I can go?"

He smiled again. The expression didn't reach his eyes. "I need to speak with my supervisors. Someone will be along to release you."

"When?"

"When you've been cleared to leave," he said shortly, and turned on his heel.

The door clicked shut behind him. A sick feeling twisted Morgan's guts. Did they really think she'd done something to cause her friend's death? Were they trying to pin the accident on one of her crewmates? A surge of helpless fear and anger washed over her. She edged back against the wall, tightening the blanket around her body and hugging the pillow. Nothing she could do but wait.

Eventually exhaustion overtook her and she fell into an uneasy sleep.

Later, she jerked awake with a gasp, panicking a couple seconds before remembering where she was and what had happened to Digger. She blinked into the dim recessed lighting and rubbed her hands over her face. How long had she slept? Five minutes? Five hours? Her wrist chron was in her locker and there wasn't one in the cell.

After stretching stiff muscles and popping a kink in her neck, she figured at least a couple of hours had passed. She eased to the edge of the cot, shoved aside the blanket and pillow and got to her feet. After using the toilet, she washed her hands and splashed lukewarm water on her face. Lack of a towel forced her to dry off with the jumpsuit's sleeves.

Morgan paced the twelve-foot cell. How long were they going to keep her here? Where were Charri and Ben and Strom? Were they still being held? Sadness and the ache in her chest returned when images of Digger flashed through her brain.

The door slid open.

She turned to face the broad-shouldered, dark-skinned man who strode into the room. He wore his hair in a gray-flecked crewcut. His piercing black eyes seemed to bore through her. He wore black dress pants and a tight-fitting tunic rather than the quasi-military fatigues worn by most of Mann-Maru Security. An odd expression crossed his face while he sized her up. She got the sense he was placing her in his mind, making connections.

"You may call me Rogan. We have much to discuss, Morgan Rahn." He nodded toward the table and two chairs. "Sit," he commanded.

She didn't move. "I already told them what happened."

Rogan crossed the room in two swift steps, grabbed her by the front of her coveralls, and growled, "How did you do it, Rahn? Tell me!"

Morgan flinched.

"Tell me!" he shouted in her face.

"I didn't do anything!" she blurted. Fear surged through her. "Let me go!" Instinctively, she swung her fist.

Rogan caught her wrist, effortlessly flipped her around into a choke hold, and twisted one of her arms behind her back. She tried to kick backward at his knee, but he shifted out of reach and jerked her arm higher. Sharp pain knifed through her shoulder. She choked off a cry and struggled anyway.

"Stop!" he roared in her ear.

Morgan froze and squeezed her eyes shut. After a second, Rogan released her and stepped back. She straightened on shaking legs, facing away from him.

"Come and sit down," he grated.

His footsteps moved away. She heard a chair scraping across the hard floor. Fabric rustled when he sat.

Slowly, Morgan turned and walked to the table, choosing to sit on the edge of the chair and meet his gaze as evenly as she could. She wasn't guilty of anything other than losing one of her best friends and she had no intention of groveling to Mann-Maru Security to prove the obvious.

The tight lines around Rogan's eyes relaxed as he studied her face. His tone changed to an almost casual friendliness. "So, tell me why you think you're so innocent."

She trusted friendliness even less than false accusations. He raised an expectant brow. She said, "Because I am."

"You're telling me you didn't wire the explosives into your suit."

"What?" She heard her voice crack on the exclamation.

"Your suit was rigged."

She stared at him.

"An igniter was wired into the power pack that ran the drill attachment. Your buddy fired it up and boom. Micro-explosives were hidden in the rim of the faceplate and on the power pack itself." Rogan shrugged. "It wouldn't have been caught by the suit's internal diagnostics. No way either of you would have seen or detected the tampering unless you knew what to look for."

Morgan sat back heavily, feeling like someone had just punched the breath out of her.

"You know anyone who wanted to see you dead?" Rogan pressed. "Enemies? Jealous lovers? I know you play some pretty rough grav-ball. You piss anyone off lately?"

She couldn't breathe, couldn't think.

"What about Drygzinski? He have any enemies?"

She shook her head mutely. Someone had tried to kill her. Someone had purposefully and maliciously tampered with her spacesuit. *I should be dead. Not Digger. Me.* A shiver ran through her. She clenched her hands into fists to stop them shaking. *What the fuck is going on?*

Rogan relaxed in his chair. "Your co-workers' stories coincide with yours," he said. "You're a lucky woman, Morgan Rahn."

She blinked and looked incredulously at him. "Lucky?" she repeated. "Are you out of your fucking mind?"

Rogan smiled tightly. "You're alive. Most people would consider that a gift."

CHAPTER THREE

"Ten freakin' hours," Morgan mumbled to herself. She trudged down the street toward her apartment building. *And for what?* The questioning had been routine and superficial. Even Rogan's accusations seemed more about getting a rise out of her than him seriously believing she had anything to do with Digger's death.

She kicked a stone as she walked and thought back to when Rogan released her from the holding cell. When she had turned away, he'd stopped her with a hand on her upper arm. "Keep your wits about you. This was probably random, but it wouldn't hurt to be cautious." Then he'd nodded, pivoted on his heel, and walked away.

What the fuck was that supposed to mean? Did he think someone might actually be out to get her? Or was it just a general caution given the situation? She was inclined to go with the latter option since she got sick to her stomach considering the alternative.

Reaching her apartment, Morgan palmed the lock and shouldered her way inside. She leaned tiredly against the wall beside the doorframe. *God, it's good to be home.*

Her flat was one room plus a bathroom. An efficiency kitchen lined the wall to the left of the doorway, leaving barely enough space for a tiny table and two chairs. At the center of the main room, an overstuffed sofa faced the entertainment center and vidscreen covering most of the wall. The bed was built into a deep niche in the rear wall. The door to the bathroom opened between the bed and the kitchen.

She shrugged out of her jacket and draped it over the back of the nearest kitchen chair.

Her computer's message queue beeped several times, breaking the silence, and announced in a low female voice, "You have four unheard messages and five missed calls, Morgan."

Morgan sighed. "Put the lists on screen." She squinted at the text. "Play last message from Dad."

"Playing message."

Vinn Rahn leaned toward the camera, his expression strained. "Morgan? Are you home yet? I tried you earlier, but you didn't pick up. I heard what happened, honey. Call me, please, and let me know you're okay."

"End message. Save or delete?" the computer asked.

"Delete. Play last message from Charri."

"Playing message, voice only."

"Morg, where the fuck are you? Call me," Charri demanded. "We're coming over, so if you're hiding out, I'll fucking kill you."

"End message. Save or delete, lover?"

Morgan smirked automatically at the flirting subroutine Digger had programmed into the computer. He'd thought a computer should at least be interesting. *Damn it, Digger, I miss you already.*

She glanced back at the list on screen. The rest of the messages were probably the same and she didn't feel like listening to them. "Delete all. Call Charri. On screen."

A quick set of beeps. A few seconds later, Charri answered. "Morgan?" Her image bobbed up and down as she walked, obviously answering on her pad and on the way to the apartment as she'd threatened.

"Yeah. I'm home," Morgan said.

Charri frowned. "You look like hell."

"Thanks."

"They didn't mess you up, did they? Those fucking bastards."

"No, no. I'm okay. Just questions."

"We're a few minutes from your place. I'm going to send Ben home, but I'm coming over, okay?"

Morgan closed her eyes and felt herself sway. "Char, all I wanna do is go to bed."

"Fine. I'm coming anyway to make sure you're okay."

"Whatever. Let yourself in."

The line cleared and the picture went gray. Morgan shook her head at Charri's stubborness then spoke to the computer. "Call Dad. On screen."

Vinn Rahn's image flickered into view.

"Hey, Dad," she said.

"You okay?" His faded gray-green gaze searched her face.

Morgan nodded. *Yeah, I'm fine, but you look tired. You've aged so much in the last few years and I probably just added another few months to that.*

"Morgan?"

She blinked. "Sorry—just wiped out."

"Charri called looking for you. Have they been holding you this whole time?"

"Yeah."

"I'm sorry, baby girl. Sorry you had to go through this. I know Digger was a good friend."

Morgan swallowed, struggling to keep what little composure she had left. "I'm okay, Dad, really."

He cocked his head, obviously seeing everything she had hoped to hide. "Get some sleep. I just needed to know you were okay."

"Thanks, Dad."

"I love you, kiddo."

"I love you too."

He signed off.

Morgan crossed to her bed, rubbing her hands through her hair. Leaning down, she unclipped the catches on her work boots, kicked them off and sat on the edge of the mattress a while, listening to the soft whirring of the air recyclers.

The door lock clicked.

She lifted her head to watch her friend slip into the apartment.

Charri hurried across the room and wrapped her into a tight hug.

She sighed and tightened her arms around Charri's waist.

"You all right?" Charri asked.

Morgan nodded into her friend's shoulder. "I miss him, Char."

"I know. I miss him too."

"I'm glad you're here."

Charri held her and rubbed her back, murmuring comforting words, and she clung to her friend and soaked up the warmth. After a while, she let Charri tuck her into bed like a child. She didn't have the energy to argue as exhaustion crept over her.

Sometime later, an insistent beeping invaded her restless dreams. She slapped blindly at the alarm, but that didn't stop the sound. Slowly, it dawned on her the noise came from the com, not the alarm. *Damn!* She rolled on her back and let the messaging system pick up the call.

Yesterday's events washed over her, leaving an ache in her chest and a vaguely sick feeling in the pit of her stomach. *I need to get up. Even though I would rather lie here all day.*

Sighing, Morgan shoved off the blankets and sat up stiffly. A groan from the living room startled her. She glanced over to see Charri rubbing her eyes and pulling a blanket around her shoulders as she sat up on the sofa.

Charri squinted at her. "Hey."

"Hey, Char," Morgan mumbled, her voice sounding rough with sleep. "Thanks for stayin'." The com beeped a reminder. She cleared her throat while she padded across the carpet. "Play new message."

The computer responded, "Playing message, voice only."

"Morgan? This is Derek Strom. Hope you're doing okay." He sounded tired and uncomfortable. "Couple of things. First, wanted to let you know that the memorial service for Digger is going to be tomorrow, fifteen hundred hours at the Christian chapel. Second, our next shift will be on the twelfth, usual time, oh-seven-hundred, so you have a couple days before we're back at it. Let me know if you need anything. Talk to you later."

After a pause, the computer asked, "Shall I repeat, save, forward, or delete this message, Morgan, dear?"

"Delete it."

Charri said, "Well, there's a smiley happy wake-up call."

Morgan pressed her lips together. She walked to the kitchen, pulled open a cupboard and grabbed a pack of coffee beans, ripped it open, and poured the beans into the coffeemaker. A second cupboard yielded a couple of prepackaged meals. She glanced at Charri. "You okay with pancakes and sausages?"

"Sure."

Morgan slid the meals into the heater and set the timer. She dug a couple of mugs and some silverware from the cupboard and put them on the table.

Charri dropped into a hard-backed chair. "So what'd they ask you? Why'd they hold you so much longer than us?"

"How long did they hold you?"

"Only a couple hours. Asked us to describe what happened. Asked about you—if you had any enemies, if you were a troublemaker, if you and Digger were fighting or something." Charri shrugged. "I told them they were crazy if they thought you had anything to do with it—that you guys were best friends."

Morgan chewed her lower lip. The timer beeped. She removed the two meals and set them on the table. The smell of food made her feel suddenly weak and shaky. Dropping into the chair across from Charri, she wrapped a pancake around a sausage. Two sausage-cakes later, her hands quit shaking.

Charri moved her plate in front of Morgan. "Here, you need this more than I do." She got up to pour the coffee, adding generous amounts of powdered cream and sweetener to each mug.

Morgan plowed through the rest of her breakfast while Charri settled in the chair with her fingers curled around the mug and slowly sipped her coffee.

Finally Morgan looked up from the plate. "What did they tell you?"

"Not a damned thing. They're investigating. Ben talked to Strom last night before I came over here. Strom was pissed because Corporate wouldn't tell him anything."

Morgan nodded thoughtfully. "They asked me the same kinds of questions, then left me waiting. A second guy came in, said his name was Rogan—must've been from headquarters. He pretty much accused me of murdering Digg. I told him I didn't do it." She got up and paced the short distance between the table and the sofa. "He said my suit had micro-explosives rigged into the tools' power pack and along the helmet's faceplate."

Charri stared at her.

Morgan twisted the gold band on her right index finger. "It wasn't an accident."

"Do they have any idea who did it? Or why?"

Morgan shrugged.

Charri said, "It just doesn't make any sense."

"Digg's dead. It should have been me. It was my fucking suit."

"It shouldn't have been either of you."

Running her fingers through her short black hair, Morgan scowled and straightened her shoulders. "Call Strom. On screen."

The com system put the call out. Her crew chief's image appeared on the vid-screen. Strom looked like he hadn't slept much, but a ghost of a smile appeared on his unshaven face. "Hey, Morgan."

"Hey. Got your message. Thanks."

He nodded and lifted a hand in greeting when he saw Charri in the background. "Hey, Char. Is Ben there too?"

Charri shook her head. "I left him home. I came over when Morgan got back last night."

"You okay, Morg?" Strom asked. "We were worried about you."

"Yeah, shook up, but okay."

"They didn't fuck you up or anything, did they? I bitched at Grohman to get your ass out of there until he finally kicked me out of his office and threatened to have me thrown in jail for harassment."

"No, just questions. You know a guy named Rogan?"

Strom shook his head. "From Corporate?"

"Probably." She gave him the short version of what Rogan had told her about the rigged suit.

Strom sighed when she finished. "I finally got Grohman to talk to me earlier this morning. If you can believe what Corporate says, they're pretty well convinced that it was, and I quote—" he made quotation marks in the air with his fingers, "—a random act of corporate terrorism."

"You believe that?" Morgan asked.

He shrugged. "Anyway, they said to be aware of heightened security at the job and probably on Base generally. But other than that, we're just going to do our jobs the way we always have."

Morgan sighed. "The more things change, the more they stay the same."

"Pretty much. Look, you guys take it easy, okay? If I hear anything I'll let you know. I'll see you at Digg's memorial tomorrow."

"Thanks, Strom."

"Talk to you ladies later."

Morgan flopped on the sofa. Leaning back against the cushions, she closed her eyes.

Charri asked, "What are you going to do today?"

"I need to go see my dad. Other than that, probably just sleep. You?"

"Hang with Ben. Maybe we'll see you later?"

"Yeah. Call me if you guys go for food."

Charri stood and stretched. "I'm gonna head, then."

"Thanks for stayin', Char."

"That's what friends are for, right?" Charri grinned. "I'm gonna get outta here so you can shower and get to your dad's. He was pretty uptight last night."

Morgan smiled tiredly. "Yeah. Sooner I get there, the better."

CHAPTER FOUR

Morgan crossed Moon Base's central plaza, wending slowly through the block-square park. Dwarf trees and perennial flowers grew in ornamental concrete planters placed along gravel walkways. Low water-use mossy grass grew between the paths. On another day, she would have taken off her shoes and roamed over the spongy, soft carpet, maybe even laid down in a quiet spot with her pad and done some writing.

She passed the vegetables growing in neat rows across a six-meter square plot, carefully cared for and cultivated by volunteers and grade school students learning about basic biology. For many of the workers on base, the green space brought a bit of Earth up to the Moon.

Morgan had never lived on Earth. She'd been there a couple of times—once as a child with her parents on a vacation she barely remembered, and once with her ex-girlfriend, Gina, during a vacation she would rather forget.

Even though she considered herself a "spacer" she was drawn to the greenness. Today, however, she passed through the park without stopping. She needed to see her father.

Her path took her to a three-story housing complex on the west side of the plaza. Her father's apartment—where she had grown up—was on the second floor. She took the closed stairwell up to the second floor and trudged down the hallway, stopping at a nondescript door with a faded welcome mat in front. She tapped the lock combination into the keypad. The door slid open and she stepped inside. "Dad?"

Familiar, comforting smells surrounded her while she hung up her jacket on a coat rack near the door. The pungent aroma of coffee wafted to her from the kitchen to her immediate right, along with whatever her dad had eaten for breakfast, and more faintly, the sweetness of his aftershave.

Her father's voice boomed from beyond the foyer. "In the living room, honey!"

She kicked off her boots and followed the voice. When she tramped into the living room, Vinn Rahn pushed himself stiffly out of his easy chair, a hand wrapped around his black metal cane. He took a step forward to greet her.

"Hey, Dad." Morgan wrapped him in a hug.

Balancing with his cane, Vinn put his free arm around her shoulders and gave her a hard squeeze. For a moment, she felt like the twelve-year-old she had been, desperately needing the comfort and reassurance of her dad's strong embrace.

"You okay? I been worried about you," he said.

Morgan nodded into his shoulder. She shook herself mentally and let go. She wiped quickly at the tears threatening to spill down her face. "Yeah, I'm good. Just a little shook up."

He gave her arm a pat. Concern and worry drew lines across his brow as he studied her.

Morgan put on her best grown-up face. "Sit down, Dad. You want some more coffee?" Without waiting for an answer, she smiled, picked up his empty cup from the end table beside his easy chair and went to the kitchen, returning with a bottle of juice for herself and a mug of steaming coffee for him. She took her usual place on the matching chair beside his, slouching into its worn depths, and stretching her feet out in front of her with a sigh.

The living room was the same as always, the furniture worn with age and use, the same faded holo photos on the walls—pictures of herself as a child, and her mother—all a silent tribute and reminder of the past.

She watched him pick up his mug and sip the hot liquid. "You want to talk about it?" he asked.

Morgan wasn't entirely sure she wanted to talk, but slowly began to relate the previous days' events. Vinn listened carefully, not interrupting, giving her hand an occasional reassuring pat. He was supportive at all the right points and never asked for more than she was willing to say. He never had. Even after Mom's death and the self-inflicted traumas of her somewhat challenging adolescence, he had never pushed, just let her work through things in her own time, on her own terms. She sipped her juice. "The last guy that came in was probably from Corporate, said his name was Rogan."

He startled, his eyes wide. "Rogan?" he repeated.

"Yeah." Morgan cocked her head. "Why?"

After a beat, his expression cleared. He shook his head and waved her off. "Just sounded familiar for a minute. Go on, what did he tell you?"

Morgan swallowed. She had to take a breath to say the next piece. The words came out flat and toneless. "My suit was sabotaged with micro-explosives. Security told Strom it was corporate terrorists."

She watched emotions flicker across her father's face. Terrorist violence had killed her mother—pirates working in the Belt, stealing ships' cargos, raiding the mining facilities for equipment and raw minerals. Mom had been in the wrong place at the wrong time, caught in the crossfire when the pirates raided the mining facility's supply depot.

"Bastards," Vinn muttered.

She sighed and continued her story, needing to get it all out. She knew she was rambling now and hated it, but couldn't stop the thoughts from tumbling out. "At first while I was sitting there, I just kept thinking it was something I'd missed, diagnostics I hadn't run. But I know I ran them. Then it turns out it wasn't anything to do with me, so there's a part of me that's really glad it wasn't my fault." She raked her fingers through her hair. "But it was still my suit Digger was wearing. If we hadn't traded, it would've been me dead. And I keep thinking maybe it should have been." She shook her head and rubbed her face tiredly with the palms of her hands. "God, I hate this." Her chest squeezed tight. She forced herself to breathe.

"I'm glad it wasn't you, Morgan."

She looked up, managing a weak smile. "Thanks."

Vinn took another sip of his coffee, set the mug carefully back down, and regarded her with gentle eyes. "What that fellow Rogan told you," he said quietly, "is a true thing. You're alive, and it's a gift. It may be hard for you to see right now, but for some reason it wasn't meant to be you in that suit. It's not your time. Somebody out here still needs you. I do. Other people do. You need to be strong for the people who still need you."

Morgan couldn't meet his concerned gaze. *You were strong for me, Dad. You were there for me even though you were falling apart too. I'll never be as strong as you, but I'll try to at least keep my shit together without freaking out on everyone.*

Vinn asked, "Did they give you a couple days off?"

"Yeah."

"Good. Spend it with your friends. Relax."

"I'll try."

He squeezed her hand. "You're gonna be okay, kiddo. Just give it some time."

CHAPTER FIVE

Shaine Wendt strolled through the wide glass doors into the personnel office of the Mann-Maru Maintenance Facility. Several rows of linked chairs lined the lobby. A handful of techs stood in line at the reception counter at the rear of the room. Others congregated in twos and threes around the perimeter. Muffled voices, the hum of office machinery, and the smell of coffee permeated the air.

She headed for the counter when a rangy, dark-skinned man waved her over. She greeted him with a smile. "Hey, Raj, how's it going?"

"It goes, it goes," he returned easily, typing into his terminal. "Looks like they finally gave you a permanent crew assignment, Shaine."

"No kidding? About time."

He gave her a rueful look and added apologetically, "With Derek Strom's crew. To replace the guy who got killed a few days ago."

She let her equipment bag slide off her shoulder and drop heavily to the floor. "Great. This oughta be a treat."

"Sorry, man. Let me grab Derek. He can brief you."

Sighing, she leaned against the counter to wait.

A few moments later, Raj led a mountain of a man to the reception counter.

Her new crew chief stood about Raj's height, but his muscular build dwarfed the thin clerk, and his voice rumbled low in his chest as he held out a massive hand. "Derek Strom."

She shook his hand briefly.

He motioned her through the swinging half-door at the end of the counter. "Come on around. Got some paperwork first, then we'll head down to meet the gang."

An hour later, Strom led her down the hallway to the separate crew ready rooms. Despite his reassurances, she wondered if she'd made a mistake accepting the assignment. Strom had reiterated what she'd heard in the news, that Drygzinski's death was an on-the-job accident. She didn't believe the story for a minute. After six years in the inner circle of Mann-Maru Security operations, she knew a cover-up when she heard it. Hell, she'd written a dozen herself. Whatever killed John "Digger" Drygzinski hadn't been an accident.

Strom said his people seemed to be handling the situation all right. Shaine thought about her experiences in Earth Guard with buddies killed in the line of duty. Some guys accepted what happened and moved on. Others reacted with anger or depression. A few freaked out. She had been one of the angry ones.

The crew chief led Shaine into the ready room assigned to his crew. To her left, she saw an entrance to the shower room, from which emanated the faint scents of soap and disinfectant. Equipment lockers and benches lined the side walls. The sealed air lock hatch was on the back wall. A row of vacuum suits and a rack of helmets hung on one side of the air lock.

Two women and a man in the midst of changing out of their street clothes stood by open lockers. Shaine caught her breath, immediately recognizing them.

Strom addressed the group with easy familiarity. "Morning, people. We got a new crewmate. This is Shaine Wendt." He pointed to the man on the right. "Ben Knight."

Shaine held a hand out as Ben finished tying his hair into a long ponytail. He grasped her hand firmly with long, strong fingers. "Hey, how's it going?"

Beside him, a feisty-looking woman with bright blue eyes and a blinding grin introduced herself. "Hi, Shaine. I'm Charri Anders. Welcome to the crew."

Shaine returned Charri's smile.

Strom nodded at the bank of lockers on the opposite side of the room and the woman facing away from them. "That's Morgan Rahn."

Morgan was stripped down to boxer shorts and a spaghetti strap tank top. An image of a scruffy, jersey-clad grav-ball player flashed through Shaine's brain when Morgan glanced over her shoulder. For a second, Morgan regarded her with a guarded expression, then turned away without a word.

Shaine stared at the flowing lines of tattoos ranging over Morgan's smoothly muscled body. Vibrant colors cascaded across the back of her left shoulder, a depiction of explosive flames dancing behind a darkened asteroid. The asteroid was engraved like a headstone "RIP 2.23.2234." A wildly colorful winged dragon swooped up from the back of her left calf. Shaine wished she could see the rest of it wrapped around the front of her thigh. Intricately woven black tribal bands wound around Morgan's left bicep.

Shaine was impressed by the painstaking, colorful detail. *Inking those had to have hurt like a bitch.*

Strom's voice pulled her out of her reverie. "You've got the green striped vac suit, Shaine. Give it a try today. If the fit's funky, we'll find you another one. Take the locker next to Morgan." He waited for her nod of confirmation and added, "Morgan, take the black suit."

Morgan's head snapped around toward Strom. Startled surprise shifted swiftly to anger. She bit off a curse and glared at him. Strom shook his head with a pained frown.

Shaine crossed to her assigned locker and set her bag down on the bench. She pressed her thumb to the sensor on the locker to open it. While methodically moving her stuff from her bag and changing, she considered the situation. Ben and Charri seemed okay, friendly enough. Pretty much the opposite of Morgan Rahn. Well. Not like she expected to be greeted with open arms by a crew who had just lost one of their people.

She glanced over at Morgan, taking in the stiff, closed-off way Morgan moved and held herself. For a brief instant, Morgan turned and met her gaze from beneath a shock of black bangs. She felt herself caught by a stormy gray ocean of emotion.

She swallowed and looked away, focusing on pulling on her bio-wired suit liner. There had been so much pain in Morgan's eyes. *I'm sorry. This really has to suck for you.*

* * *

Morgan closed her locker, took a deep breath and gritted her teeth. The room was empty without Digger's usual morning grumbles. Ops had wasted no time assigning a replacement. She had expected it would just be the four of them today and maybe the rest of the shift cycle. She didn't want someone taking Digger's spot on the crew. Not yet. It was too soon. She wanted time to get used to his absence.

She moved around the bench to the vacuum suits hanging in an orderly row, helmets and gloves lined up on the shelf above. Her boots remained attached to Digger's suit from when she had worn it last week. She didn't like that their equipment had been set out as though nothing had happened, that someone else had been checking out their things, putting everything back in place. She felt violated by the intrusion, even more so because she didn't know or trust the hands that had handled her gear.

Her stomach roiled uneasily as she regarded the black striped suit and helmet. *Christ, what if this suit is rigged now? What if it wasn't random and it was really me they were trying to kill? What if they decided to try again?* For a second she saw Digger's ruined face behind the shattered helmet, saw him staring at her with dead, empty eyes. *Fuck, fuck, fuck!*

She shot an angry glance at Strom. What the hell was he thinking, making her wear Digger's vac suit? How could he so casually throw that order out? *Take the black one,* she thought acidly.

Did he really think she wouldn't care? Couldn't he have just gotten her a different one? Gritting her teeth, she lifted Digger's suit off the hook. *Just put it on and get it over with.*

Stepping into the legs, she worked her feet into the attached boots, then twisted to pull the bulky torso over her shoulders and push her arms inside. By the time she got the suit-liner leads plugged in, Ben had joined her to slip into his own suit.

Morgan grabbed her helmet—Digger's helmet—and settled it forcefully onto her shoulders, letting the neck seals snap into place. The life support system kicked in and a breath of air fanned down over her face. The headgear still carried the lingering scent of Digger's aftershave. She blinked hard to stop the tears. *Damn it! I am not going to start crying like a freakin' baby!* Clenching her jaw, she started to lift a hand to swipe at her eyes, remembered she wore the sealed helmet and let her arm fall back limply to her side. She jammed her hands into the gloves, sealing them with angry motions, and shuffled to the air lock.

It was going to be a long shift.

CHAPTER SIX

Morgan joined Ben and Charri that evening for dinner. Her intention had been to go home after her shift and curl up with a book, but Charri ragged at her until she agreed to go home with them. She sat on a stool at the bar separating the tiny kitchen from the living room and sipped from a bottle of beer while Charri put a pizza in the oven.

Charri set the timer and leaned against the counter. "I really didn't think Strom would make you wear Digg's suit," she commented.

Morgan scowled. "I know. I figured he'd have just gotten a different one for me, instead of making me wear Digg's again. Probably Ops wouldn't give him a replacement." She took a long swallow from the bottle. "I just about peed my pants when I kicked in the fuser the first time, waiting for the damned thing to blow up."

"You didn't really think it'd happen again, did you?"

"Why not? Get the job done right this time around."

"Now you're being morbid."

"Of course I'm being morbid. I think I have a right to be."

Ben padded out of the bedroom, shirtless and wearing loose, worn sweats. He passed into the kitchen, grabbing a beer from the refrigerator on the way. He slid up behind Charri. Long arms wrapped around her shoulders. She leaned into him with a sigh. "Sure sucked not having Digg there today," he said quietly.

Charri nodded.

Ben gave Charri a squeeze and kissed her hair before wandering into the living room. He scooped the remote off the coffee table and turned on the entertainment center. After a few minutes, he called, "Hey, you guys should see this."

"See what, hon?" Charri asked.

"Another mining facility in the Belt got hit."

Morgan turned to face the screen.

A ticker ran across the bottom of the screen, subtitling the voice-over from the reporter. "—have not determined who was behind the destruction, though pirate activity is suspected. Mann-Maru Universal Industries reports nineteen workers injured, four confirmed dead. Three remain missing. I've just been told we will have Mann-Maru CEO Tarm Maruchek on the line shortly to give a statement."

Scenes of the attacked complex flashed behind the reporter. Morgan recognized the wreckage of an ore processing plant. A close-up showed a conveyor belt melted into a twisted metal ribbon. Personnel in bright orange vac suits floated around the damaged site. Emergency skiffs flooded the area with spotlights. The stark outline of a construction crane with a broken boom rose out of the debris like a dead tree against the blackness of space.

Her fingers closed around the beer bottle. The destruction on screen brought back haunting memories of a similar scene. She had been in the darkness of her childhood bedroom. Clinging to the cold metal frame around the single round window, she'd held herself on tiptoe, watching the emergency vehicles move slowly around the wreckage of the mining facility where her family lived. Her father's muffled sobs sounded from the living room. She remembered thinking she should be crying too. But she couldn't— not right then—and instead stared out the window, feeling only painful emptiness.

"Hey." Charri's hands settled on her shoulders.

Morgan blinked away the visions and dragged in a shaky breath. "I'm okay. Just…remembering."

Charri hugged her. "You want Ben to turn it off?"

"No. I want to know what's going on."

The timer beeped. Charri gave her a pat and said, "Go sit down."

Morgan slid off the stool and wandered over to drop into the far corner of the sofa.

Charri joined them, pushing Ben's feet off the coffee table and putting down the pizza before settling between Morgan and Ben.

Morgan took a slice, chewing slowly while she watched the images scroll across the screen. The reporter continued to repeat what they already knew, which wasn't much. The attack on the mining outpost had happened the previous day. In-system emergency personnel and an armored Earth Guard division had just arrived at the facility.

If Earth Guard is involved, maybe they're expecting a second go-round. Terrorist violence against the mega-corporation had been increasing steadily since Mann-Maru announced the discovery of a new ore processing technology that would give them an even greater monopoly on asteroid mining.

Morgan hated that innocent people were caught in the middle of the fight. System authorities were never quite able to stop the violence. She didn't necessarily agree with the hard-core conspiracy theorists who believed the terrorist attacks were a political and financial ploy for the benefit of Mann-Maru, but neither was she certain there wasn't a kernel of truth to the speculation.

The scene behind the reporter shifted to a split video feed. On the left, a continuing shot of the ongoing cleanup operations in the Belt. On the right, the camera zoomed in on a distinguished, middle-aged man in a formal business suit. Morgan recognized Tarm Maruchek, CEO and owner of Mann-Maru Universal Industries, gazing calmly into the camera through deep-set, gunmetal-blue eyes.

The young reporter straightened and focused on the camera. "This is Raston Fuller with System Forty News. I'm here right now with Mann-Maru CEO Tarm Maruchek. Mr. Maruchek, thank you for sparing us a few minutes of your time."

"Of course."

"Can you give us an up-to-date status on what's happening at Facility 2333?"

Maruchek nodded. "Yes. The facility has been secured. The damage was primarily external, centering on the automated areas of the processing plant. Personnel quarters were not affected so loss of life was mitigated. My own security personnel and Earth Guard are investigating the situation. I hope to have more information shortly."

Ben glowered at the screen. "Yeah, more information he'll twist around to say whatever he wants us to hear."

Morgan agreed. *Never trust Corporate because it's all about the bottom line. Always has been, always will be. Fuck the little guy. What do the CEOs care, as long as they get their profits?*

The reporter continued, "We've gotten word of a recent accident at Moon Base where a dock maintenance worker was killed. Can you tell us anything about that, Mr. Maruchek?"

Maruchek hesitated a split second. Morgan could have sworn she saw a flicker of actual emotion on his face. He said, "Our internal security is still investigating that incident, Raston. At this time it appears to be some kind of failure of the suit's helmet seal. We've never seen anything like it, to be honest."

Morgan blinked in shock. "What?"

Maruchek continued, "We're working with the helmet and suit's manufacturer to try to understand what happened."

"You fucking lying bastard!" Morgan hissed.

"Unbelievable," Ben breathed.

"There have been a lot of rumors on the net suggesting foul play around the incident, and pointing to terrorist infiltration."

"There are always rumors," Maruchek responded evenly. "In this case, they are unfounded."

"Unfounded my ass!" Morgan exploded.

"The issue appears to have been a fault in the locking mechanism in the neck seal," Maruchek continued.

"I can't listen to anymore of his crap." Ben flipped the channel.

Shaking her head, Morgan fell back into the cushions. "How can he lie like that?" she asked. "I saw the explosion. We all saw what it did to Digg."

Charri looked from her to Ben with an incredulous expression. "You guys didn't think Maruchek's PR people were going to let him tell the truth, did you? They're going to play it down and shove it under the rug. That's what they always do."

"Doesn't make it right," Morgan said.

"Of course not," Charri agreed. "But there isn't anything you can do about it, so why get all worked up?"

Morgan lifted her head and met Charri's even gaze with a raised eyebrow. "Because it makes me feel so fucking good?"

Charri rolled her eyes.

Ben laughed and started flipping through channels, finally settling on a grav-ball game.

Morgan thought about her own team, mulling over what they were going to do without Digger. "You think Carlis will play for Digger next week?" she asked.

Ben made a face. "Next week, probably. But he won't stick around. You guys are gonna have to find a regular."

"That's what Ally thought, too. I don't know who we're gonna get, though. Maybe Tyke Springler?"

Ben shook his head. "The Dawgs need a decent defensive player. Springler's a center and you guys have that covered. What about Joe Marconn?"

Morgan said, "Ally talked to him yesterday. He said he's done playing league ball. Only other player I know who's not already on a team is Ally's ex-girlfriend, and I am not playing with that bitch, no matter how good she thinks she is."

Charri asked, "What about Shaine? Think she plays? Strom said she's ex-Earth Guard, so she's probably good in null-grav."

Morgan looked down at her hands. *I don't know if I'm ready for that.*

Ben said, "She seems pretty okay."

"I think she's nice." Charri smirked and nudged Morgan's foot. "Not to mention easy on the eyes."

Morgan snorted. Charri had a one-track mind. *What is it about married women that turns them instantly into matchmakers?* "Give it up, Char."

Charri ignored her. "Wonder why she's got a bio-mech leg, though? Was she wounded in the EG?"

Ben put in, "She said that's why she got out—medical discharge."

"When'd she tell you that?" Charri asked.

He shrugged. "You guys were in the showers."

Morgan considered the tall redhead who had joined their crew. Shaine hadn't said much. Of course, what had there been to say, other than the occasional work-related comment or question? Working without Digger felt strange—empty and too quiet. She hadn't given a thought to Shaine's looks, nor had she given more than passing consideration to the prosthetic on Shaine's right leg. The detachable bionic limb was barely noticeable, anyway. She shrugged inwardly. Without Digger, Shaine just wasn't that important.

CHAPTER SEVEN

"Four down, one to go," Charri announced with a sigh, hanging her vac suit in its place on the ready room's back wall. "Glad this week is almost over."

Morgan flipped her towel over the door of her locker, silently agreeing, although she had to admit work was getting back to normal. She pulled on a long-sleeved T-shirt, fished in her bag for a pair of clean socks and sat on the bench. At least she no longer expected Digger to show up, or prefaced every other thought with what Digg would do or say.

Shaine Wendt had proved herself a good mechanic and easy to get along with. Not that they'd talked all that much, but at least the conversations hadn't been too strained.

Ben strode out of the shower room. "Hey, you guys," he called. "Don't forget my band's playing tonight over at Tranquility."

Morgan flicked a glance over her shoulder. Ben had a towel wrapped around his waist and used another to dry his hair.

Shaine Wendt followed a couple of steps behind him wearing green boxer shorts and a tight gray tank top. Shaine crossed the floor, her loose gait accented by a barely noticeable limp. She combed her fingers through wet red hair, ordering it haphazardly, and pulled open the locker next to Morgan's.

"Shaine, you should come to the club," Charri said.

Shaine dropped her towel on the bench. "What kind of music?"

Ben grinned. "Hard-core speed thrash."

"Sounds like fun."

"Serious slammin'," Ben confirmed. "Just ask Morgan. Last time she came out, she was feeling it for a freakin' week."

Morgan smirked. "I think I had bruises on my bruises."

He laughed. "Poor baby," he teased. "Admit you had a good time."

"Yeah, yeah." She flipped him off and joined the laughter.

* * *

Club Tranquility was the only large-scale entertainment complex on Moon Base providing a public venue for dancing and live shows. The building took up nearly an entire block. Inside, neon lights scrolled across black walls in vivid patterns, and multicolored tiles flickered under the dance floor in front of a raised, full-sized stage. To the right of the stage, a nine-meter wide, clear-walled cube rose to the ceiling. Fitted with a zero-gravity generator, the cube created a freeform 3-D dance space.

Morgan and Charri paused just inside the club's entrance. Morgan shoved her hands into her pockets, suddenly not sure if she wanted to stay. Her stomach clenched. She couldn't remember the last time she'd been out to see Ben's band without Digger at her side.

It was so easy to picture Digger laughing and drinking, purposely obnoxious, all the more so when she rolled her eyes. They'd both loved the adrenaline rush of whipping through the wild slam-dance patterns in the null-grav field. She and Digg had been in the middle of just about every brawl started by overeager slammers in the cube, always managing to slip out of the fray before the crap hit the fan. *Damn, we had a good time. But tonight it won't be the same.*

She shook her head. *Quit being a fucking baby.* Straightening her shoulders, she turned toward the bar. "Come on, Char. I need a drink."

Charri grinned. "I'll get the first round."

Beer bottle in hand, Morgan followed her friend toward the stage. Ben and his band always reserved space up front for their partners and friends. She and Charri exchanged greetings with the half-dozen men and women already settled in and claimed a hi-top table for themselves.

Morgan leaned against the table while Charri perched on a stool across from her.

"You okay?" Charri asked.

Morgan waggled her hand. "Managing. What about you? And Ben?"

"We're okay. I've been worried about you."

Morgan studied the bubbles rising slowly in her glass. "I'm all right." She ran her hand through her hair and let her gaze slide across the dance floor, past the bar, toward the entrance where patrons arrived in a steady stream. She recognized many of them—people from other maintenance crews, from the grav-ball teams, and band groupies.

A group of dock mechanics rambled into the club—Digger's buddies and hers. They wore the band's T-shirts like a uniform. Some had ripped off the sleeves or cut open the necks. All wore work boots and cargo pants with the legs cut off at the knees.

Part of her expected Digger to come swaggering in with them. The knowledge that he wouldn't be there threatened to overwhelm her. She shoved the feeling forcefully aside. *I am not going to fall apart. I'm going to hang with my friends and I'm going to do it for Digg. He'd kick my ass if I didn't go out there and party for him.* She finished half her beer in a silent toast and continued her perusal of the growing audience.

Morgan blinked when Shaine Wendt swaggered into the club. "Jesus."

Shaine paused just past the end of the bar. Low-cut black pants hugged her hips and long legs. A cropped black sleeveless vest left plenty of bare skin across her middle, and was zipped up barely past indecent. Her red hair stood up in short, unruly spikes. She met Morgan's wide-eyed stare, lifted a hand in greeting and started across the floor.

Morgan forced herself to look away. *Okay, that's not what I expected.*

Shaine sauntered up to the table. "Hey, guys."

"Hey, Shaine. Wow." Charri whistled as she gave the tall woman a once-over.

Shaine grinned and made a half-embarrassed shrug. "Guess I kinda overdressed, huh?"

Holy shit, Shaine. Showing enough skin? Morgan managed a weak smile. *You're not supposed to look that hot. And I'm not supposed to notice.* She slammed back the rest of her drink. "I'll be back," she said shortly.

She turned and headed to the bar.

* * *

Frowning, Shaine watched until Morgan crossed the dance floor. "What's her problem?"

Charri shrugged, a thoughtful look on her face. "Not entirely certain," she admitted.

A server came over. Shaine ordered a beer and a round for Charri and Morgan on the assumption that Morgan would return. She watched Morgan talking to the group at the bar. One of the guys threw a beefy arm around her shoulders. Morgan exchanged hugs with several others.

Charri said, "I'm glad you decided to come out tonight, Shaine."

Shaine nodded. "Thanks. Not sure if Morgan is so glad I showed up, though."

"Don't worry about Morgan. It's kinda tough for her tonight without Digger here. Once the music starts they'll get her up in the null-grav cube and she'll work it out."

Shaine asked, "Morgan and Digger were really close?"

"Yeah. Digg was kind of like her big brother. He kept an eye on her, kept her feet on the ground. Digg was always out with us on nights like this."

"It's tough losing a good friend."

"Yeah."

Shaine sipped her beer. A handful of faces and names came to mind. *Adam Sharrick. Perr Gaston. Joey Marris. Tanya Hauer.* How many times had she wished she'd died with her squadmates? How many more times had she wondered why her life had been spared? Acceptance was easier now, but she would never forget them. She let out a long breath. "So, does Ben's band play here often?"

Charri seemed relieved by the subject change. She went into a glowing description of the band and a little of their history.

Morgan wandered back a while later with another beer and perched on a stool. She looked at the full bottle on the table in front of her. "That for me?" she asked, surprised.

Shaine nodded. "Yeah. Figured you'd be back."

"Thanks." Morgan met her gaze with a quick smile.

On stage, the lights went black and the background music cut off. A momentary hush fell across the club. A second later the air exploded with a deafening rush of sound and blinding flashes of light. Heavily rhythmic opening notes ripped into the crowd. The dark crunch of the rhythm section underlined the lead guitar's scream. The lead singer tromped up front and leaned over the edge of the stage, snarling into a handheld microphone, growling out angry lyrics.

The music vibrated through Shaine's body. She grinned. Ben hadn't exaggerated when he'd said the band was tight. Nightwalker was rock solid. The darkness and anger in the words and rhythms whipped around her, bringing back her years in the EG when this kind of music had been the soundtrack for her world.

She saw Morgan close her eyes and lean back, basking in the cacophony. Peaceful relief slid across the woman's face. She wondered if the anger in the music soothed Morgan's soul the way it soothed her own.

"Morgan, hey!" Two guys rushed up to the table. Each grabbed Morgan by an arm. "Come on! Let's slam!"

Grinning, Morgan slid off the stool and allowed them to pull her across the dance floor to the zero-grav cube. The threesome kicked off from the handles around the entry hatch, weaving into the chaotic crush of bodies diving and spinning around the zero-gravity space.

Shaine watched Morgan weave through the dancers twisting and catapulting with reckless abandon. At least three dozen "slammers" clustered in the upper half of the cube. She studied their movements, picking out the fast-shifting pattern as the dancers used each other to propel themselves within the sphere they created.

Morgan drove toward the center of the action, spinning, pivoting, launching herself and others back and forth.

Damn, she's good.

The band rocked through the first two sets. Morgan and her friends came and went from the null-g cube, sometimes joining her and Charri at the table, sometimes the gang at the bar. Alcohol flowed freely.

Shaine turned down a couple of invites to join the slammers in the cube, preferring to sit back and watch. *Typical thrasher crowd*, she observed, knowing a band like Nightwalker appealed to a specific audience. Either you liked the music, or you hated it. And if you hated it, you didn't put yourself through four hours of ear-ripping guitars and drums.

Toward the end of the final set, Morgan returned to the table for a break. Charri passed her a glass of water. Morgan gulped the water, then got a beer from one of the staff. She ran a hand through tousled, sweat-dampened hair and grinned.

Shaine lifted her bottle in mute greeting.

Morgan shifted her attention to the stage, nodding her head while she mouthed the lyrics.

After the song finished, the lead singer yelled, "Thanks for stickin' with us tonight! You guys fuckin' rock! We got time for one more tune. This is for Digger. We miss you, ya bastard!"

The song cranked up with a shriek of feedback.

Morgan stood and grabbed Shaine's arm. "Come on, you gotta slam the last tune."

Shaine protested, "I haven't done this in ten years."

Morgan tugged at her. "Come on!"

Hoping she wouldn't make a fool of herself, Shaine followed Morgan to the cube.

She and Morgan ducked through the hatch and kicked off toward the top. As they reached the outer ring of dancers Morgan gripped her wrist with one hand, while at the same time catching the hand of another slammer who swung them into the fray.

Morgan cast her free, laughing when she twisted around to be pulled further into the slam sphere by a tall woman with a shaved head.

Shaine struggled to orient herself for a second or two before her instincts kicked in. It may have been a few years since she'd been in null gravity, and longer since she'd participated in a slam sphere, but her body remembered.

Bass notes thrummed through her chest. Her pulse sped up to match the driving, frantic rhythm. Adrenaline surged through her veins. She let herself be pulled and passed through the outside of the slam pattern. Out of the corner of her eye, she saw Morgan flip and twist within the inner group of slammers. She grabbed the arms of another fellow and launched herself in that direction.

She caught up to Morgan, clasping wrists with her when their paths crossed. Morgan grinned and released her, trading directions as they spun away from each other.

Shaine did a backflip and righted herself in time to see Morgan thrown back toward her. A heavyset, muscular guy crossed Morgan's path, out of the pattern. Morgan slammed roughly into him, her shoulder and elbow digging into his chest.

"Fuckin' bitch, watch where you're going!" His boots connected with her middle.

Morgan flew backward, arms flailing.

Shaine took someone's hand to get her moving in Morgan's direction. She managed to swing through several dancers to catch her. They floated in sync for a few seconds. "You okay?" she yelled above the music.

Morgan nodded, grimacing while she rubbed a hand across her ribs. "Yeah, but I'm gonna smack that bastard if I catch him!"

One of Morgan's buddies dove toward them, his arms outstretched. "Here ya go, girls!"

He caught Shaine and Morgan by the wrists and flipped them back the way he'd come. Laughing, she and Morgan split up again, weaving back into the pattern.

Shaine glanced over to see the big guy from earlier headed in Morgan's direction. She could tell by Morgan's determined expression that she'd seen him too.

Morgan shifted her path, driving hard to intercept him.

Shaine kicked off someone's shoulder. Stretching her body, she slid between Morgan and the man just before they collided. She saw a glint of metal in her peripheral vision and reflexively knocked the guy's switchblade aside as she grabbed Morgan around the waist.

Morgan twisted in her grasp. "What the fuck are you doing?"

Shaine tightened her grip and bounced them down the wall to the hatch, ducking and half-dragging Morgan with her out of the cube. She stumbled when she hit gravity, struggling to keep her balance while supporting her own weight and Morgan's.

"Jesus, Shaine!"

Steadying herself and Morgan, Shaine asked, "Are you okay?"

Morgan gave her a confused look. "Of course I am. What the fuck did you do that for?"

"He had a knife in his hand."

"Who?"

"The guy you were going at had a knife. He was about to use it on you."

Morgan said, "I didn't see anything."

"I knocked it away." Shaine glanced around. Nobody had followed them out of the cube. She let her hands fall back to her sides.

The band finished their set with a thunderous ending. "Rock on, people! We love ya, Digger! We miss you!"

Morgan glanced toward the stage. The lights went black.

Shaine touched her shoulder. "Come on." Keeping half an eye on the crowd and looking for the man with the knife, she led Morgan to the tables.

Charri studied her and Morgan curiously as they approached. "What happened?"

"Shaine was overreacting," Morgan said.

Shaine bristled. "The man had a knife, and you would have gotten it in the stomach."

Charri raised a brow. "A knife?"

"Yes," Shaine said shortly.

"We should tell security," Charri said.

Shaine rolled her eyes. "You really think either the weapon or the man will still be around by the time security shows up? Besides, he never actually touched her."

"But you saw the knife, right?"

Shaine sighed, suddenly wanting the whole thing to go away. *I don't do this shit anymore.* "I saw it. I knocked it away and pulled Morgan out of there. It's done."

Charri held her gaze a long moment. Shaine was certain the little blonde would start asking questions for which she had no answers. Instead, Charri got up. "Let's go home."

Morgan said, "I've had enough for one night," and walked with Charri toward the door.

Following another quick glance around for the knife wielder, Shaine went with them, thinking it might be a good idea to make sure the guy didn't show up outside. She and the other two women walked together until they reached the Central Park Plaza. Charri headed toward the apartment she shared with Ben in the west quarter of the dome.

Shaine and Morgan turned east. Morgan scuffed along with her hands shoved deep in her pockets and her head down.

Walking beside Morgan, Shaine pondered the incident in the cube. Why did the guy pull a knife? *You play in the slam cube, you should expect to get slammed.* That was the whole fucking point. Besides, he'd been out of sync when Morgan ran into him the first time. She shook her head. Some people were just idiots.

She alternately scanned the darkened streets and mulled over her reaction.

She had acted without thought to the perceived danger. She didn't question her reflexes. She'd seen the knife. He'd been in a position to use it. *If I had been armed, if the threat had been more than a small knife, if he'd actually gotten to Morgan…* A slew of scenarios flashed through her brain. *I could have killed him as easily as I knocked him aside. Broken his neck, shattered his windpipe, used his own weapon against him.* In this case, there'd been no need to do more and she'd acted accordingly. Inwardly, she sighed. *Changing jobs isn't going to change me. Mechanic, undercover security agent, or commando, I'm still a trained protector and a trained killer.*

Morgan shot a glance at her and said quietly, "Usually, it's Digger walking my sorry ass home."

Shaine heard resigned sadness in Morgan's tone. "Sounds like he was a good guy."

"Yeah."

"I'm sorry I didn't know him."

Morgan nodded. Her gaze focused on the duracrete under her feet. "This is my stop," she said, gesturing vaguely at a four-story living complex.

Shaine slowed to a stop at the short front stairway.

Morgan ran a hand back through her hair. "Um, thanks for walking with me."

Shaine shrugged. "Not a problem. It was on my way. See ya tomorrow."

"Sure. See you tomorrow, Shaine." Morgan gave her an unsure half-smile, turned, and trudged up the stairs.

Shaine waited for the doors to slide shut before continuing home. She figured she'd probably fall asleep with that image of Morgan in her head, looking up at her with sad eyes half-hidden behind dark bangs. She sighed. *Damn.*

CHAPTER EIGHT

Morgan faced her tasks the following morning with grim determination and a large dose of painkillers. She ached from the top of her head to the tips of her toes. She had managed to collect a full set of bruises from the previous night's slamming, the worst a boot-sized discoloration across her upper stomach.

She was still pissed off she hadn't gotten the chance to beat the crap out of the idiot who kicked her. She wasn't sure what to make of the whole incident. Shaine had insisted the guy had a knife, but she hadn't seen it. In any case, the incident happened so quickly, they were outside the cube before she'd even had time to react. This morning, Shaine had made no mention of last night's events other than to compliment Ben on his band and say she had a good time.

She sighed and pushed the thoughts away, turning her focus on her work.

Morgan clumped across the hull of the ship and knelt over an access panel. She spun the hand-sized release and clipped the hatch securely against the hull. Several layers of wires, piping and insulation ran beneath the plating. She isolated the path of the primary starboard thruster control. The optic fiber bundle appeared intact where it passed through the access panel. She used a tracer to register the control's ID signal and stood up to follow its path under the hull. The indicator stopped abruptly some four meters from the hatch. She swung the tracer in a slow arc around the point where the signal ended. Sighing, she traded the tracer for her pad, and marked the position on the ship's blueprint. "That's about all I can do with that," she muttered to herself.

Shaine's voice crackled inside her helmet. "What'cha got, Morgan?"

"Broken lead. Gonna have to pull hull plating to get to it."

"So much for a quick fix, huh? System diagnostics are fine so far—I've got a couple more components to test, but it looks like you found the problem."

"Yeah." Morgan toggled her com volume up. "Hey, Strom, I've got a broken lead under the hull plating. You're gonna need to clear the repair with Ops."

"Roger that," Strom replied. "We have to replace some plating on the forward port side anyway. Mark the sections that need removal."

"Right. Shaine still has a couple more things to check."

"I need you to head forward when you're done. Come to midship, panel 308, and start working your way around and aft from there. We need to do a full hull check on this piece of junk. Shaine can start her check aft when she's done."

"Roger that." Morgan headed back to the open access hatch. "Hey, Shaine, you get that last part?"

"Yeah, I'll be on the hull check in a few."

"Okay." She knelt to reseal the hatch.

A couple seconds later, Shaine asked, "Hey, Morgan, you want to go to the Afterburner after shift?"

Morgan blinked. *What?*

"I was thinking about a burger," Shaine continued.

The vaguely queasy feeling in her stomach made the thought of food less than appealing. "I think I'm still hungover."

"You'll feel better if you eat something."

"That's debatable."

Shaine laughed. "So, you wanna go for a burger?"

"Sure, why not?" *Did she just ask me out?* "I'm heading up front." Morgan unclipped her pad from her belt, checked her position on the ship's blueprint and started forward and to port.

Her thoughts drifted while she surveyed the hull plating visually and used her pad to scan for escaping gases. Strom had paired her and Shaine on work detail most of the week. She didn't mind, even though she missed Digger and his constant pissing and moaning and laughing at his own bad jokes. Shaine wasn't Digger. The woman wasn't loud or obnoxious. She knew her stuff and didn't blather on about nothing just to hear herself talk.

Morgan heard the click of the com system flipping channels. Charri's voice interrupted her thoughts. "Did I hear Shaine ask you out?"

Morgan glanced at her heads-up display to make sure they were on a private channel. "No," she replied flatly.

Charri laughed.

Morgan knelt to take a closer look at a scrape on the hull. Seeing that the damage didn't reach into the insulating coating underneath, she stood and continued her search. "For the record, Little Miss Nosy, she didn't ask me to dinner. She asked if I wanted to go to the Afterburner for a burger. That's not dinner, that's just grabbing something to eat."

"Are you going?"

"Why not? Food's better than what I've got at my place."

Charri laughed again. "Uh-huh. Company's better, too."

"You're a pain in the ass."

"I think she likes you."

"And I think you're nuts." Morgan clicked off, effectively ending the conversation.

Grabbing a burger after work is not a damned dinner date. Besides, I'm not looking for a new girlfriend. I still haven't recovered from the last one. Shaking her head, she focused on finishing her work.

CHAPTER NINE

Shaine and Morgan made their way through the Afterburner's bustling after-work crowd and claimed a booth off to the side. Vidscreens lined the walls, playing various news and sports feeds, or set up for live trivia games. A long, rectangular bar split the room between the restaurant in front and the pool and holo-games tables in back.

Shaine initiated the menu screen on the wall. "What do you want to drink?" she asked.

"Dark beer, whatever they have on tap."

Shaine punched in the order for two drafts, and added her request for a burger and fries. She sent Morgan a questioning glance. "Food?"

A wan grin twisted Morgan's lips. "I'm trying to decide how much food's a good idea," she admitted.

Shaine grinned. "Still fighting that hangover, huh?"

"A little. Order me a burger and fries, and I'll see how it goes."

"I can always just get you ripped again so you won't notice," Shaine teased.

"Such a comedian."

Shaine answered Morgan's grin with a smile of her own. She felt like a connection had been made, the possibility for friendship solidified. She finished ordering, tapped off the menu, and leaned back in the corner of her seat, resting an arm across the back of the low booth.

Morgan leaned forward with her elbows on the table, idly glancing up at one of the video monitors and twisting the gold band on her right hand.

"How long have you and Charri and Ben worked together?" Shaine asked.

Morgan looked at her and considered for a moment. "I think it's been almost seven years. I knew Charri before that, though. We've been friends since middle school."

"Quite a history between you guys." Shaine hesitated before asking, "Was Digger with you all that time, too?"

"Yeah. He was." Morgan's eyes darkened. She looked at her hands. "We played grav-ball for a few years before we were working together."

Shaine noticed the emotions flickering across Morgan's face. She reached across the table and laid a hand over Morgan's, lightly squeezing the thin fingers that felt cold to her touch. "I'm really sorry, Morgan."

Morgan met her gaze a second. "Thanks."

A waiter brought their drinks.

Shaine sipped hers slowly, watching Morgan do the same, catching her fleeting glances and meeting them with a steady gaze. She sensed Morgan's unease, but wasn't sure how to read it. She studied the gold band on Morgan's finger and the unconscious way she played with it. Intricate, spiraling patterns decorated the thick metal. "That's a beautiful ring."

Morgan smiled. Her fingers stilled. "My mom's wedding ring," she said. She shrugged, a flush rising on her cheeks. "It keeps her with me, you know?"

"Yeah, I do." Shaine reached inside the neck of her shirt and pulled out a dull silver chain strung with five military dog tags. She leaned forward, holding the blue-tinged titanium tags so Morgan could see. "One's mine, the other ones belonged to my squadmates who didn't make it."

She frowned at the onslaught of dark memories—flying debris and screams and deafening explosions lighting the jungle around her. She still felt her panic when the narrow rock ledge she lay on gave way, and the excruciating pain for those few seconds before she blacked out. Taking a breath, she blinked away the visions and dropped the chain back under her shirt.

Morgan touched her arm tentatively. "I'm sorry," she said.

Shaine caught Morgan's hand and held it lightly, twining their fingers together in a motion that felt much more natural than it should have. Morgan didn't pull away.

We've both had losses, Shaine thought, feeling that for both of them, the pain seemed to lie pretty close to the surface. She studied Morgan's hand, so small against her own, yet not delicate. Morgan's nails were cut short. Strong tendons stood out against her skin, callouses raised on her palm. Morgan's sleeve slid up. A series of precise, faded scars sliced across the inside of her left wrist.

Shaine's gaze flashed up to Morgan's face.

Morgan swallowed, her expression haunted. She mumbled, "It was a long time ago." She managed a weak smile. "I'm all better now."

Shaine gripped Morgan's hand more tightly. *It may have been a long time ago, but something hurt you so badly you felt like you needed to hurt yourself. Who are you? I want to know.* In the past week, she had seen anger and sorrow in those eyes.

On the job, Morgan was quietly confident, and very competent. Last night, she'd noticed Morgan's happiness and relaxed contentedness. The more pieces she saw, the more she was drawn in. *Like the proverbial moth to the flame.*

She and Morgan remained silent a while longer.

Morgan ran a thumb over a jagged, raised scar across the back of Shaine's hand.

Shaine caught her breath at the light caress. Tingles ran up her arm and down her spine.

"Tell me how you got it?" Morgan asked. "I mean, if you don't mind my asking."

Shaine smiled slowly. *Yeah, that's a good, safe story*, she thought, relieved Morgan wasn't asking about her artificial leg. That was a story she wasn't ready to tell. She smirked. "You wouldn't believe me if I told you," she said.

"Try me."

"Okay." Shaine took a second to collect her thoughts. "After I got out of Earth Guard, I got a job at Mann-Maru working entry-level security at the headquarters compound in New York City."

Morgan gave an impressed whistle. "You worked planet-side?"

Shaine nodded. "Yeah. Anyway, I was on duty at the outer doors of Mann-Maru's corporate headquarters, which is pretty much the most boring job in the galaxy. It's like being a glorified bellboy. I was out there with another guard. It was late afternoon, hot, humid, and miserable. It was all we could do just to stay halfway alert. Suddenly, out of nowhere, this guy races past me full-out and this woman behind him is screaming, 'He stole my purse! He stole my purse!' So I took off after him. After about half a block I managed to grab him by the back of his shirt and took him down. He twisted around under me and swung a knife at me. I kept him from slicing my face, but he got my hand. I smacked his lights out before I even realized I was bleeding." She grinned at Morgan's wide-eyed stare. "Damned serrated edge—there was blood all over the place, but it looked a lot worse than it was. Anyway, I got the nice lady's bag back and I got a date on top of it." She laughed and cocked her head. "So, do you believe me?"

Morgan shook her head, laughing. "I'm not sure if I should or not. You really got a date?"

Shaine held up her hands in mock submission. "Okay, I admit it. I didn't get a date. The lady was old enough to be my grandmother. But the rest of it is true."

Morgan rolled her eyes. "Ha."

Shaine laughed and sipped her beer. She shot Morgan a challenging look. "If I saved you from getting your purse stolen, would you date me?"

"First off, I don't carry a purse," Morgan pointed out dryly before grinning. "Yeah. Yeah, you'd get a date." Her face flushed and she looked down.

Shaine chuckled.

The waiter arrived with their burgers and fries and another round of beer. Conversation came in spurts while she and Morgan ate and kept to mundane topics.

After another round of beer, Morgan leaned back in her chair, turning the heavy glass slowly on the tabletop. "Can I ask a question?"

Shaine wondered where Morgan was headed. "Sure, ask away."

"Did that guy really have a knife when you grabbed me out of the cube?"

Shaine took a sip from her beer. "I saw the metal flash in his hand."

"You were going to keep me from going after him, though, even before that."

Shaine heard the accusation in Morgan's tone and nodded slowly. "Yeah."

"Why? He deserved to be smacked."

"Yeah, he did. But—" Shaine shrugged helplessly. "I don't know." She couldn't explain, not even to herself. She'd jumped in because it felt right. "I didn't think about it, I just did it."

Morgan looked at her doubtfully.

Shaine ducked her head. "I'm sorry."

After a moment, Morgan waved it off. "Hey, don't worry about it. You probably saved me a trip to the infirmary. Thank you."

Shaine managed a sheepish smile. "You'd have been okay. I probably overreacted." *You wouldn't have gotten killed. Hurt, probably, but not killed.* Shaking her head, she changed the subject. "Where'd you learn to slam like that? Pretty damned impressive. Especially in your inebriated state," she teased.

Morgan laughed. "Yeah, yeah, I grew up here and in the Belt, so I spent a lot of time in zero-g. And I played a lot of grav-ball in school."

"You still play." Shaine saw realization dawn.

"That night in the bar," Morgan said with a curious half-smile. "That was you, wasn't it?"

"Yeah."

"You play ball?"

Shaine made a face. "It's been a long time."

Morgan chewed her lip before her words came out in a tumble of rapidfire syllables, ending on an uneasy, questioning look. "Um, well, would you want to? I mean, 'cause of Digg—we could use another guy on the team. You know, if you wanted to just try it out or something."

Play grav-ball with Morgan? Oh, twist my rubber arm. But is she serious, or just being nice? God, I feel like a damned teenager. "Yeah, I'll play, long as you guys don't mind me having to catch up a bit. Sounds like a lot of fun."

Morgan grinned. "Slammin'."

The conversation continued to flow easily, covering sports, music, current events and living on Moon Base. She found more points in common with Morgan than not. She could have sat there half the night, but when Morgan started trying hard not to yawn, she realized that she, too, was exhausted from the week. She offered to walk Morgan home.

They set a leisurely pace through the streets under the Moon Base dome, wandering through the park, taking the long way around. Shaine thought it was a good way to extend the evening, which she'd very much enjoyed. She glanced at the wiry woman beside her.

Morgan had her hands shoved deep into her pants pockets. *She walks like a spacer,* Shaine thought, recognizing the smooth, almost bouncing stride she'd seen used by so many of her buddies in the Guard.

When Morgan's long bangs drifted down over her eyes, she flipped them back with a casual shake of her head. Shaine's fingers flexed. She imagined what it would feel like to run her fingers through Morgan's silky black hair. Without thinking, she draped an arm around Morgan's shoulders.

The dark head snapped up, but after a moment Morgan wrapped her arm loosely around Shaine's waist, leaning into her while they strolled.

Shaine smiled contentedly, comfortable having Morgan close. *I really like this. I really like her. I really like how this feels. It's been a long time.*

They arrived at Morgan's apartment building and stopped at the bottom of the entryway stairs. Shaine slid around to face Morgan, her hands resting on Morgan's shoulders. She found herself searching Morgan's eyes for a reaction. Her pulse pounded in her ears.

The corners of Morgan's mouth lifted into a shy smile.

Shaine said, "I had a good time tonight." Her voice sounded breathless.

"Me too."

I don't want this evening to end. I just want to hold you, to touch you. God, I can't believe I'm thinking—and feeling—like this. Shaine found her voice, hoping she didn't sound as desperate as she suddenly felt. "Can I call you tomorrow?"

"Yeah."

Shaine gently brushed baby-fine bangs back from Morgan's eyes. She heard Morgan's sharp intake of breath. Morgan's lips were soft against hers. Warm, sweet breath puffed over her face as they exchanged tentative kisses and Morgan's arms wound around her waist.

Shaine held her tightly for long minutes, nuzzling her hair.

Morgan rested her head against Shaine's shoulder.

Shaine didn't have words for what she felt, unnerved by the onslaught of raw emotion. But she knew that somehow, holding Morgan Rahn felt right.

CHAPTER TEN

After changing into loose shorts and a sleep shirt, Morgan paced around her apartment in a daze until she finally flopped on the sofa and closed her eyes. She could still imagine the warmth of Shaine's solid body under her hands, taste the softness of her lips.

I am not looking for a girlfriend, she reminded herself. She shook her head and laughed. *Who am I kidding? God, if she doesn't call me, I'll call her.*

Over the course of the evening, she'd found herself drawn further and further in, fascinated by the woman across the table. She had sensed nothing shallow or pretentious about Shaine Wendt. *It's her eyes*, she decided. *I don't know how you could fake that kind of intensity.*

She was relieved to connect with someone who wasn't playing games with her, someone who wasn't going to use her and toss her away. Shaine was different than Gina. Worlds different. *I feel safe with her.* She ran their conversations through her head.

Shaine had alluded to some rough times in Earth Guard. She hadn't said much, but Morgan got the feeling there was a lot of emotion and pain hidden just under the surface. *Like when she showed me the dog tags from her friends. What a heavy burden to bear.*

Morgan chewed her lip. Shaine had been trying to share, letting her know she understood about Digger and her mom. *Damn. So intense.*

Too wired to sleep, Morgan grabbed the comp pad from the end table and stretched out on the sofa. She logged in, thinking some writing or reading might settle her brain.

Charri's avatar popped up on her screen almost immediately. The 3-D image of a pink and magenta-striped jungle cat purred at her. Violet cat eyes blinked, and a deep alto voice growled out of the tiny speaker. "You're up late, Morgan."

Morgan laughed in good-natured consternation and engaged her own avatar as she spoke into the pickup, "Hey, Charri." She knew on her friend's screen, her blue winged dragon spoke in hushed, sibilant tones. "What are you doing lurking around the net?"

The magenta tiger chuckled. "How was dinner?"

Morgan sighed heavily, purposely trying to sound bored. "Come on, it was burgers and beer after work, not freakin' dinner."

"Yeah, yeah. So spill."

Morgan snickered. She enjoyed pulling Charri's chain. "We ate, we talked, she's gonna play on the ball team, and we made out like teenagers in the street."

"What? Oh, my God! Morgan!"

Morgan laughed.

"I am calling you. We need to talk."

Two seconds later the com system pinged. Morgan acknowledged, "Video on, main screen." She laughed at Charri's incredulous expression. "What?" she asked innocently.

"I told you so! Told you she liked you!"

Morgan folded her arms behind her head. "Yeah, whatever, Char."

"How in the hell did you get from 'it's not dinner' to kissing in the street?"

"I don't know. It just happened." Morgan shook her head. "I didn't expect the night to go that way. But Shaine's—" She hesitated, trying to find words. She finally settled on sounding like an idiot. "She's really great."

Charri's eyes narrowed. "Call me overprotective, but you're okay, right?"

Morgan couldn't stop the blush or the grin. "I'm good. I really like her." She shrugged helplessly. "I don't think I can explain it."

For a long moment, Charri studied her face. Finally, she snickered. "One date and you're whipped," she accused.

Morgan sighed. "Yeah, probably."

"I hope this works out, Morgan. I really, really don't want to see you getting destroyed again."

Morgan's smile faltered. "Yeah, I know."

"You're gonna see her tomorrow, right?"

Morgan burst out laughing.

* * *

Shaine hummed contentedly while she tapped her key code into the lock on her apartment door and walked through. She knew she had a stupid grin on her face. She felt like she'd floated the two blocks between Morgan's apartment and her own. It was insane, and she didn't care.

"Lights." As she glanced at the com center to check for messages, the vid-screen blinked with an incoming call. She didn't recognize the calling code. Maybe it was Morgan? She grinned. "Take call," she said to the voice recognition system.

The screen cleared, showing a dark-skinned man with a graying crewcut and cold black eyes.

Shaine blinked, her breath stopping as dread instantly replaced the warm excitement she'd been feeling. There was no good reason for Duncan Rogan, head of Mann-Maru Security, to contact her. Only bad ones. Her stomach clenched. "Rogan." Schooling her expression to remain empty, she stepped in front of the screen, her shoulders automatically straightening.

"Wendt." His voice rumbled in his chest. "I have a job for you."

She took a long breath. "I don't do that anymore. I'm a mechanic, remember?"

His black eyes flashed a warning. "You'll be providing protection without the target's knowledge."

She glared at him. "No."

"I am not asking, Wendt."

Her hands curled into fists at her sides. "There must be somebody besides me who can handle your dirty work for you."

"Not someone who's already in place, and not with your—affinity—for the subject."

"And if I refuse?"

"Believe me, Wendt, this is an offer you just can't refuse." He smiled smugly. "Don't even think you can argue with me."

"Bastard." She closed her eyes. After a moment, she met his expectant gaze. No point arguing a losing battle. He owned her life and they both knew it. "Fine. So tell me what I'm doing."

"I need you to play bodyguard for a few days. Your mark does not know she's in danger, nor should she know you're guarding her. I expect your assignment will be precautionary only, but the situation could escalate."

"Who am I babysitting?" *Probably some freaking high-ranking client of Maruchek's who's shown up unexpectedly. Wonderful.*

Rogan smiled coldly. "You'll be protecting Morgan Rahn."

Shaine blinked again. "Morgan?" Her stomach plummeted. All the warning bells in her head went off at once. "Why?" she demanded.

"You don't need to know why. Just make sure she stays alive, Wendt. She is important. I don't care how you cover it. Just do it. There are security cameras in her building. You'll have access to those feeds. I'm sending the live links now."

"I'm not your fucking security bitch anymore. You've got half a dozen agents you could use for this, Rogan. Use one of them."

"She knows you. There is an established level of trust. I need someone in place when she's working and someone who can keep an eye on her when she's not. You are the obvious choice." He gave her a darkly amused look. "In any case, I imagine you'll enjoy spending more time with Ms. Rahn, yes?"

Shaine felt herself flush. *Fucking bastard.* She forced down her anger. "Are there any other mission parameters I should be aware of? For instance, why is Morgan a target?"

"I told you, that is information you don't need to know."

She walked away to pace, her thoughts in motion. After a few seconds, she turned to the vid-screen. "The incident that took out her crewmate and the guy at the club—are they related?"

Rogan shook his head. "We're working that angle, but I don't think so."

"Great. Who's after her, Rogan?"

He smiled tightly. "Just do the job. I am not going to tell you more over an unsecured line. Keep her alive, Wendt." He killed the connection.

Shaine dropped heavily onto the sofa. "Fuck you, Rogan." Her fists clenched and unclenched. Rogan would never leave her alone, never let her go. She groaned and leaned her head back, closing her eyes. *I'm living a lie.*

She'd talked Rogan into letting her retrain as a maintenance worker. In her mind, she'd walked away from doing undercover security work, walked away from the icy, empty life of a corporate hitman. She thought she'd have her life back. She thought she could be a normal person. But Mann-Maru Security still owned her. She would have no life of her own, not as long as Rogan thought she might be useful. And once she wasn't useful she'd probably just be dead.

The com beeped. She opened her eyes to squint at the screen. An icon flashed in the upper right corner. Data package incoming, probably the links and access codes to the security feeds Rogan promised.

Shaine grabbed the comp pad off the coffee table and tapped a couple of commands to link into her main system feeds. The vid-screen on the wall duplicated itself on the pad. She opened the message icon. The contents were what she expected, a set of links to Morgan's apartment building's cameras.

She opened each link in sequence, her attention split between the pad screen and the main vid-screen in front of her. Each link opened a separate camera feed. The first view showed the stairs going into Morgan's building and a bit of the street out front. The second showed an empty hallway lined with doors. A third window, then a fourth popped up, mostly hidden behind the first two. She tapped them to the front.

Two camera views crossed each other, one from each end of Morgan's studio apartment. A wide-angle shot included the kitchen, looking toward the living room, the door into a bathroom, and the bed built into the back wall. The second camera looked back at the apartment's entrance and the kitchen. Both feeds had icons allowing her to pan left and right, up and down, and zoom. There was an audio feed as well, but she left it off.

Shaine saw Morgan sprawled on her stomach on the overstuffed sofa, propped on her elbows and leaning over a comp pad while she scribbled intently with a glowing lime-green stylus. She wore gray shorts and an oversized shirt. Her feet were bare.

The living room camera caught Morgan from the front. Her eyes remained hidden by her bangs as she looked down, but her hair didn't hide her wide grin. She stopped writing, said something, paused, and replied before going back to her writing.

Talking to someone online, Shaine decided. She almost reached for the zoom icon to see the avatar on Morgan's screen and wondered briefly what Morgan used as a net persona. She shook her head abruptly. *Fuck. I should not be seeing this. This is wrong on so many levels.* But she couldn't tear her eyes away from the woman on the screen.

Her brain frantically worked the puzzle while she watched. Why was Rogan concerned with Morgan Rahn? Something Morgan knew? Something she'd seen? Something to do with the incident that had taken her friend Digger's life? Rogan's interest made no sense. What would a line mechanic know that could possibly be a threat or cause her to be threatened?

Shaine cracked her knuckles one by one. The whole situation sucked. Rogan said Morgan couldn't know she was being stalked or targeted. Which meant she'd have to lie about her intentions. Of course, the truth didn't sound any better. *Gee, can I spend some time with you because I'm supposed to be guarding you? And it's easier to do in person than from my place, where I'm just a voyeur.* She supposed she could come up with a plausible excuse not to meet Morgan, which would eliminate having to say anything at all. *But I really want to see her.*

She played back Rogan's words in her head, trying to come up with any pieces he'd left out. There had to be a connection.

Morgan said her dad worked for Mann-Maru for decades—was considered a "lifer." Maybe that was the tie-in? But she'd gotten the impression Morgan's dad had been a line worker, too, never in the kind of position that could be a threat to anyone.

Shaine scowled. She had an ace up her sleeve—a friend she had avoided since she left her security position. If she wanted answers, she could trust only one person: Kyle Ellerand.

Resigning herself to old patterns, she keyed in an encrypted line and tapped his calling code into her pad.

After a longish pause, her mousy little intel source appeared on-screen, greeting her with a wide smile as he brushed his hair out of his eyes. "Hey, Wendt, long time no see."

She couldn't help smiling back. "Hey, Kyle, how's it hangin'?"

He smirked. "Probably better than yours, if you're actually calling me," he observed.

"What, I can't just call an old friend?"

"Not on an encrypted line out of the blue."

She chuckled. "Yeah, yeah. So what's Rogan got going?"

"Not much that I'm aware of. Nothing anyone is up in arms about, anyway. Just same old, same old. Pirates out in the Belt again. Why? What have you heard?"

"Does the name Morgan Rahn mean anything to you?"

He thought a second, then turned to an off-screen monitor. She heard the clicking of his fingers on a keyboard. "She's part of that crew who lost a guy on Moon Base. Why?"

"Rogan informed me I'm supposed to keep an eye on her. For some reason, she's become a target. He wouldn't say who was after her, or why. I just got assigned to her crew last week. Could be Rogan's intervention, could be coincidence. I need to know what's going on."

Ellerand had been scanning the console to his right while she spoke. Absently, he flipped his hair out of his eyes again. "Hmm… Interesting…there's an exchange between Maruchek and Rogan about the security report on that incident being leaked. Maruchek is furious about names and photos showing up in the report, but that's all there is. No follow-up." He poked around some more. "Nothing else on the subject. No other mention of a Morgan

Rahn, either. If there were any related conversations, they've been cleaned. I'd have to look closer to be sure."

"If they're deleting and cleaning up behind themselves, there's something going on."

"I agree." He reached for a keyboard and started working. Shaine waited, watching his expression shift. After a few minutes, he turned a curious look on her. "Uh, Shaine, does Morgan Rahn look familiar to you?" he asked slowly.

"I've never met her before now, if that's what you mean. Why?"

"I think I've found the problem. Take a look at this." The screen shifted to two photos side by side.

Shaine's heart stopped. "Holy fucking shit," she breathed.

On the left was a forty-year-old press photo of Tarm Maruchek and his wife, now long dead. On the right, Morgan Rahn's corporate ID picture. Morgan could have been Arella Maruchek's twin. Same eyes, same face, same expression. *Damn!* How had she not seen it before? How many times she had seen holos of Maruchek's dead wife in his office, on his desk, on the wall. Was Morgan some long-lost relative? She took a breath, trying to settle her thoughts.

Ellerand's fingers flew over his pad, pulling data. When he looked up, his expression showed a mix of wonder and disbelief. "Okay, I may be jumping to conclusions here, but it all fits. Arella Maruchek was murdered by a sniper twenty-eight years ago. She was pregnant at the time and it was reported both she and the baby were killed. There was a lot of hush-hush around the incident and a closed casket funeral. Never found the sniper."

Shaine stared at him. "Morgan's the baby."

Ellerand nodded. "I'd put money on it. Rogan and Maruchek are either afraid word will get out, or they know it already has."

Fucking hell. It's a sure bet Morgan has no idea. Does she even know she's adopted? "Find out what's going on, Kyle. I've got a bad feeling."

He studied her and finally nodded. "I'll get back to you. Give me a day." He closed the connection.

Shaine sat back on the sofa with a heavy sigh and closed her eyes. She had no doubt Morgan was Tarm Maruchek's daughter. Too many coincidences for it to be anything but true. How did she get involved in this shit? Could she not live a normal life just for a little while? *I kissed Tarm Maruchek's daughter. And I enjoyed every moment of it. And I want to do it again.*

Her stomach clenched. She tasted bile at the back of her throat. *I just cannot get away from these people.* Part of her wanted to lash out and start breaking heads, another part wanted to curl up in a fetal ball and wait until it was over. A third part wanted to grab Morgan and run off with her. She opened her eyes. Her gaze slid automatically to the camera feeds from Morgan's apartment.

Morgan laughed. She set aside the pad and rolled effortlessly off the couch onto her feet. After a brief sojourn to the bathroom, she crossed to the bed and curled up in a colorful quilt, wrapping herself around her pillow. She reached up and tapped a control over her head to kill the lights. Washed in the green of the night vision cameras, Morgan looked like a child with just the top of her dark head and her nose poking out of her warm burrow.

Shaine wanted to reach out to touch Morgan, to hold her, while at the same time sickened that she was even watching. She sighed heavily, knowing she wasn't going to sleep tonight. *You don't know the storm that's coming, Morgan Rahn. And I'm sorry you're going to get caught in the middle of it.*

CHAPTER ELEVEN

Morgan hummed to herself as she threw a change of clothes into her small pack. She dug through a drawer for matching socks, grabbed her workout sneakers from the corner where she'd kicked them and sat down on the edge of the bed to pull them on.

As promised, Shaine had called. They were getting together after she finished her routine at the gym. Initially, Shaine had sounded more reserved than she'd expected, but that didn't last long. They'd made no decisions on what they would do—dinner, maybe a movie at Shaine's place, or wander over to Rose's for a drink.

Morgan didn't care one way or another. She laughed inwardly at the giddy feeling in her stomach. The thought of spending time with Shaine made her smile, and the thought of how it felt to kiss Shaine sent shivers up and down her spine. Yeah, the possibility of a relationship was sudden and unexpected, but good.

She left her apartment, jogging down the emergency stairwell to the lobby and pattering down the half-flight of stairs to the street. She glanced overhead while she strolled down the lane.

Earth shone brightly against a black sky salted with stars, the velvet of space marred only by the dome's scratched and dust-weathered surface.

She sauntered down the street, letting her brain take its own meandering path as her feet headed automatically toward the gym.

Last night, Charri had teased her relentlessly and for once, she hadn't really cared. Typically with the expected teasing, Charri had worked in her fair share of cautionary warnings. "Are you being too trusting? Are you really okay with this? She didn't push herself on you?"

No, yes, and no. Even if I said that about Gina, too. Morgan shuddered. She had to trust that Shaine wasn't Gina. Shaine may have her own issues, but she didn't appear manipulative or controlling.

She still felt sick when she thought about the way Gina had wrapped her in lies, and how she'd actually believed it all. Shaine was ex-EG, a workmate, and she truly believed Shaine was a "what you see is what you get" kind of person. *I can't be that wrong, can I? I'd have learned after Gina, right?*

Besides, how could she be wrong about a woman who kissed her like that? Even at the beginning, Gina had been so much more aggressive and dominating. There'd been no deep emotion in their intimacy. Gina had been all about making Gina feel good, even when trying to convince her she truly cared.

Morgan shook her head. No, she truly didn't believe Shaine would hurt her that way.

She wondered idly if this was the beginning of an actual relationship, a friendship with benefits, or just a friendship. She chewed on the idea a while, studying her feet while she paced easily down the street. What did she want? More than just a friend, certainly. But something serious? She wasn't sure she was ready to take that step. She'd finally gotten her balance back after the whole blowup with Gina and wasn't sure she wanted to jump back into the fire.

She strolled down the familiar street, her hands stuck into the pockets of her shorts. There wasn't much traffic in the residential areas, only the occasional person coming and going. The ever-present background hum of life support rumbled in her ears. She felt the slight movement of flat-tasting recycled air against her skin. Her footsteps crunched lightly on the pavement.

A couple of low-powered hover-bikes cruised past her—one a personal transport, another pulling a small delivery cart painted with the gaudy logo of a grocery outlet. She nodded to a young couple passing in the opposite direction. She was vaguely aware of someone walking behind her, but she didn't turn and look.

At the corner, Morgan took a right. Residential housing units flanked either side of the street. She barely made note of the anonymous, flat-topped, two- and three-story buildings. The gym was on the next block, on the bottom floor of a short strip of connected storefronts.

The growling, high-pitched whine of a motor erupted onto the quiet street, echoing starkly off the buildings. Startled, Morgan looked up. A black hover-car with tinted windows slewed around the corner just ahead, spraying gray duracrete dust as it headed right toward her.

She skipped to the side. "Stupid fucker, slow down!"

The car approached her, engine roaring.

Morgan backpedaled. She sensed a flash of movement to her side. An instant later pain exploded across the backs of her shoulders. She stumbled and fell forward as a heavy, bruising weight dropped onto her back. Pinned facedown on the ground, she gasped for breath.

The hover-car fishtailed sideways and hissed to a stop a couple feet away.

Panicking, she shifted under her attacker's weight, trying to wrench herself free.

A muffled voice snapped, "Just grab her!"

Morgan fought, but the guy on her back had her good and pinned. Something connected across the back of her head, slamming her nose and chin into the pavement. She saw stars and desperately blinked away the pain. A knife appeared at the edge of her vision.

Suddenly, the man holding her jerked violently and cried out.

A sharp jolt of electricity snapped through her, taking her breath away.

He jerked again with a choked scream and collapsed forward, the knife in his hand slicing down across her cheek as his dead weight slumped across her back.

The hover-car took off with a roar, spitting dust and gravel.

Heart pounding, tasting blood and grit, Morgan twisted free of her attacker's body.

"Morgan!"

Her head snapped up. She saw Shaine running toward her with a gun in one hand.

Shaine dropped to her knees at her side. The man lying beside her groaned and started to get up. Shaine's fist connected with his face. He crumpled and went limp.

Morgan raised her hand to her cheek. Her fingertips came away coated with blood. Her breath came in panting gulps. She managed to get to a half-seated, half-lying position. More blood dripped down her chin. *Aw, fuck*, she thought, and looked up. "Shaine?"

Shaine shoved the gun into her waistband and pulled off her sweatshirt. She pressed the garment to the bleeding gash on Morgan's face. A sharp gaze swept the street before focusing on her. "We gotta get out of here. Think you can walk?"

Morgan nodded jerkily. "Yeah." She looked at the man lying beside her. "What about—"

Shaine took Morgan's hand and put it firmly against the sweatshirt pressed to her cheek. "Zap charge," she said shortly. "He'll live. Can you hold this?"

Shaine didn't wait for a response. Easing to her feet, she helped Morgan stand.

Morgan swayed. Shaine's arm slid firmly around her waist. She was aware of Shaine's concerned attention, and she nodded when she'd gained her footing.

Shaine grabbed the gym bag she'd dropped and shouldered it. Keeping a supporting arm around her waist, Shaine led her away from the scene. "We'll go to my place. It's closer."

Morgan didn't argue, concentrating instead on putting one foot in front of the other. Still in shock, she tried to process that someone had just tried to—what? Kidnap her? Kill her?

By the time she and Shaine reached the building, blood had seeped through the sweatshirt's thick fabric. They took an elevator to the second floor. Shaine's door was the first one in the hallway. She guided her into the tiny kitchen area.

Morgan felt her knees collapse. She more or less fell onto a chair at a green plastic table.

"Whoa. Hang on there, Morgan."

Gentle hands on her shoulders steadied her and leaned her against the chair's back.

"Stay here a second. I'm going to get the med kit."

Morgan nodded. *Like I'm in any shape to be going anywhere.* Sticky wetness dripped slowly down the back of her hand and wrist. Her arm shook with fatigue from holding the impromptu compress against the wound, but she knew if she took it away, there would be a mess. At least her nose wasn't bleeding anymore, but her chin stung where she'd scraped it on the pavement. She figured that wound was probably bleeding too.

She closed her eyes, forcing herself to breathe deeply and slowly, taking the time to assess other hurts. With her free hand, she gingerly touched the goose egg forming on the back of her head. Her shoulders ached—an insistent throbbing just above her shoulder blades where she'd intitially been hit. She let her hand drop back to her lap. Exhaustion took over as the adrenaline faded.

"Morgan?"

She jerked alert, wincing with the movement and blinking hard to focus.

Shaine grabbed the other chair, pulling it around and perching on the edge of the seat, her knees touching Morgan's. She opened a substantial looking first-aid kit. Sitting back, she hesitated, studying her face.

Her vision tunneling, Morgan lost herself in the intense green gaze.

After a beat, Shaine gently removed Morgan's fingers from the cloth compress. "I have it," she said softly. She eased the cloth from the wound and assessed the cut. "Still bleeding a little," she murmured. "Could probably use a stitch or two. Good scrape on your chin, too." She paused. "It might scar."

Morgan shrugged. *What was another scar?*

Shaine cleaned, taped and sealed the gash and the scraped skin on her chin.

The antiseptic spray stung. Morgan caught her breath at the shock.

Shaine murmured an apology. Deft fingers dabbed away the extra liquid and sprayed sealant over the wounds before taping gauze over the whole thing. She used some dampened pads to wipe the blood from around Morgan's nose, gently feeling for a break. "Think it's okay. Stopped bleeding, at least. A little swollen." She sat back. "Better?"

Morgan tentatively touched the bandage on her cheek. "Yeah. I think so." She moved her jaw and winced.

Shaine smoothed the bangs back from her eyes.

She swallowed. Her eyes fluttered shut at the warmth of Shaine's touch.

Shaine stood. "Um, I should find you a clean shirt or something and you can wash up."

Morgan looked down. Blood splattered the front of her shirt, stained her arms and the backs of her hands.

"Come on, I'll grab you a washcloth and towel." Shaine helped Morgan to her feet and guided her toward the bathroom. Shaine paused just outside the door to grab a towel and washcloth out of the linen closet and set them on the edge of the sink. "Soap's there—anything else you need, just let me know."

Morgan took a breath. "Okay. Thanks."

Shaine nodded and closed the bathroom door.

Morgan stood in front of the small sink. The fluorescent light over the mirror glared at her. She turned on the tap, letting the water run over her fingers. Pink rivulets ran down the drain. On autopilot, she washed her hands and forearms and eased the bloodstained shirt over her head, balling up the thin fabric and dropping it on the floor at her feet.

The motions made her head spin. She stood for a few moments, hanging on to the edge of the cool metal basin, letting the dizziness and nausea pass, waiting for the pounding in her head to subside. Slowly, she washed the rest of the blood from her face and arms, careful to avoid Shaine's handiwork, wincing when she got too close to her aching and bruised nose. *You look like Frankenstein's monster.* She twisted to study the line of bruises forming across her upper back. Her attacker must have hit her with a piece of pipe or a crowbar or something. The bruises hurt like a bitch, but at least they weren't bleeding.

As she closed the tap, she heard a soft knock on the door and Shaine's disembodied voice. "Hey, I think this should fit." The door eased open. Shaine held out a dark blue tunic. Her gaze tracked across Morgan's bared back, taking in the red and purple mottled skin. Their eyes met in the mirror. Shaine swallowed. A quick series of emotions flickered across her face and her voice came out in a cracked whisper. "You—um—need any help?"

Morgan shook her head slowly. "No, I'm okay." She took the shirt from Shaine. Their fingers touched briefly and lingered a second before Shaine nodded and backed out of the bathroom, pulling the door shut behind her.

Morgan glanced at her reflection in the mirror. *I'm in shock.* Her gray eyes seemed too wide, her skin too pale. She looked away and pulled Shaine's tunic carefully over her head. The long-sleeved shirt was roomy, soft and comfortable. Retrieving her bloodied clothes from the floor, she let herself out of the bathroom.

Shaine puttered around in the kitchen, packing things back into the med kit. She looked up when Morgan entered. "Feeling better?" she asked.

"I think so."

"Here, I can take that." Shaine stepped across the room to take the shirt from her hands, hesitated an instant, and gently wrapped her in an embrace.

Morgan sighed. She leaned into Shaine, resting her head on Shaine's chest. She didn't understand what was happening, and for just a moment neither did she care. Warm, strong fingers combed gently through her hair. She clung to the strength of Shaine's muscular form against hers.

Shaine's voice rumbled softly in her ear. "You sure you're okay?"

Morgan took a long, steadying breath. "Yeah. Yeah, I'll be okay." She cocked her head to give Shaine a questioning look when a thought occurred to her. "Should it worry me this is the second time in three days you've saved my ass from guys with knives?"

Shaine's breath caught. A cold, blank expression slid over her face. After a beat she muttered, "Yes. It probably should." She turned abruptly and crossed the kitchen to put the bloodied clothing into the compact washing unit, slapping buttons to kick off the cycle.

Surprised and confused by Shaine's sudden change of mood, Morgan watched the woman's brusque motions and the stiff set to her shoulders. A vaguely sick wave pulled at her stomach. She said slowly, "I guess maybe I should call Moon Base Security to report the attack."

Shaine's head snapped around. "No!"

Morgan blinked.

Shaine dropped her gaze, took a long breath, and ran her hands through her hair. "No," she repeated quietly. "There won't be anything for them to see, anyway. Just—" She stopped, sighed, and shoved her hands in her pants pockets. "Aw, fuck."

"Shaine, what's going on?" Morgan asked warily. The ache in her stomach ratcheted up a notch.

Shaine regarded her bleakly. "Welcome to my fucking nightmare," she said. "Look, this is crazy, but your life is in danger."

"What?"

Shaine motioned tiredly toward the tiny living room. "Let's sit down."

"I don't think so."

Shaine sighed and ran her hands through her hair again. "The head of Mann-Maru Security called me when I got home last night. He used to be my boss. He ordered me to keep an eye on you and keep you alive. He didn't tell me why."

Morgan's pulse started pounding in her ears. "I thought you quit Security."

Shaine sounded defensive and angry. "I did quit. I didn't ask for this assignment and I don't have any choice. You don't turn down Tarm Maruchek's right-hand man when he tells you to do something, even when it's no longer in your job description."

Morgan said nothing for a long time, trying to decide if she should believe Shaine. She tasted bile. Her head throbbed and her knees felt weak. She backed up until she leaned against the bathroom doorframe, putting a distance between them. *This is insane. My life is in danger? What the fuck. She's no different than Gina, after all. I do not fucking need this.*

"Morgan."

She looked at Shaine from across the room and saw tired resignation, frustration, regret.

Shaine said quietly, "Please, just wait before you leave, okay? Let me call Rogan. I'm not making this shit up."

Rogan? That was the name of the corporate guy who'd interrogated her after Digger's death. Realizing Shaine waited silently for a response, Morgan nodded reluctantly.

Shaine crossed the room to the keypad on her desk. She tapped in a calling code, which scrolled across the main vid-screen.

After a few moments, the screen cleared, and a tall black man with a graying crewcut appeared on the screen. Piercing black eyes took in the scene—Shaine standing in front of the camera and Morgan in the background with a bandage across her cheek.

Rogan raised an eyebrow at Shaine, his expression stony. "That didn't take long," he commented. He nodded toward Morgan. "So much for secrecy?"

Shaine's lips thinned. "Secrecy ends when the shit starts hitting the fan. Two guys. One on foot, one in a hover-car. I zapped the guy on foot. The other one got away. I need to get Morgan to a safe zone."

Rogan looked past Shaine to focus on Morgan. "You're all right, Ms. Rahn?" he asked.

Morgan gave him a wary look. "I'm okay," she said. She touched the bandage on her cheek, her gaze shifting from the screen to Shaine and back to Rogan. "I want to know what's going on."

Rogan nodded. "Yes. You do need to know. But it is not my place to tell you." He returned his focus to Shaine. "You know Johann Kries?"

Shaine nodded.

"Good. Expect him within the hour. Mr. Maruchek will want to see both of you."

Morgan stepped forward. "Wait a minute," she interrupted. "I'm not going anywhere with anyone. Not until I know why."

Rogan smiled, not quite pulling off the false expression of concern. "Ms. Rahn, I realize this must be disturbing to you, but please believe we have your best interests in mind. Mr. Maruchek does not want any harm to come to you. Ms. Wendt will see that it doesn't. There is more happening than I can discuss at this time." Another flash of a smile lasting only an instant before he ordered Shaine, "Wendt, keep her safe. Your life depends on it." He cut the transmission, leaving a blank screen.

Morgan felt as though the rug had been pulled out from under her.

Shaine glanced down and checked her chron. She looked at Morgan. "If there's anything you need from your place, we should get it now," she said shortly.

"What the fuck, Shaine?" Tension and fear boiled over into anger. "Have you been following me around since you signed on to my crew? Was dinner last night just a convenient way to keep track of me?"

Shaine's expression turned hard, her voice cold. "I told you. He called me when I got home. That's when I knew."

"Yeah, and you did such a phenomenal job protecting me," Morgan snapped.

"You're fucking standing there, aren't you?"

"Fuck you." Morgan spun toward the door, intending to walk out. A long arm snaked out as she brushed past Shaine. A hand closed around her bicep, stopping her. She glared into flashing green eyes. "Let me go."

After a beat, Shaine dropped her gaze. The broad shoulders fell, but she didn't release her hold. "I can't," she said quietly.

Morgan jerked her arm free, wincing when the motion pulled the bruised muscles across her upper back. She glared at Shaine, expecting anger in return, but the woman's expression only showed regret, resignation and hurt.

Shaine whispered, "I did not lie to you."

Morgan closed her eyes. She wanted to believe those words. She truly did.

"I swear to you, Morgan. Please."

Morgan reacted to the desperate tone and swallowed hard. She felt her anger seep away.

Shaine's arms slid around her, gently pulling her close.

She nodded into Shaine's shoulder, her arms wrapping tightly around Shaine's waist. *Damn, don't let me be wrong about this.*

CHAPTER TWELVE

As expected, Rogan's agent buzzed Shaine's apartment almost exactly an hour later. Morgan was impressed by the promptness. She watched silently as Shaine went to the door, tapping the intercom when she reached it. "Yeah?"

"Kries."

Shaine palmed the lock and moved to the side of the door. She held a small laser pistol drawn and ready.

A compact, muscular man walked into the room. Though Shaine loomed over him by at least a head, Johann Kries seemed to take up at least as much space as her. He scanned the room, stopping briefly on Morgan before returning to Shaine. A slight smile pulled up the edges of his wide mouth. "Wendt. Long time," he said. His voice growled deeply in his chest. "Didn't know Rogan still had you on staff."

Shaine scowled. She shoved her gun into a holster at the small of her back. "He doesn't. I got dragged into this assignment."

Kries snorted. "Kicking and screaming, huh?" He shot her a grin. "Rogan said you're headed to Earth. Shuttle's on standby, so we need to go."

Morgan stood up from the sofa, shouldering her duffel bag. Shaine motioned her to follow Kries while she brought up the rear, pausing to lock the door behind them.

He hustled them out to a sleek, silver hover-car with tinted windows.

Shaine opened the back door for Morgan, then folded into the cramped seat beside her.

Morgan sank into the seat as Kries stomped on the accelerator and guided the hover-car through the Moon Base streets, out the primary air locks, and across the Moon's gray surface to the public spaceport ten kilometers away.

Morgan watched out the windows as the car quickly ate up the distance. The spaceport was perhaps a third the size of the main Moon Base dome. Kries piloted through the public air lock opening into a circular central plaza. Around the circumference of the dome, several shuttle companies had their own sealed passenger terminals accessible through secondary air locks. The larger passenger shuttles were docked on the dome's exterior, connected by umbilical walkways to the terminal.

The hover-car pulled up beside an air lock opening to a private docking space with the Mann-Maru corporate logo painted on the door. Kries got out, tapped a code into the sealed entrance and stood for a retinal scan. After a moment, the hatch slid open. He motioned for Shaine and Morgan to get out of the hover-car and follow him into the docking bay.

A midsized shuttle waited at the center of the sealed bay. A boarding ramp extended down from an open hatch amidships.

Kries said, "Go in and get settled." He pulled a communicator from his pocket. "Captain, your passengers are here." He nodded at Shaine. "Safe flight, ladies. Good luck." He turned on his heel and let himself out of the private terminal, sealing the hatch behind him.

Morgan let out an airy whistle as she took in the details of the mirror finished silver and white detailing, the pristine condition of the hull. "Jesus. Nothing like overkill." Though the vessel looked similar to the early Earth-orbit shuttles circa 2000, this ship had more elegant lines. The short wings were sharper, flatter and more swept back than the originals. The cockpit had a larger front viewport.

Shaine shrugged. "Yeah. C'mon."

Morgan let Shaine lead the way up the boarding ramp and into the passenger compartment. The interior was finished in rich dark wood, the floors covered in thick, dark brown carpeting. No portholes, but an oversized vid-screen covered most of the far wall, showing a live exterior view. Oversized leather recliners shared space with small cocktail tables. Plush sofas lined the outside walls. She followed Shaine toward a pair of recliners placed on either side of a cocktail table at the rear of the cabin.

Shaine stowed their bags in a wide storage locker built into the wall while Morgan settled into one of the chairs. She leaned her head back against the soft leather and closed her eyes, letting a slow wave of exhaustion roll over her. It had definitely become a long damned day.

She heard Shaine drop into the seat beside her and opened her eyes to see the woman reach to her right and pull out the safety harness hidden in the side of the chair. The light webbing unrolled across her upper body and clipped at the top and bottom to inset hooks on the opposite side.

Morgan sighed. *Nice. Like I would ever have thought to look for crash webbing in a lounge chair.* After a moment, she located her restraints and pulled the safety harness into place. She wondered how many times Shaine had been in shuttles like this one. She seemed so comfortable, as though she belonged here.

Morgan ran what she knew about Shaine's past through her mind and realized it wasn't much. Rogan, the head of Mann-Maru corporate security, had been Shaine's boss, which suggested Shaine had held a powerful position, especially given the way the two interacted. It certainly pointed to a higher rank than she'd suggested in the story about the purse snatcher.

Rogan's threat to Shaine hadn't gone unnoticed either. Morgan questioned Shaine's role in Mann-Maru's Security Department. She got the distinct sense that Shaine's involvement hadn't been on the periphery. If Shaine had gone that high up the corporate security ladder, what did it say about the woman? A vague shudder slid down her spine.

Morgan didn't trust corporate bureaucracy. It seemed to her the bottom line always fell to the profit margin and to hell with the workers. The politics was crap, always had been, and probably always would be. But a person had to make a living, right? And she, like her dad before her, would spend her life more or less owned by Mann-Maru. Of all the mega-corporations, Mann-Maru was probably the best of the bunch, she thought. Certainly, they were the biggest. They paid the highest wages. On Moon Base, Mann-Maru was almost the only option, anyway, since they owned and ran most of the primary facilities and operations.

The com system beeped for attention. The pilot's cultured voice came over the speakers. "We have launch clearance and will be taking off momentarily. Please strap into your seats and prepare for departure. I will let you know when it's safe to remove your restraints. Thank you."

Shaine shifted and leaned back into the soft leather seat. Morgan wished she felt as comfortable as her counterpart in the extravagant surroundings.

The hum of the engines shifted to a growl.

Morgan looked past Shaine to the vid-screen on the starboard wall. The outside view showed the external bay door rolling open. The shuttle taxied slowly out of the sealed docking area, the sun painting its black shadow onto the flat gray plain. Beyond the runway, dark gray peaks of a distant mountain range created a jagged horizon against the velvet blackness of space.

The flooring vibrated more strongly as the engines revved. *I'm going to Earth*, Morgan thought, slightly disbelieving. She'd only been there twice before in her life. Given the situation, she wasn't sure if she should be excited, scared, or angry. In the last three hours she'd been attacked and injured, learned someone was trying to kill her, been told that for some reason the CEO of Mann-Maru cared about her safety, and discovered the woman she was beginning to really like wasn't quite who or what she seemed.

What have I gotten myself into, or caught up in? Will I get answers when we get to Earth? The ship vibrated roughly. Morgan closed her eyes as the shuttle shot away from the ground. G-forces pinned her into the cushions for several seconds before the engines settled into a steady hum under her feet. She opened her eyes.

A few minutes later, the pilot announced they could move freely around the cabin.

Morgan released the safety harness, but remained seated.

Shaine got up. She crossed to the small bar against the wall and ducked behind it, coming up a few seconds later holding two bottles of juice. "Want one?" she asked. "There are sandwiches in the cooler, too."

Morgan asked, "Are you supposed to be back there?"

Shaine grinned. "Hey, if Rogan and Maruchek are going to drag my ass around the system without asking, then I'm gonna have lunch on them. Besides, I'm hungry." She grabbed two wrapped sandwiches, poked around until she'd found a plate, knife and fork, and brought her stash back to the table between the two lounge chairs. Popping the tops of the juice bottles, she handed one to Morgan. She set one sandwich on the plate with the silverware, and started unwrapping the other sandwich.

Morgan studied the sandwich she'd been given. She looked across the table at Shaine. "Why would someone be trying to kill me? And why would your old boss or the CEO of Mann-Maru give a flying fuck about it?"

Shaine chewed a bite of her sandwich. She spoke slowly without looking up. "I'm not sure. Rogan wouldn't tell me anything."

Morgan regarded Shaine a long moment, trying to read the suddenly expressionless face. *If you can't look at me, you're lying.* "Don't bullshit me."

Shaine's gaze snapped up and met Morgan's before she looked away again. "I'm not lying. Rogan's being a bastard and not talking to me. I've got a guess about what might be going on, but I don't want to say anything until I get some answers first."

Morgan stared at Shaine for another couple of seconds. *No, you're a lot more certain than you're admitting. I'm not stupid.* Shaine had seemed so open last night, so readable, her intentions pretty much right out there, her emotions and vulnerabilities so close to the surface. Now she had closed down, obviously hiding her thoughts.

Morgan sighed and sipped the juice. Finally setting down the bottle, she unwrapped her sandwich. How in the hell did she manage to be so absolutely inept at reading the women in her life? She attempted to open her mouth wide enough to take a bite. Pain seared through her cheek and jaw. Making an annoyed hiss, she ripped off a small piece of bread with her fingers and chewed gingerly on it.

Shaine said, "That's why I brought you the silverware."

Morgan smiled sheepishly. "Right."

She remained silent awhile, working on her juice and sandwich.

Shaine finished first and leaned back in her chair with a sigh. She stretched her arms over her head and groaned when she let her long limbs flop down.

Morgan watched silently, appreciating the view despite the fact her head still spun from the rapid pace of events. On top of everything else, she still ached from Digger's death. Each day at work had gotten easier without him. By the end of the week, she'd managed to pull on the black striped vac suit without wondering if her power pack might blow up in her face. She'd even almost stopped thinking about how Digger would have done something, what he would have said, or what he would have thought. And each day, Shaine had been there, not trying to fill Digger's shoes, not doing anything but her job. She was a solid, quiet presence lending her support to the crew.

Morgan knew she hadn't wanted to like Shaine. The first couple days, she'd resented Shaine for taking Digger's place. Now she wasn't sure what she felt. *Who are you, really? And how much are you hiding?* Last night, she'd thought she was getting a sense of Shaine. Then again, how much could she read into an evening or a kiss?

At dinner, Shaine had said she didn't want to work security anymore. Morgan wanted to believe her, but doubt ate at her. Too many unanswered questions floated around her mind. Rogan told them she was in danger. But from whom? And why? *I'm a damned mechanic. I don't know anyone important.* She wasn't a troublemaker. Fights in the bar or during grav-ball games didn't count. She'd never even been arrested. Well, okay, not since she was a teenager. What would anyone want from her? And why would Rogan keep it hushed up?

The thought of Rogan raised the hairs on the back of her neck. She sensed something dangerous about the man. She didn't trust him and she didn't like him. Not only that, the antagonism between him and Shaine had been obvious.

Damn, it, why won't Shaine tell me what she's thinking? Shaine had as much as said she had suspicions. It pissed her off that Shaine wouldn't share. She found it difficult to believe Shaine acted completely in the dark. Did this threat have something to do with Digger's death? She wasn't a suspect. Rogan had told her so in the interrogation room. She shivered. Was Rogan lying? Could he possibly believe she'd been somehow involved? Or had she actually been the target of a less-than-random terrorist act?

Morgan glanced over to where Shaine leaned back in her chair staring at the ceiling, her expression far away, gaze focused inward. She had so many questions. If she asked, would she get a response? If she got a response, would it be one she wanted to hear? She scowled, realizing there was really only one way to find out. She wrapped her courage around herself and asked into the silence, "So when you used to work for Rogan, what did you do? How did you end up working for him?"

Shaine sighed and closed her eyes. "It's a long story, starting back when I was in Earth Guard."

"We've got time," Morgan offered.

Shaine took a long breath. She didn't open her eyes. Her words came out slowly, as though she were telling someone else's story. "About a year into my stint in Earth Guard I got assigned to a unit doing patrols out in the Belt. That's where I ran into Rogan the first time." She paused and opened her eyes to glance at Morgan, who nodded for her to go on. She closed her eyes again. "Remember when there was all that pirate activity out in the Belt maybe ten, twelve years ago?"

Morgan said quietly, "My mother was killed in one of the early raids."

Shaine swallowed visibly. "God. I'm sorry," she whispered.

"Thank you. Go on, though."

"My ship was using Mann-Maru's primary mining facility as a base of operations, since that was easier than going back and forth from the Moon Base Guard Station. Rogan was Maruchek's head of Security even back then. He and my CO were running the whole anti-pirate operation. I was a squad leader. Most of the time it was just routine patrols.

"On one mission, though, we were down deep in a pirate holding in an abandoned mining facility, setting charges so when they blew, the whole thing would just collapse in on itself. Because of the high iron content of the rock, we were out of radio contact with our base ship, so we didn't know the pirates were incoming. It was a bad fight. I made it out with one of my guys, but that was it. We lost four men.

"When we got to the surface, the main facility was compromised—no air—and we figured we were pretty well screwed. We only had about an hour of air left in our tanks. We called for an emergency pick up and hoped for a lot of luck. By the time the EG responders reached us, we were half-conscious and sucking backwash. We detonated the charges as we left.

"Anyway, Rogan noticed me when he and my CO debriefed us. I got a rank promotion for my so-called 'bravery' and started working a lot more closely with him and my CO. Not long after that I entered Special Ops training. Was a commando for six years. When I got out of the Guard, I had to find a job, and there were a lot of security positions open with Mann-Maru. It was familiar work, so I applied. Didn't take long for Rogan to recognize me. I ended up working with his covert corporate security group."

Morgan asked, "What's covert security?"

Shaine mulled over her question before she replied. "Spying on the competition, spying on employees suspected of passing information to the competition, making sure the information was either recovered or destroyed, ensuring no further information changed hands."

Morgan processed what she'd been told. It was no real secret that big corporations like Mann-Maru were practically laws unto themselves. There were regulations governing corporate power, but the fact that they operated outside the law was simply a given. Especially out in the Belt. Earth Guard patrolled there, but Earth Guard wasn't a police force. Security in the Belt was primarily up to the corporations mining there. Because of that, most corporations ran their security like private militias. Mann-Maru wasn't as bad as some. But she had no illusions about the kind of work Shaine had probably been involved in.

She got the feeling Shaine wasn't going to expand on her rather limited summary, so she jumped to the next question. "How'd you end up being a mechanic, then?"

Shaine rubbed her hands over her face. "I tried to quit Security. Thing is, I know too much and Rogan sees me as a liability. I think he would have just killed me, but he probably figured he'd be able to use me at some point." A bitter smile twisted her lips. "Why throw away a valuable asset, you know?" She shrugged at Morgan's widened eyes. "Anyway, we settled on a compromise. I got training to be a mechanic, and he gets to keep me under his thumb and make sure I don't stab him in the back."

"But you wanted out."

"Yeah. I couldn't do it anymore." Shaine hesitated. Morgan thought she was going to say more. The woman seemed lost in thought before she shook her head and continued in a matter-of-fact tone. "I've been a mechanic for about three years, mostly out in the Belt. I got transferred to Moon Base about a month ago." She shrugged. "And that's about it. Life was beginning to feel something like normal. I ended up on your crew. And then I got a call from Rogan last night, telling me to keep you alive. And here we are."

Morgan sat silently a few moments. She watched Shaine stare at the ceiling, furrows across her brow, clearly caught in something dark and uncomfortable, frustration and resignation slipping across her face. She asked, "He really just called you last night?"

Shaine turned her head, focusing clouded green eyes on her. A hint of hurt appeared in her expression. "I walked in the door and the com buzzed," she replied tiredly. "And no, my asking you to dinner had nothing to do with any of this mess. That was just me. No ulterior motives. Just me. And you." She kept their gazes locked together.

Morgan smiled. "I'm glad."

Shaine returned the smile. "Me too." She got to her feet and stretched before walking toward the oversized sofa under the vidscreen. "Come sit with me. Might as well be comfortable, huh?"

Morgan shrugged. "Sure."

Shaine settled into the corner of the sofa. With a hopeful expression, she patted her lap.

Morgan pushed to her feet and crossed to take the offered hand.

Shaine grinned and guided her down. "C'mere."

Morgan settled sideways in Shaine's lap.

Shaine wrapped an arm around Morgan's shoulders, cradling her. She gave her a squeeze. "Comfy?"

"Yeah." Sighing, Morgan relaxed into the warmth of Shaine's embrace. A voice in the back of her head warned her off and she purposefully ignored it. It felt good to have Shaine's arms around her, felt to have someone to hold onto. Despite the niggling doubts, she trusted Shaine. She didn't understand why, but she was too tired to question her instincts.

She closed her eyes against the dull pounding in her head. Her jaw and upper back still throbbed, reminding her of the close call she'd had only hours ago. She shivered. It was one thing to have someone come after her in a bar fight or on the grav-ball court, but entirely different when she never even saw it coming, and even more disconcerting because she could see no apparent reason for the attack. What did they want from her? None of it made any sense. She sighed.

Shaine murmured, "You okay?"

"I don't like not knowing what's happening."

Shaine hugged her closer and nuzzled her hair. "I wish I knew more, too."

Morgan tipped up her head. "Seriously, Shaine, is there anything at all you can tell me? I know you have at least a hunch."

"But that's all it is. A hunch. I don't want to start making stuff up when I could be way far off."

"And I don't want to go into this situation completely clueless."

Shaine was silent for several moments. Finally, she said slowly, "You bear a striking resemblance to someone in Maruchek's family. That could be why you've been targeted."

"Mistaken identity?"

"Possibly. I honestly don't know yet."

Morgan nodded slowly and returned her head to Shaine's shoulder. It wasn't exactly an answer, but it was something. For the moment, she had to be satisfied.

Shaine hugged her closer again. "It'll be okay, Morgan."

Morgan wasn't sure she believed the sentiment, but she didn't have the energy to argue. Shaine's arm was a comforting weight around her shoulders, Shaine's breath warm against her hair. She closed her eyes and turned her face into the soft fabric of Shaine's tunic, letting exhaustion overtake her, just for a while.

CHAPTER THIRTEEN

The landing on Earth was quick and mostly smooth. The shuttle hit the ground with a roar and a bit of a bounce before it taxied to a halt and the pilot announced passengers were allowed to remove their crash webbing.

Rubbing the sleep out of her eyes, Morgan yawned and stretched as Shaine crossed the cabin and keyed open the pressure hatch.

Shaine looked over her shoulder. "You ready?" she asked.

Morgan shrugged. What choice did she have?

Shaine gave her an encouraging grin and stepped out onto the lowered boarding ramp.

Morgan followed. The acrid engine fumes washed over her. She stepped into nearly blinding sunlight and stopped, blinking and squinting into the glare.

Thick summer heat closed around her. Gasping, she fought down panic. Her brain insisted she was fine even as she fought to suck in the heavy, exhaust-tainted atmosphere. *I'm drowning!* There was so much air and it was so rich, so unlike the scrubbed air on Moon Base. She stood at the top of the ramp clutching the hatch frame, forcing air through her lungs. She relaxed when she started to catch her breath. Her eyes remained squinted nearly closed against the glare, but she smiled at the warmth of real sunlight on her face. Slowly, she opened her eyes. Shaine stood a couple steps below her, grinning and holding out a hand she automatically reached out to clasp.

The metal just to her right hissed loudly. Burning pain seared across her bicep.

Shaine barked, "Down!" and dove at her, tackling her back into the cabin.

Laser blasts peppered the hull around the hatch. She watched a handful spray overhead and burn holes into the carpeting.

"Get back!" Shaine pushed her further into the compartment before swinging around on a knee and firing a small laser pistol through the entryway.

Morgan lay on her back, blinking at the ceiling. Her arm stung. She turned her head to see the charred fabric of her shirt. Her gaze tracked to the door. Shaine alternately ducked behind the hatch and then forward, returning shots. She started to sit up.

Shaine caught the motion peripherally and snapped, "Stay the fuck down!"

Morgan obeyed without question, startled at the fierceness of the order. Her heart pounded against her ribs.

After a few seconds silence dropped around them. Shaine remained kneeling at the side of the hatch, her body completely still, waiting. Seconds passed. A minute. Finally a shout came from outside. "Wendt, stand down! You're clear!"

Another moment and Shaine's shoulders relaxed a fraction. Slowly, she stood.

Morgan started to do the same, but stopped when Shaine held a hand flat and shook her head sharply.

Shaine eased around the corner, still wary. Taking a look outside, she completely relaxed. She turned back toward Morgan, shoving the pistol into a holster at the small of her back. Her expression shifted in an instant from cold business to worried concern. "Are you okay?"

Morgan eased to a sitting position and touched the throbbing burn on her upper arm. "I think—"

"Fuck." Shaine dropped into a crouch beside her, gently easing the burnt fabric from the wound. "This is my fault," she growled angrily. "Should have seen it coming. Fuck."

Morgan frowned. "It's not bad," she murmured. "You couldn't have known."

Shaine's green eyes flared. "I should have." She stood and helped Morgan to her feet, keeping a supportive arm wrapped firmly around her waist.

Rogan appeared at the hatch, a dark, menacing shadow framed in sunlight.

Shaine sent him a furious glare. "Nice reception," she snapped. "Ever fucking hear of clearing the area?"

"The problem has been eliminated," he returned blandly. "Come. Mr. Maruchek is anxious to speak to Ms. Rahn."

Morgan held her injured arm against her chest, leaning into the arc of Shaine's arm. She turned an angry frown on Rogan. "And I'm anxious to know why I'm getting attacked and shot at," she said.

Shaine added, "We need to see a medic."

Rogan's gaze rolled past Shaine, then up and down Morgan. He nodded curtly. "Of course. Come." He turned on his heel and headed down the ramp.

Shaine sighed, shook her head, and gave Morgan a gentle squeeze as they stepped onto the boarding ramp and walked down to the steaming duracrete surface.

A nondescript hover-car waited for them several meters away. Rogan ushered her and Shaine into the car, slammed the door shut with a bit more force than necessary, and got into the front passenger seat. The car accelerated with a lurch, pushing the occupants into the plush leather seats as it powered forward to take the sky lanes into the city.

Morgan closed her eyes against the pain radiating from the burn on her upper arm. At least it wasn't bleeding, but it stung like hell.

Shaine patted her leg. "Welcome to Earth."

Morgan shot her a dark look. "Thrilled to be here."

A short while later, Morgan marched down the hallway beside Shaine while they followed Duncan Rogan toward Tarm

Maruchek's personal office suite. The group had stopped in the small corporate infirmary and she now sported a bandage over the stinging laser burn on her arm, and a fresh coat of Nu-Skin over the cut across her left cheek. She was beginning to feel like a pincushion. Or a punching bag.

On the other hand, the various pains served to take her mind off the fact that she was about to be thrust into the presence of one of the most powerful men in the System who, for some bizarre reason, had an interest in her. Shaine had said she looked like someone in Tarm Maruchek's family, but she didn't see why that would make her particularly interesting. She ran into people every day who reminded her of someone else. There had to be some kind of mistake. This was Tarm Maruchek. Not Joe-on-the-Street. Was there some kind of ulterior motive?

Morgan thought of the less than truthful statements Tarm Maruchek had made to the media about Digger's death, claiming the suit had been defective and they were working with the manufacturer. *I don't know what you want from me, but I know I'm not going to be bought by your face-saving lies. Digger deserves better than that.* Of course, if she actually came up with the guts to defy Maruchek, it would probably just get her killed more quickly. She was glad of Shaine's confident presence at her side. At least Shaine didn't seem intimidated by these men.

The door to Maruchek's corporate office opened when she, Shaine, and Rogan approached. Rogan halted and waved them forward.

Morgan walked in a half step behind Shaine and stopped at her side. She got an immediate impression of expensive functionality from the room—dark wood, plush carpeting, leather and chrome.

Tarm Maruchek stood in front of a monstrous mahogany desk in the back of the room. She felt the man's gaze assessing her with an intensity that made her uneasy. Maruchek wasn't a large man, but he was well built and wore a conservative gray business suit. He had impeccably styled hair graying at the temples. His intense blue eyes seemed to stare right through her.

He came forward and stopped in front of her. Strong, well-manicured fingers reached out and took her hands between his in a strong grip.

Startled, Morgan backed up a half step and pulled her hands away. She felt the brush of Shaine's fingers on her arm, steadying her.

After a long, uncomfortable pause, Maruchek took a step back as well, but his gaze did not leave her face. He said quietly, "I have waited a long time to see you in person."

Morgan regarded him, her wariness settling into a vague, self-protective anger simmering in the pit of her stomach. "Why?" she demanded. "I don't know you. What do you want with me?"

Maruchek gestured toward a grouping of comfortable furniture. "Please, let's sit down. We have a great deal to talk about."

Rogan said sharply, "Wendt, let's go. I have a job for you."

Morgan looked at Shaine, who raised a questioning brow, an unspoken check to see if she would be all right. She managed an uneasy smile. She sensed Shaine's reluctance to leave with Rogan, but as much as she had no idea what was happening, she wasn't afraid of the man standing in front of her. She gave a slight nod.

Shaine smiled and brushed a hand over her arm a second time in a reassuring touch. She turned to follow Rogan from the room.

The door slid shut, leaving Morgan to face Tarm Maruchek.

He motioned again at the small grouping of overstuffed leather furniture crowding a slate-topped coffee table. Morgan moved carefully to stand in front of the loveseat. Maruchek smiled. "Please, sit down." He waited until she perched on the edge of the sofa and lowered himself gracefully into one of the chairs across from her.

Morgan sat stiffly, her feet flat on the floor, her hands on her knees. She continued to watch Maruchek warily, wondering what he could possibly want from her.

He poured tea from a shiny black and white tea service and set a cup in front of her. Taking the other cup for himself, he settled back in his chair.

Morgan didn't take the tea. She just wished he would get on with it.

Maruchek's expression slid between stony seriousness and openly curious assessment of her. He sipped his tea. "We have much to discuss, Morgan Rahn."

"I don't even know you."

A flicker of something looking to Morgan almost like sadness crossed his face. "No," he said, "you don't." He studied her.

She looked down at her hands, unease bubbling up the back of her throat. She wanted to scream, *Just tell me what the fuck is going on!*

"There is so much to say and it's difficult to know where to start." He stood abruptly. "You are my daughter," he said.

Morgan blinked. "What?"

He made an impatient flick of his hand and repeated, "You are my daughter."

Morgan stared up at him. "I think you've got the wrong person. My father is Vinn Rahn. My mother was Elise Rahn."

Maruchek walked away from her. He spoke without turning. "You know you were adopted?" he asked.

Morgan glared at his back. *Of course I know. It's not a secret. I always knew. It doesn't matter.* Anger seeped through her unease. "What do you want?" she demanded.

Maruchek turned to face her, his expression flat and unreadable. "You don't believe me."

"Why should I? It's ridiculous."

His gaze bored into hers. "Believe me or don't, but I speak the truth. I am your biological father. Your birth mother, my wife Arella, was murdered. She was seven months pregnant with you. The medics were able to save you, but not Arella. Your life was in danger. My enemies had already kidnapped your brother Garren and there were ongoing threats. I couldn't save my wife. I barely saved my son. I was terrified I wouldn't be able to save you, so I let you go."

Morgan sent him a disbelieving glare. "You expect me to believe one of the most powerful men in the known universe would give up a child because he was afraid for her life?" She choked on a bark of laughter. "I may be a lowly mechanic, but I'm not an idiot. I don't know what you're playing at, but you can stop now."

Maruchek stiffened in anger, though his voice remained even. "If you don't believe me, ask Vinn Rahn." He nodded toward the com console behind his desk.

Morgan glowered at him. *I don't care who you are, you don't have the right to mess with me and my family.* She raised her chin, challenging him. "Why come and find me now? If I'm supposed to be your long-lost daughter, why wait thirty years to bother to contact me?"

Maruchek's expression went hard and steely. He said sharply, "Because until now you weren't in danger. Have you not noticed there have been attempts on your life?"

Morgan surged to her feet and touched her dully aching cheek. She was also aware of the stinging burn on her arm. "So I have you to thank for this?" she shot at him.

He softened. "I am truly sorry for that, Morgan. That's why I had Rogan send Wendt to help you. It was all I could do before I could get you to safety."

"Yeah, it was real safe getting off your shuttle," she said.

Maruchek flinched. "I'm sorry," he repeated quietly.

She stared at him for a long moment, caught by the tone of his voice. Could he really be telling the truth? His story seemed too much to believe, too convenient. She shook her head and caught her breath as a thought smacked her between the eyes. A surge of panic rose into her throat. "When Digger's control unit exploded and his suit ruptured, that wasn't terrorists, it was an attack really meant for me?"

Maruchek shook his head quickly. "No. No. As best we can tell, the incident was random terrorism. The suit had been tampered with, yes, but it wasn't targeted at you particularly. The attacks on you happened after that."

She shivered, tucking her hands into her pockets. "It still makes no sense. How do you get from a random incident to attacks on me personally? I still think you have the wrong person. Or someone does."

"No. You are the target because of who you are." Maruchek walked past the cluster of furniture to perch on the edge of his desk. "Internal reports of the incident that killed your crewmate were smuggled out of my organization. The reports contained names, personal background, and photos of everyone in your work crew. My enemies—one specific person, actually—saw your photo and made the connection that turned you into a target. The media has not been provided photos or identifying information of you or your crew."

"Someone made a connection from a photo," Morgan repeated doubtfully.

Maruchek reached behind himself and picked up a holo frame from his desk. He crossed to where she stood and handed her the holo. "You are the spitting image of your mother."

Morgan took the heavy chrome frame, carefully not touching his hand, and tilted it to bring the holo into focus. She stared, incredulous.

The smiling image could have been her. The woman in the holo was a bit older than she was now. Her black hair fell in gentle waves around her shoulders instead of being cropped short. But the eyes and the lines of the woman's face—she sucked in a ragged breath. It was like looking at her reflection in a mirror.

The photo had been taken on Earth. The ocean and a fair blue sky framed the background. Dark strands of the woman's hair whipped behind her in a strong breeze as she smiled at the camera with an open, relaxed expression.

Morgan glanced at Maruchek. She had no words. *This can't be!* Her gaze returned to the holo. She wanted to believe it was fake—somehow Maruchek had fabricated the photo and the story—but deep down, she knew he hadn't. After a long time, she handed the frame back to him.

Maruchek took the frame without speaking, setting it carefully on his desk. When he turned back to her, he raised a dark brow. "Now do you believe me?" he asked.

Morgan chewed her lower lip. "I don't know." Taking a long breath, she tried to process the information.

"Your mother was—" A com chirped loudly. Maruchek pulled a small unit from his pocket. "Maruchek."

"Mr. Maruchek, there's an update from Facility 2333. Would you like to take the call in your office?"

"No. I'll take it in the security office." He killed the connection and looked at Morgan. "Please, make yourself comfortable. This shouldn't take long."

Morgan nodded, startled by his abrupt departure. She stood motionless as the door snicked shut behind him. *Make myself comfortable. Yeah. Right.* She found herself moving to the huge mahogany desk and picking up the holo again to stare at the woman by the ocean.

She'd never considered that she might resemble another person. *I've never looked like anyone before.* She bore no resemblance to either of her adoptive parents and until this moment, she'd never thought it strange. She never expected to look like them.

She noticed a second holo frame on the desk, a cube with photos on four sides. She set down the frame gently and picked up the cube.

The first holo in the cube was a more formal image of the woman who looked so much like her. The woman wore a mid-length black dress, lacy and cut much lower than she would've ever considered wearing. If she'd ever consider wearing a dress, which she wouldn't. The woman smiled at the camera, but her eyes were guarded.

Morgan turned the cube in her fingers. The next holo showed a young man in his later twenties, perhaps a formal graduation photo. His dark hair was pulled tightly into a ponytail at the nape of his neck. She sensed a seriousness about him, in the intensity of his eyes and the tight line of his mouth. He had Maruchek's strong jawline and the same piercing gaze.

The third side of the cube contained a holo of the woman playing with a dark-eyed, dark-haired toddler. Both sat cross-legged on a white carpeted floor with a pile of colorful geometric blocks between them. The boy laughed with delight, holding a bright yellow triangle up toward the camera. The woman appeared to be as delighted as the child.

Morgan turned to the last holo: an image of the boy again, this time as an adolescent, grinning as he sat astride a black air-bike. He wore dark glasses and his shaggy hair fell past broadening shoulders.

She had to assume the holos were Maruchek's wife and son. She could see the resemblance between father and son, even mother and son, but it wasn't the uncanny likeness between his wife and herself. She frowned, not quite able to come to terms with thinking of the woman as her mother. But unless Maruchek had gone through an awful lot of bother to create these photos and set up the whole situation, what other explanation could there be? And why would he go through that kind of work to lie to her?

Slowly, she put the holo cube on the desk.

Had her parents known about Maruchek? How could they live with a secret like that? And how could they not have told her, if they did know? Or had Maruchek hung the knowledge around their necks like an albatross, holding threats over their heads in exchange for their silence? After all, Rogan was doing something similar to Shaine.

Morgan turned to the com console behind Maruchek's desk. She needed to talk to her father. Maruchek had offered, after all, so it wasn't like she'd be stealing com time. She leaned over and tapped open a line, typing in the familiar code. The screen went from black to gray with a small spinning icon. The words "transmitting com signal" scrolled slowly across the screen in blue script. A second later, her father's image shimmered into motion as he picked up the call.

"Morgan?" Vinn Rahn's ruddy face broke into a wide grin when he recognized her.

"Hey, Dad."

"Hey, kiddo. I called you earlier but you didn't answer, and I was getting worried since you didn't stop by yesterday, either. Where are you?"

"I'm on Earth, actually."

"Earth?" he repeated. Vinn blinked unbelievingly and shook his head. "How the hell did you get there?"

Morgan read his expression as a mix of worry and relief. She spread her hands, trying to find a reasonable explanation to give him. "The trip was kind of last minute," she said.

He nodded. "I just wanted to make sure you were okay." His eyes narrowed. "What happened to your face?"

Morgan touched her cheek. "Um, it was an accident. I'm okay." She hesitated and finally blurted, "I'm in Tarm Maruchek's office, Dad."

The color drained from Vinn's face. A long silence ensued while he scanned the room behind her. Morgan saw his panic as he searched for words. Realization hit like a blow to her stomach. She could barely find the breath to whisper, "You knew, didn't you?"

A long beat. He nodded mutely.

She slumped against the desk. Pain stung her arm and throbbed along her cheek, but those minor hurts were nothing compared to the ache in her chest stealing the breath from her lungs and threatening to bring her to her knees. *How could you do this to me?* "Why didn't you tell me?" she asked.

Vinn rubbed his forehead. He avoided her gaze, regret etching deep lines on his face. "Morgan, honey, I'm sorry," he rasped. "We were going to, someday, but it never came up. And then, it just didn't seem to matter." He shrugged helplessly. "As the time passed, it just didn't seem right to worry you. Me and your mom loved you, Morgan. I love you. Just—we didn't want you to get hurt." He sighed. Failure showed in the shadows behind his eyes and in the bowed line of his shoulders.

"But how? Dad, how did it happen? I need to understand."

He looked away again, the heavy weight of past decisions clearly bearing down on him. Morgan thought he seemed suddenly so much older and so tired. She hated to see him hurting.

He sat heavily in the chair she knew stood at the side of the table beside the com console. The automated camera followed his movement. His gaze turned inward when he spoke. "You know your mom had a miscarriage when we were working in the Belt."

Morgan nodded slowly.

He continued, "That was true, but the timing was different from what we told you." He rubbed his forehead again.

Morgan wanted to shout, *Just tell me!* She fought her impatience, knowing it was a hard story for her father to tell as much as it was a hard story for her to hear.

His voice cracked roughly. "The morning your mom miscarried—that was a terrible day. I don't know my heart has ever hurt so much, Morgan, except when she died. We were both so devastated. I stayed with her all day into the night. Your mom was so sad, she cried and cried.

"And then a man came to our hospital room. He was a big, tall, dark-skinned man. He had Mann-Maru Security credentials and said he couldn't explain, but there was a baby girl who'd just been born and needed a family. He was very apologetic. He asked if we would take her and adopt her as our own. I think your mom just saw it as a way to bring back the baby girl she'd lost. We agreed. There was never any question, really. The nurse brought us the most beautiful baby girl we'd ever seen. And that was you, Morgan." Tears rolled down his lined cheeks. He swiped at them. "I only spoke to Mr. Maruchek once, at a worker's rally on Moon Base. He seemed to know me and asked if my daughter was well. That was all, but I knew." He spread apart his hands. "I don't know what else to tell you. I love you more than life. So did your mom."

Morgan wiped at her eyes, rubbing wet tracks from her face. She couldn't find the words to express the emotions washing over her—disbelief, anger, sadness, understanding, love, forgiveness. So many things. Finally she looked up. "I love you, Dad," she managed hoarsely.

"Morgan—"

She shook her head, cutting him off, suddenly unable to continue the conversation. "I have to go," she whispered. "I'll call again." She cut the connection without waiting for a reply.

She didn't know how long she stood there staring at the blank screen, seeing nothing but the images in her mind of her mother— the only mother she'd ever known—and her dad, their life on Moon Base, the stints in the Belt when she was a older, the last one ending with her mom's funeral. Then it was just her and her dad on Moon Base, struggling to move on.

And now what? Did the truth change anything? Did it change everything? Or did it only create complications? Slowly, she padded across the thick carpet to the loveseat and sank onto it, emotionally and physically exhausted. She leaned back her head and stared at the ceiling, wishing she were in her quiet apartment on the Moon.

CHAPTER FOURTEEN

Shaine followed Rogan through the maze of hallways toward the suite of workrooms she always thought of as "Security Central." Rogan's office was accessible from the outer hallway as well as from inside the hub. They entered from outside rather than parading through the main Security center, which told her Rogan didn't want her presence widely known. Not a good sign.

He waited for her to precede him into the stark, dimly lit office. A com console and computer center took up most of the desk at the center of the room. A worktable with a lamp hung over it was tucked into the back corner. All the furniture and surfaces were black lacquer against flat black walls. Recessed lighting threw soft illumination into an alcove on the far wall where a single sculpture rested—a silver, geometrically styled figure of a naked running man with a spear in throwing position.

Shaine sprawled into the austere chair in front of the desk and casually stretched her feet out in front of her.

Her former boss gave her an annoyed look, but said nothing as he eased his bulky frame into the leather chair behind his desk. He picked up a comp pad, removed a data chip from a pocket inside his jacket and plugged it in. "I have a job for you, Wendt."

Shaine raised a brow. "You're so short-staffed you need me to do your dirty work, Rogan?"

He met her gaze coldly. "You're just so good at what you do best," he replied smoothly.

She glowered at him. *I am not that person anymore. I am not your fucking assassin.* She said aloud, "Tell me what's going on with Morgan."

"You haven't figured it out yet?" Rogan looked disappointed.

"She's Maruchek's daughter. The one everyone thought was killed with Arella." She was surprised at how even her voice sounded. "That doesn't tell me why someone wants her dead, or who's doing the hunting." She glanced at the photo on the pad he handed her. "Tyr Charun?"

He nodded.

Shaine dug through her brain for knowledge of the man. His company was Mann-Maru's biggest competitor in the market. Tyr Charun and Tarm Maruchek had a decades-long history of adversarial relations. The two men were polar opposites and mixed like fire and liquid propellant. She had only met Charun once. Her dislike of him had been immediate and palpable.

From what she knew, Charun was a devious little scumbag whose greatest skill was making money. He had no conscience and no work ethic other than having everyone else do his bidding. Most of the press he got was in the gossip rags because he lived fast and loose, hung out with the famous and fabulously wealthy, and went through women like water. He had always been high on the list of Rogan's people to keep an eye on.

She frowned. She was still missing something. "So Charun's a bastard. What does he have to do with Morgan?"

"Charun couldn't have Arella Maruchek for himself, so he had her murdered. Now that he knows about Morgan Rahn, he doesn't want Tarm to have a daughter, either. Especially one who reminds Charun so much of Arella. Charun needs to be eliminated. Immediately."

Shaine dropped the pad on the edge of his desk and shook her head. "No. No way." She stood in a fast, fluid movement. "No."

"It's not up for debate."

"Find someone else."

"You're the best."

"I'm not suicidal."

Rogan smiled smugly. "Think about it this way, Wendt. If someone doesn't eliminate Charun, it's only a matter of time before you lose your girlfriend. He is obsessed."

"If I refuse?"

"Then you live with the result, knowing you could have stopped your girlfriend's death. Or I can put a hit out on you, since you can no longer be trusted."

Shaine ground her teeth, anger surging up and nearly choking her. She leaned over his desk, her fingers spread on the cold black surface. "Fucking bastard!" she growled. She wanted to strangle the son of a bitch.

Rogan sat without flinching, calmly waiting her out.

After a few seconds and a handful of calming breaths, she dropped into the chair. He had her by the balls. He knew it and she knew it. "Okay. Fine. You win."

"I never doubted it."

Shaine's jaw clenched. "And Morgan's not my girlfriend."

He shrugged. "I don't really care who you sleep with, Wendt. Plans are already in motion. Be here at Central Ops at oh-six-hundred. Your second is Cord Barill. Ellerand is handling intel."

Shaine stood. She knew Barill and trusted him. At least he was smart enough to stay out of her way. "Am I dismissed, then?"

He gestured to the door. "Go. Your girlfriend is staying with you in the main guest suite. I assume you remember the way."

She glowered at him and walked out, wishing she had the option to slam the door behind her. Instead, it slid shut behind her with a barely audible hiss. She walked fifteen meters down the hall and stopped at another door. She lifted a hand and slapped it against the palm reader.

An instant later, the plain white door slid open and a friendly voice greeted her. "Hey, Wendt. I was wondering when you'd get here."

She stalked into an office cluttered with computers, comp pads, monitors and electronic bits and pieces. Kyle Ellerand perched on a rolling stool in the midst of the chaos. His dishwater blond hair hung near his shoulders, uncombed and in dire need of a trim. Small round glasses nearly hid his eyes. His black uniform looked as though he'd slept in it all week.

Shaine scowled at him. "We need to talk."

He grinned. "Rogan being less than forthcoming?" he asked.

A rolling chair stood near the door. Shaine grabbed the stack of papers on the seat and dropped them on a nearby counter. She flopped into the chair and skated it toward her friend. "Rogan's a fucking bastard," she said flatly. She glanced at the scattered bits and pieces around the room. A smile slid across her lips when she considered the man watching her. "It's good to see you, by the way."

Ellerand laughed. "Glad you haven't changed, hardass."

"Ha." She sobered. "Fill me in. Tyr Charun wants Morgan dead. What's the whole story?"

He nodded, grabbed something off the desk and flipped it to her. She snagged the tiny data chip one-handed out of the air. He said, "Everything you probably want to know, a lot of crap you probably don't. But I'll give you the highlights. You really got yourself into the middle of it, didn't you?"

She rolled her eyes. "We were right about Morgan being Tarm's lost child."

He nodded. "Does she know?"

Shaine shook her head. "Unless Maruchek told her in the last hour, she doesn't." She looked down thoughtfully for a few moments and asked, "What else do you know?"

"We were right about the security leak from the crew incident. That's where Charun found out about her. According to the moles we have in Charun's organization, he's nuts over the whole thing. The story is that he and Maruchek were both in love with Arella before Maruchek married her. Arella was an obsession for Charun. That's a lot of why Rogan figures it was Charun behind Arella's assassination, even if they were never able to nail him. The crazy bastard even commed Maruchek a day ago to ask him how his children were."

"Are you fucking serious? Crazy is right. Tell me more about the leak."

Ellerand shrugged. "Pretty standard stupidity. The security report got leaked, complete with photos IDing the whole crew. I've been digging. Seems a clerk who'd been bought off by one of the big media conglomerates got hold of it. She insists the file was on a public access site. Turns out the report was accessible for about as long as it took her to find it and download it locally. Then it disappeared from the public server space. The trace file was left behind."

"Who put it out there?"

"There wasn't a digital signature on the file, but it had the original encrypted security access level. Only a few people with that level of access." He grinned and tossed her a pad. "I've narrowed it down to two likely suspects, which I marked."

She scanned through the list of names on the screen, grinning ferally when she recognized the two marked names. "Alik Asai and Lissa Hedding. Gee. Such a surprise. My two favorite people in the world."

Ellerand laughed. "I'd personally put my money on Hedding."

"She still hasn't gotten bored with kissing up to Maruchek?"

"Not that I've noticed." He smirked. "I haven't been able to pin anything on her yet, though. Been through all her electronic communications, net links, everything. Asai's too. Rogan's got both of them under physical surveillance. I don't think he's come up with anything either. At least, nothing he's let anyone know about."

Shaine nodded. *Internal security leak. How in the hell did Rogan let that slip?* The issue now was if either Asai or Hedding were involved, Morgan was in danger, even here in the compound. *Fuck, fuck, fuck.* What was Rogan thinking, bringing her here? Even if he thought he had a handle on his potential leaks, she needed to know what other security measures he had in place around Morgan. Rogan was good, but his first priority would always be Tarm Maruchek. Anything else—anyone else—came second.

"Rogan's got a plan up his sleeve," Ellerand added. "He and Cord Barill were holed up in his office earlier today for a few hours. I couldn't pick up a lot of what they were doing. They're keeping it close to the vest and off-line, probably until we meet tomorrow. What I gave you is history, background, updated intel on Charun, and a copy of the security report."

"Any additional security around Morgan right now?"

He shook his head. "No. I imagine he's counting on your presence to keep her safe for the moment." He swiveled around, reaching up to tap long fingers across a series of open windows on a monitor. Live video feeds shifted from window to window while he worked until, satisfied, he scanned the feeds a few moments and swiveled back around to Shaine. He considered her with a curious expression.

She noted the screens he watched had various views from inside the guest suite where Morgan Rahn stood at the window, staring out at the sunset skyline. *Damn, she looks good.*

He asked, "What's she like?"

Shaine grinned. "You'd like her, Kyle."

He cocked his head and studied her. "You're whipped," he accused.

She shrugged, unable to deny the obvious.

"When I see you up in the suite, I'll kill the surveillance."

Laughing, Shaine got to her feet. "Thanks, buddy."

CHAPTER FIFTEEN

Ten minutes later, Shaine came to an oversized wooden door at the end of a long hallway. She palmed the lock, expecting she had been cleared to enter. The heavy door opened with a click, slid aside into the wall, and silently shut behind her when she passed into the entry foyer.

She stood a moment, her gaze scanning the room, reality and memory overlapping. The last time she'd been in the penthouse suite she'd been working low-level security, standing guard outside the door for one of Maruchek's "less trustworthy" business associates.

She noted the décor hadn't changed much. The entry foyer opened into an atrium with a high ceiling and a wide, domed skylight. Stylized imitations of ancient Italian frescoes covered the upper two-thirds of the walls. Swirled pink and cream marble tiles covered the floors and the bottom third of the walls. A single matching marble pedestal table rested at the center of the rotunda, supporting a heavy crystalline vase filled with heavily scented hyacinths, white roses, and tiny purple flowerets.

Beyond the foyer, the atrium opened into the main living room done in beige, cream, mauve and ivory. The bare tile gave way to plush white carpeting and overstuffed sofas and chairs. An ornate chandelier hung presumptuously from the center of the ceiling. Off the living room, heavy wooden doors opened to the bedrooms and a small library. A solid glass wall overlooked the jagged New York City skyline.

Shaine walked across the floor, her boot steps echoing on the tile.

Morgan sat on the sofa in the living room, facing away from the entrance, her head bowed so she looked down at her lap. Her dark hair contrasted with the lightly colored fabric.

Shaine felt her heart rate pick up. Morgan seemed so small and alone, sitting in the corner of the huge cream-colored sofa. She wondered what Maruchek had told Morgan when they were alone. She thought about the gut-level guess she'd made yesterday—that Morgan was Maruchek's lost child. She was glad her intuition was still working, but the fact that Morgan was Maruchek's kid made everything that much more difficult.

If Charun was truly behind the attempts on Morgan's life, then Rogan was right when he'd said the only way to keep Morgan safe was to eliminate Charun. The man was sick at best—insanely dangerous at worst. The fact they'd never been able to pin Arella's murder on him meant there would be no help from the authorities. She would be on her own. She felt angry that Rogan had decided to play games instead of just telling her up front what was happening. And she worried about how Morgan was going to deal with the situation.

She wondered for the hundredth time if she should have told Morgan what she'd suspected. But what if she had been wrong? Then she'd have freaked out Morgan for nothing. Damn. What if Maruchek hadn't told her? Morgan had a right to know what was happening.

Then again, would Morgan even tell her what Maruchek had said? Morgan barely knew her. She barely knew Morgan. Rogan had called Morgan her girlfriend. Part of her scoffed at the idea. But she couldn't deny either the physical attraction or the underlying and unexplainable something seeming to tie Morgan so tightly to her heart and mind.

Whatever happened, she knew in the core of her being she would, at the very least, remove this threat to Morgan's life.

Shaine shook her head slowly. She was out of her mind. Would Morgan even trust her after all the intrigue and the lies? Would Morgan trust her when she found out she was going to assassinate Tyr Charun? Her thoughts turned dark. *I can't blame her if she just kicks my ass out of the room. She probably thinks I've somehow set her up, or knew she was being set up. Hell, she's probably better off without me anyway.* She took a deep breath, squared her shoulders, and entered the living room.

Morgan didn't seem to notice her.

"Morgan?"

Slowly the dark head came up. Morgan half-turned, focusing haunted eyes on her. "Hey."

Shaine perched on the arm of the sofa beside the woman. "You okay?"

Morgan shrugged, grimacing when the motion jostled her arm and back. "Not sure," she said quietly, her hands clasped together as she leaned forward with her elbows on her knees.

Shaine wanted to slide down beside Morgan and put an arm around her, but instead remained a safe arm's length away. "Did Maruchek tell you what's going on?" she asked, careful to keep her voice even, not demanding and not prying.

Morgan shrugged. "Some of it. Most of it." She looked down at her hands, playing with her mother's ring. "It's insane."

Shaine nodded her agreement. *Do I tell her what I know? Do I tell her I'm going to kill a man to keep her safe? Damn it.* She pushed restlessly to her feet, pacing across the room to the windows. The lowering orange glow of the sunset backlit the dark city skyline.

She felt anger swell inside her again. She had been railroaded into this position. Not that she wouldn't do anything in her power to keep Morgan alive and well. It was the principle of the thing. Rogan considered her an assassin. What would Morgan think, knowing she intended to kill a man in cold blood to save her life? She watched the flashing lights of a shuttle cross the sky. She was a killer. She didn't want to be, but the training and instincts went bone deep.

Shaine paced back to the sofa, acutely aware of Morgan watching her with eyes the color of storm clouds. She wanted to wrap her arms around Morgan and make the hurt go away. Maybe holding Morgan would help make the pain in her chest go away, she thought. But she was afraid to invade Morgan's space, not wanting to frighten her into bolting. How in the hell could she possibly explain what she had to do? How could she justify her work as an assassin to Morgan? Hell, she couldn't even justify it to herself right now.

She found herself standing beside the sofa.

Morgan asked quietly, "What did Rogan tell you?"

Shaine shook her head and choked on a dry laugh. "Rogan told me if I wanted to keep you and me alive for any length of time, I need to eliminate a man named Tyr Charun."

"Eliminate?"

"Eliminate. Kill. Terminate. Whatever you want to call it."

"And you're going to do it?"

"Yes."

Morgan stared at her a second and looked away.

"Morgan?" Shaine ventured.

Morgan met her questioning gaze.

"I won't let Tyr Charun hurt you. I will take him out if it'll keep you safe." Shaine swallowed, feeling the need to say more, but the words eluded her. Her heart pounded against her ribcage and made it hard to breathe. She took another step toward Morgan, but stopped when Morgan took a choking breath and closed her eyes.

"He's my father," Morgan whispered. "Maruchek's my biological father."

Shaine's breath caught in her throat. Even though she'd known, Morgan's admission came as a shock, and the pain behind the words hit her like a gut punch.

Morgan seemed to shrink into herself where she sat, her shoulders hunching as her head bowed. She shook with silent tears.

Shaine took two steps to reach Morgan's side, sat beside her, and wrapped her arms around the weeping woman's shoulders.

When Morgan didn't pull away, she tucked Morgan's head against her chest and rubbed gentle circles on her back.

Morgan relaxed.

Tears soaked through her shirt's light material. Shaine rocked gently and whispered into Morgan's hair, "It's gonna be okay, babe, it'll be okay."

But she didn't know if anything really would be okay and she didn't know what else she could say. Her thoughts reeled. When they'd had dinner, Morgan talked about her parents and her life growing up on Moon Base and in the Belt, making it obvious how close she and her dad had gotten after her mom died. It had to be a mind-blowing shock to have her assumptions about who she was shot to hell and back. She held Morgan tightly and hoped her attempt to comfort was enough.

After a bit, Morgan spoke softly, as much to herself as to Shaine, whispering into her shoulder. She didn't look up, didn't shift away from the embrace, just spoke as though the words needed to come out. "Maruchek hid me away. He said he was afraid his enemies would get to me. His wife was killed—she was pregnant with me. The doctors saved me. My mom and dad, they were working in the Belt. Mom miscarried. Dad said Rogan asked them to take me." She glanced up with wide eyes. "I called him," she said. "I called my dad while I was in Maruchek's office. They knew and they never told me. Dad said they always meant to tell me. They just never got around to it." She dragged in a ragged breath. "Everyone thinks they're doing the right thing, and I'm the one who ends up having to deal with all their damned secrets."

Shaine ran gentle fingers through the feathery, fine black hair. "Your folks were better parents than Maruchek would have been."

Morgan eased back and looked at her with a sad smile. "They were."

Shaine nodded. She and Morgan sat quietly for a long time. She found herself staring at Morgan's profile, truly seeing the resemblance between Morgan and Arella Maruchek. She finally shook her head. "Damn, Morgan, you really could be Arella's double."

Morgan shot her an alarmed look. "You knew?" she asked.

Shaine sighed. "I suspected after I talked to Rogan that first day. But I didn't know and he didn't tell me, and I didn't want to make any assumptions." She shrugged regretfully. "So I didn't say anything to you."

Morgan chewed her lip. "A heads-up might have been nice."

"I'm sorry."

Morgan absently traced her fingers along the line of Shaine's collarbone, ending in a light touch on the soft fabric of her shirt. "I still don't understand why this guy would want to kill me. Maruchek didn't really talk about it."

Shaine sat back in the soft cushions, keeping an arm around Morgan, who settled against her. "I'll tell you as much as I know," she offered. "Tyr Charun. He's the owner and CEO of InterSys Enterprises. He's a megalomaniacal nut job. Charun and Maruchek have been at each other's throats for years, on a business and a personal level. Rogan and Maruchek have always suspected Charun of being behind Arella's murder. The man was obsessed with Arella. Never forgave Maruchek for winning her heart. Never forgave her for not choosing him. Since you look so much like Arella, it seems he's transferred his obsession to you."

"That's downright creepy."

"I won't argue."

Morgan sighed, curled closer, and gave her a squeeze. The room fell silent a while before Morgan said, "Rogan doesn't seem to like you much."

"Yeah. He doesn't appreciate that I developed a conscience."

"I'm sorry you got dragged into all this crap. I know you don't want to be involved."

Shaine shrugged, managing a tight grin. "For you, Morgan, it's worth it."

Morgan protested, "You hardly even know me."

Shaine's grin broadened. She waited until Morgan met her gaze. "I know you well enough to know I want to keep you around to know you better," she replied easily, lifting a suggestive brow.

Morgan managed a tired-looking smile. "Well, all in all, I can't think of anyone I'd rather have guarding my body," she mumbled. Apparently realizing what had just come out of her mouth, she looked down, blushing all the way to her hairline.

Shaine grinned. "So, you hungry?"

"Um, sure."

"Personally, I'm starved. Let's use up some of Maruchek's hospitality and enjoy a decent meal and some expensive beer on the house."

Two good-sized steaks, a pile of thick-cut, skin-on fries, and a couple of dark beers later, Shaine and Morgan relaxed at the small table they'd positioned against the windows overlooking the interior gardens. The luxury of having real meat and fresh potatoes instead of processed protein and flash-frozen, ready-to-eat substitutes was a wonderful treat.

Morgan popped the tops of two more bottles of beer, and after passing one to Shaine, sipped contently at her own.

Shaine kept the conversation light through dinner. By mutual, unspoken agreement, neither she nor Morgan made mention of Maruchek, Rogan or the issues at hand. Eventually, they moved from the table to the comfort of the big sofa in the living room. Now she pulled the coffee table closer so she could put her feet up and tugged Morgan down next to her. She slid an arm around Morgan's shoulders.

Morgan leaned close and put her feet up too, sighing as she sank into the cushions.

Shaine smiled. "Yeah, you know, I think—"

The door buzzed long and loud, as though someone leaned on the call button.

Morgan started to get up, but Shaine shook her head, motioning her to stay put. "I got it," she said, swinging her feet to the floor and standing in a graceful motion. With a grim twist of her lips, she pulled the pistol from the holster at the small of her back.

Morgan's eyes widened.

She shrugged. "From here on in, I'm not taking any chances," she said flatly, starting toward the entry foyer.

The front door slid open before she got halfway to the marble atrium. A tall blond woman—Lissa Hedding—stepped through into the suite.

Shaine leveled her pistol. "Something I can help you with?"

Lissa stopped short with a frown. She wore a clean-cut, navy blue pantsuit with a close-fitting jacket. Her hair was pulled into a tight ponytail at the nape of her neck. She glared at Shaine, nodding with distaste at the gun. "Is that really necessary, Wendt?" she demanded.

Shaine didn't shift her aim, merely raised a brow. "I don't know, Lissa. Is it?"

"No. It is not."

Shaine waited a long second before flicking on the safety and lowering the gun. "Next time, wait until someone answers the door," she snapped. "What do you want?"

Lissa nodded in the direction of the living room where Morgan stood behind the sofa. "I came to speak with Morgan," she said, brushing dismissively past Shaine.

Shaine resisted the urge to body-slam the bitch to the floor and settled for simply glowering as she followed her old rival into the next room.

Lissa strode around the sofa, approaching Morgan with her hand outstretched, a wide smile on her face. "Ms. Rahn, I'm so pleased to meet you."

Morgan pointedly shoved her hands in her pockets and just nodded.

Lissa ignored the slight and continued unperturbed. "Your father asked me to stop by and introduce myself. I'm Lissa Hedding, your father's personal assistant. I want to assure you if there is anything you need, all you have to do is call my com." She reached into her breast pocket and retrieved a clear plastic card, handing it to Morgan, who tucked it into a pants pocket without looking at it. Lissa went on, "Call anytime. If I'm not available, there will always be someone on staff who can help you."

Morgan nodded. "Sure," she said.

Shaine came around the side of the sofa, purposefully positioning herself a half-step in front of Morgan.

Lissa sent a dark look her way before returning her attention to Morgan. "Your father asked me to invite you to join him for breakfast tomorrow morning. I can send someone at eight o'clock to escort you."

Shaine said, "I'll bring her."

Lissa's expression turned almost gleeful. "Rogan said he'll see you at oh-six-hundred, Wendt. So I'll send someone."

"Rogan can wait."

"You assume too much," Lissa snapped.

Shaine let her lips stretch into a feral grin. "You assume I care. Was there anything else, Lissa?" she added sweetly.

The tall blonde squared her shoulders and turned a bright smile on Morgan. "I'm very glad to meet you, Morgan. Remember, if there's anything you need, let me know." With that, she turned and left. The door snicked shut behind her.

Shaine stalked to the door and spent about three minutes tapping command codes into the security panel before returning to the living room. "The only people who should be able to get through that door without you physically unlocking it and letting them in are you, me, Maruchek and Rogan," she said.

Morgan nodded.

Shaine saw the unease in Morgan's expression and wished she could take it away. But they were in this situation now and the only thing she could offer was to protect, and hopefully, to give Morgan the strength to keep moving forward. She let her practical commando persona slide to the forefront, pulled the pistol out of its holster and held the weapon in the palm of her hand. She turned a questioning look on Morgan. "Ever handled one of these before?" she asked.

Morgan shook her head. "No."

Shaine nodded. "It's okay, no issues. This is the easiest gun there is." She shifted so she stood behind Morgan and wrapped her arms around her. She closed Morgan's fingers around the pistol in a two-handed grip and moved Morgan's first finger over a small catch just forward of the stock. "This is your safety. Off, you can shoot." She guided Morgan's finger. "On, the trigger is locked." She felt Morgan stiffen. *Aw, crap, I'm scaring the hell out of her.* She took a breath and gently bumped the back of Morgan's knee with hers. "Relax," she teased.

Morgan glanced back at her. "Easy for you to say."

For a second, Shaine leaned her head on Morgan's shoulder. "I know," she murmured. "I know. I'm sorry, Morgan. I really am. I just want you to be safe."

Morgan took a deep breath, straightening her shoulders. "It's okay. I'm okay." She steadied her grip on the pistol. "Now what?"

Shaine couldn't help grinning. Morgan was a tough cookie. She guided Morgan's arms higher and adjusted her grip. "Now, you just point and pull the trigger," she said. "You probably won't hit anything, but it doesn't matter. A shot can buy you enough time to duck."

Morgan turned at the last word, giving Shaine a half-panicked, wide-eyed stare.

Shaine let her hands drop. "I'm sorry. That was dumb," she said with a sigh. She added, "Honestly, most untrained civilians with guns can't hit the side of a shuttle. I just don't want to lie to you."

Morgan swallowed, dropped her arms, and held the pistol loosely at her side. Slowly, she put the weapon on the coffee table.

Shaine said uneasily, "Look, Morgan, you're probably not going to need it. I just—" She stopped and tried again, "I don't mean to scare you. I'm probably being paranoid."

Morgan faced her. "Maybe. Maybe not." She shook her head. "This is so insane."

"That it is." Shaine regarded Morgan in silence and finally looked at the sofa. "Come on, may as well sit, huh?"

Morgan shrugged.

Shaine almost reached down to pick up the pistol and return the weapon to its holster, but stopped the motion. *Just leave it.* She dropped into the corner of the sofa.

Morgan slid in close, curling a leg under her body.

Shaine rested an arm loosely around Morgan's shoulders and leaned her head back against the cushions, closing her eyes.

Morgan asked, "Any idea what happens next?"

Shaine considered. She didn't like that she wasn't in control of the situation, didn't like that she was just a pawn in Rogan's game, but the situation would change tomorrow. Once she and Ellerand joined the mission planning, they would take over. If an operation was going to come together to take out Charun, she and Ellerand would run it, the way it always had been.

"Rogan said he has a plan and I'll find out about that tomorrow," she said. "Other than that, I'm not sure yet."

After a pause, Morgan asked, "What does it mean, really, if technically Maruchek's my father? Legally, it doesn't mean anything—not unless one or the other of us decided to make something of it. I sure as hell won't. I don't want his money." She raised and dropped a hand, clearly frustrated. "I don't want my life to change. Things are fine just the way they are. And what about my dad? It's not like I'm going to walk away from him just because Maruchek's my birth father. Besides, what could Maruchek possibly want with me, anyway? Am I supposed to suddenly be part of his life?" She sighed. "Where does this leave me, Shaine?"

Shaine wished she could come up with an intelligent and helpful response. "I don't know. Talk to Maruchek tomorrow. Just ask him. He's a reasonable guy, really. A lot more reasonable than Rogan. I don't see Maruchek trying to force you into doing anything."

"But he can force you into killing someone."

"That's different."

Morgan shifted, turning a serious look on her. "How? How is it different? He and Rogan are manipulating you. He can do the same thing to me."

Shaine shook her head. "No. You don't know any deep, dark company secrets. I do. With the knowledge I have, I could do a hell of a lot of damage to Maruchek's reputation, the company's reputation, and probably get both him and Rogan put in jail for some of the crap they've pulled. All you can do is tell the world you're his long-lost daughter. It'd be news for about a week, and then they'd just shove it under the table."

Morgan took a long breath. "When you put it that way, it's kind of insignificant, isn't it?" she asked quietly.

Shaine squeezed Morgan's hand. "Not insignificant," she countered. "Just not as damning."

Morgan said nothing. She stared down at their clasped hands. After a time, she tilted her head to glance up. "So, really, what it comes down to is in order for either of us to have our lives back, you need to kill Charun. How do you do that without getting thrown in jail?"

"That's why they call it 'covert.' I won't leave enough behind for the authorities to trace me. As for the press and the media frenzy, that's not my problem. I play cold-blooded killer and we all live happily ever after until Rogan finds another reason to drag me in again." She couldn't quite keep the bitterness out of her tone.

"Don't sacrifice your soul for me, Shaine. I'd rather see you just walk away."

Shaine swallowed down the anger and shrugged. "I can't walk away. And honestly, Morgan, I couldn't live with myself if I didn't do everything in my power to make you safe. I don't understand it, and I know we hardly even know each other, but…" She hesitated, fighting for the words to express what she felt. "I can't let them hurt you. Even if you just walk away from me afterward, I can't."

Morgan whispered, "I won't walk away, Shaine."

Shaine stared helplessly into stormy depths of emotion. Her heart ached, making it hard to breathe and her world tunneled. She ran her fingers lightly against Morgan's bandaged cheek and traced her lips. *I need you. I don't know what's happening to me, but I swear I'd die for you.*

Morgan sighed at the touch. Her eyes fluttered closed.

Shaine leaned down to kiss her slowly, Morgan's mouth soft and warm under hers. Sensations exploded through her, Morgan's fingers twisted strongly into her hair, pulling her closer, deepening the kiss. She dragged Morgan's body over hers, her hands sliding under Morgan's shirt, finding the softness of skin.

Morgan shifted, pressing a leg between Shaine's.

Shaine groaned into Morgan's mouth, "Oh, God."

Morgan rocked against her, making Shaine's hips surge in turn. Morgan breathed, "Please…"

Shaine didn't think. She gathered Morgan into her arms and carried her into the bedroom, laying her on the bed. Morgan reached up to pull her down, but Shaine backed away, lifting a finger. "One second," she murmured.

She stripped off her shirt, then her boots, shimmying out of her pants and underwear, stopping as her fingers touched the synthetic skin below her right knee. She straightened, standing naked in front of Morgan, and suddenly remembered her prosthetic leg. She swallowed, almost overcome by the panic she hadn't felt in so long. "My leg," she whispered.

"Doesn't matter," Morgan said softly, and held a hand out to her. "Come on."

Sighing with relief, she climbed naked onto the bed. She covered Morgan's body with her own, leaning down to capture

Morgan's lips, groaning as Morgan's tongue met hers. For long moments they explored each other's mouths, letting the heat build between them until they had to break the kiss to breathe.

Shaine sat back, sliding her fingers under the hem of Morgan's shirt, reveling in the silky feel of her skin. Morgan wordlessly helped her pull it off and toss it aside on the floor. She placed a line of kisses down Morgan's stomach, then wriggled down and very deliberately began removing Morgan's boots and socks. She slid her hands up the loose fabric of Morgan's worn cargo pants, over slender hips to the waistband and teased the warm skin, sliding her fingertips against softness and bringing goose bumps to Morgan's flesh. Looking up to hold Morgan's heated gaze, she undid the catch and pulled Morgan's pants and underwear down and off.

Morgan propped herself up on her elbows, watching Shaine's seduction with expectant, half-lidded eyes.

Shaine grinned and crawled on the bed like a predatory cat, taking her time and kissing her way up Morgan's legs, tracing the outlines of the dragon tattoo on Morgan's thigh with the tip of her tongue. Morgan's body twitched beneath her.

She eased her long frame over Morgan's, hissing softly at the feel of hot skin on skin, feeling need and desire igniting, sending sharp jolts to her groin. Morgan's hands slid up her back, hot trails on her skin. She rested her weight on her elbows and studied Morgan's face. "You are beautiful," she whispered.

A still silence fell between them.

Shaine lost herself in Morgan's eyes, in the depths of need. She traced the smooth planes of Morgan's face and ran her fingers through the straight dark hair falling in feathery layers. She let Morgan's hair slide through her fingers as she kissed the woman's closed eyelids, her forehead.

Slowly, she eased down, trailing kisses along Morgan's jaw, down the neck, into the hollow between pert breasts. Morgan shuddered under her. She felt strong hands clutching at her shoulders when Morgan's body arched up.

She kissed Morgan's breasts, teased and sucked at the nipples until Morgan moaned. She slid down further, touching, tasting the smooth, flat planes of Morgan's stomach, letting her hands trail along narrow hips, tracing lines down the long thighs.

Forcing herself not to hurry, Shaine finally slid her fingers into the warm wetness at Morgan's core.

Morgan whimpered at the touch.

Shaine shuddered with need. It had been so long, so long since she'd wanted anyone like this. So long since anyone had made her care this much or need this much.

She explored with gentle fingers. Morgan squirmed and thrust against her, pushing for more, nails scraping her back and shoulders until she finally slid inside again. Morgan gasped, an incoherent moan escaping her lips.

Shaine felt a groan rise in her throat. She rubbed her cheek against the taught, smooth skin of Morgan's stomach as hot, wet muscles tightened around her fingers. She thrust slowly in and out, forcing a rhythm and moving harder and faster, more desperately until Morgan's hips spasmed up against her and she cried out, clutching at her with desperate hands, and finally going limp beneath her.

Shaine groaned and wrapped her arms tightly around Morgan's middle. Her heart felt as though it would explode inside her chest. She ached with emotions she was afraid to identify, and buried her face into Morgan's warm, sweat-dampened skin, not wanting to show the tears she knew were sliding down her cheeks, not sure why she cried in the first place.

Morgan's hands caressed her hair, rubbed light circles along her back and shoulders. "Shaine," she whispered. "Hey, come up here."

After a moment, Shaine took a long, shaky breath and shimmied up to lie face-to-face with Morgan. She smiled and kissed Morgan softly.

Morgan studied her face. Gentle fingers wiped away the dampness of her tears while soft lips traced the tracks they'd left. Morgan ran strong fingers through her thick hair, then traced feather-light caresses along the line of her neck and shoulder.

Shaine sighed, shivering at Morgan's touch. She allowed Morgan to roll them over and continue her silent caresses. Morgan's hands moved along her strong curves. Morgan's lips and teeth and tongue explored her skin.

She responded to Morgan's touch, emotion building inside her like a volcano waiting to erupt. Morgan's hands moved slowly downward, while that hot mouth suckled her taut nipples and firm breasts. She gasped when strong fingers found her need. She thrust against Morgan's sure strokes until release came in a rush of sensation that left her reeling, clinging to Morgan as a point of solidity in a whirl of cascading emotions that left her dizzy.

She and Morgan lay entangled for long minutes. She breathed in Morgan's scent. They snuggled together, encircled in each other's arms.

Shaine gazed into Morgan's eyes. She wanted to understand what was happening to her, wanted to understand what made her feel like she never wanted to leave this moment in time or the woman who made her feel things she never even knew existed. But her brain had shut down, and all she ran on now was pure animal instinct, an instinct telling her the connection between her and Morgan was true and right, even if she found it overwhelming.

She shivered, her body reacting to the cool air cycling over her hot, damp skin. Swallowing, she eased back from her lover, getting a startled look in response. She kissed Morgan's mouth. "Hang on," she whispered, "I'm cold." She crawled down to the foot of the bed to snag the comforter and pulled it up over Morgan and herself. "Here," she murmured, nudging Morgan to rest her head on her shoulder and carefully tucking the soft material around them.

Morgan's body molded against hers, relaxed and sated, an arm draped comfortably over her middle.

Shaine closed her eyes with a long sigh, reveling in the feel of Morgan's heat. *I want this. I need her. God, I can't lose this. I have to stop Charun. I have to give us our time. Then maybe I can finally have my life back, and Morgan's life too.*

But for right now, they had the night and she planned on making the most of it.

* * *

Morgan didn't remember falling asleep, but she woke with a gut-wrenching shock of adrenaline, disoriented and lost. She sat up in a panic, ready to bolt before her brain caught up with her reactions and she remembered where she was. Sensation washed over her, visceral memories of Shaine's body beneath her, memories of skin and heat and need. She squeezed her eyes shut, forcing herself to start breathing normally again. Blinking, she unclenched her fingers from the comforter's thick fabric.

Beside her, Shaine mumbled and shifted in sleep, wrapping an arm a little tighter around her hips. A well of emotion bubbled in her chest. She automatically tamped her feelings down.

The chron on the nightstand read 5:39 a.m. In just a few hours she was supposed to be having breakfast with Tarm Maruchek. Her birth father. She felt sick. *This can't be real. How could my whole life be one long lie?* She rubbed her hands over her face and squeezed her eyes shut again. *What the fuck—I don't want to deal with this.*

"Morgan."

She opened her eyes to look into Shaine's dark green gaze.

"It'll work out," Shaine said softly.

Morgan swallowed. "Will it?" she whispered hoarsely.

Shaine smiled. "It will," she said. "Come on, sleep a while more, okay?"

Morgan took a long breath, nodded slowly, and let Shaine pull her under the covers.

"You're going to be okay," Shaine whispered into her hair. "Sleep now. Close your eyes."

Morgan turned her cheek against the warm soft skin of Shaine's breast and inhaled her lover's scent. She closed her eyes. *Safe here.* The strength of Shaine's arms wrapped around her was comforting. Maybe everything would be all right. Maybe there was a way to make it all right. She fell back asleep with the gentle motion of Shaine rubbing her back and continuing to whisper reassurances into her hair.

* * *

Morgan blinked awake to the sound of water running and the sweet, fresh smell of soap. Rolling over, she untangled herself from the bedding. The mattress was still warm where Shaine had slept beside her. She smiled and stretched, rubbing the sleep out of her eyes. The chron on the nightstand showed 6:40 a.m. She hadn't heard an alarm and wondered if it'd gone off, or if Shaine was one of those people who just got up without one. She wasn't.

And she really needed to use the bathroom, she realized. She sat up and scooted off the bed, shivering as she padded naked to the bathroom. Fortunately, the bathroom was filled with warm steam. She paused when she walked in, staring for a long moment at the shadow behind the frosted glass shower door, feeling the slow burn of desire wash through her body.

Motion behind the glass stopped. "Morgan?"

"Uh, yeah. Hey. Gotta pee." She rolled her eyes, feeling her face flush. *Idiot, do your business and get out before you embarrass yourself anymore.* "Um, I didn't hear you get up."

Shaine chuckled and spluttered water. "You were out cold."

"I guess."

Morgan finished and stood. The toilet flushed automatically and she hesitated while listening to the shower run. She knew what she wanted to do, but wasn't sure if she would be welcomed.

The frosted glass door cracked open, letting out a waft of fragrant heat. Shaine peered at her with a seductive grin. "You coming in or not?" she asked.

Morgan grinned. She hoped the hot water would hold out.

CHAPTER SIXTEEN

"You're late, Wendt."

"So fire me." Shaine strolled into the bustling security control room at just past oh-eight-hundred hours. She'd already escorted Morgan to the entrance of the indoor conservatory where she was supposed to meet Tarm Maruchek for breakfast. She smiled sweetly at Rogan's glowering visage. "I was playing bodyguard."

Rogan glared at her for a long second. He snapped, "My office. Ten minutes. Brief with Ellerand first." He turned on his heel and stalked away.

She grinned and looked around the busy room, realizing all eyes were on her. She shrugged. *Let 'em look.*

The familiarity of her surroundings struck her. She recognized most of the faces behind the monitors and workstations as dedicated security officers, mostly good eggs. Some offered tentative smiles of greeting, others disinterested glances, a few blatantly hostile glares. She ignored everyone and turned to the one person in the room she considered a friend.

Kyle Ellerand rolled his chair back from a cluttered row of monitors and keyboards similar to the mess in his office. His space in the main room took up the greater part of the far corner. Comp pads, handwritten and printed sheets of notes, and a half dozen coffee mugs covered the counter for three meters. He motioned for her to join him at his workstation.

Shaine perched on a rolling stool beside him. Most of the room returned to their work.

Ellerand flashed her a grin. "Hey, Wendt. Sleep well last night?"

Shaine smirked. "Like a baby, Kyle. So what've you got for me?"

He made a rueful face. He tapped at the keyboard, reached over to one of the touch-screen monitors, and shifted a couple of the windows around. "You can say what you want about Charun, but you gotta admit the man is a paranoid fucker and he runs a tight ship. Right now he seems to be hunkering down for the long haul. He's holed up in the desert compound. So if you're going to take him out, you're gonna have to do it from the inside."

He tapped on the screen and stretched one of the windows with a flick of his finger. The window still only took up a quarter of the monitor. Shaine didn't mind. She understood and respected Ellerand's need to keep his information close.

She squinted. "Blueprints of the compound?"

"They're a little out of date, but it's a start. I haven't had a chance to go over them closely yet. Just got my hands on 'em last night."

"You're good, Ellerand."

He scratched his head. "Yeah, well." He cleared the screen. "I'll send ya an upload of everything I have. I've got some ideas on how to tackle this."

"Good, thanks."

He nodded surreptitiously at one of his monitors.

Shaine followed his gaze to a live surveillance feed boxed in a corner of the monitor, opposite the one where the blueprints were displayed. The video stream showed a tropical scene and a woman strolling slowly through it. Even at a distance she recognized Morgan's slim figure moving through the conservatory.

Ellerand said, "I got her covered, okay?"

Shaine smiled, feeling a sense of relief at knowing Morgan wasn't on her own. "Thanks." She nodded toward the office. "I'd better get in there before he blows a gasket."

Ellerand grinned. "Yeah, he's pretty uptight. And Lissa Hedding is seriously pissed with you, by the way."

Shaine snorted. "Good. Bitch."

Ellerand threw his head back and laughed.

Shaine grinned and headed to Rogan's office, figuring it would be an interesting day.

* * *

Morgan stood at the entry to the gardens, missing Shaine's presence at her side. She glanced behind her at the empty hallway, trying to shake off her unease, angry at herself for feeling that way. *Jesus, Morgan. Get the fuck over it. You don't need Shaine holding your hand.* She shook herself mentally, took a long breath and looked into the expansiveness of the indoor garden.

A path of stepping stones led toward the center of the conservatory. She picked her way slowly along. Towering palm trees bordered the trail, reaching toward the clear ceiling some four stories above. The warm, mossy-smelling air clung damply against her skin.

Behind the line of palms, other tropical trees and thick foliage grew in landscaped terraces and rocky outcroppings where springs and waterfalls gurgled into small pools. Vines with gigantic leaves hung haphazardly between the trees. Brilliant flowers bloomed around ponds filled with fish and small reptiles. Birdcalls echoed and blended with the low buzzing of insects. Leaves rustled in a light man-made breeze while butterflies fluttered lazily on the currents. She peered around in wide-eyed wonder. She'd been in the botanical garden at Luna City on the moon a few times, but it was barely a quarter the size of this space and certainly didn't have anywhere near the variety or quality of foliage. From where she walked, still near the outer edge of the conservatory, she couldn't see the other side through the vegetation.

She marveled at the lavish amounts of water, heat and energy a conservatory like this required. Only on Earth could someone get away with this kind of excessive use of environmental commodities.

She walked until she reached the center of the conservatory where a multilevel patio was built into a terraced rock plateau. A waterfall at the far side splashed into a shallow pool. Tucked against a craggy rock wall, a glass-topped table and four wrought-iron chairs were shaded by tropical ferns and foliage.

A tray with a chrome thermal carafe, a pitcher of ice water and glasses, and a set of heavy earthen pottery mugs and saucers were arranged on the table. She noticed a small setting of lawn furniture off to the side, including a love seat/glider and several well-padded chairs with wrought-iron drink tables scattered among them.

Morgan looked around, but she appeared to be alone. Enticed by the strong aroma of coffee, she poured herself a mug, adding generous dollops of cream and sugar from a matching service. She brought her steaming coffee to an overstuffed patio chair and settled in. Breathing in the heady, rich scent, she sipped from the mug, relaxing as the warm liquid slid down her throat. She forced herself to wait quietly for Tarm Maruchek.

Minutes passed. Morgan finished her coffee and thought about getting another cup. She was beginning to get impatient when she finally heard footsteps on the flagstones. She looked up to see Maruchek striding toward her. His expression went from serious and lost in his thoughts to smiling and relaxed as he caught her gaze. Even his posture changed—his shoulders dropping and his stride easing by the time he reached the patio.

"Morgan, good morning. I see you found the coffee," he said.

"I did. It's good." She almost rolled her eyes at the way she sounded so bright and intelligent...not.

Maruchek poured himself a cup. "Need a warm-up?" he asked amiably.

"Um, sure. But I can get it." She started to stand.

He waved her back down, walked over and took her empty mug from her hands. "Sugar and cream?" he asked.

Morgan nodded. "Please."

He nodded and quickly fixed her coffee, returned the mug to

her and settled into a chair with his own mug. He took the time to savor a couple of sips before he turned his gaze onto her. "You slept well, I hope?" he asked.

Morgan ducked her head to hide the flush as visions of Shaine danced through her brain. "Fine, yes, thank you," she managed. "This place is incredible."

Maruchek smiled. "It is, isn't it? Feel free to spend as much time here as you'd like while you're visiting." He continued sipping his coffee. "Breakfast should be out shortly." He observed her over the rim of his mug. "I still can't get over how much you look like your mother," he said quietly. "It's really quite amazing."

Morgan had no idea how to respond.

Maruchek smiled sadly. "You know, you don't need to look so shell-shocked. You have nothing to fear from me."

Her stomach clenched. Didn't she? A week ago nobody was trying to kill her. She set her mug on the ground at her feet. A hundred thoughts and emotions rushed through her brain. His casual familiarity grated against her nerves. He didn't know her. She resented how he easily commented on her likeness to a woman he said was her mother, whom she didn't remember and never would. Part of her wanted to believe his sincerity, but another part wanted to scream accusations at him for the lies he'd told about what happened to Digger.

Maruchek set his mug on the table at his side. "You spoke with your father yesterday."

Morgan nodded. "I needed to talk to him."

"And he told you I was not lying?"

Cold bitterness in the pit of her stomach replaced the comforting warmth of the coffee. "I think I'd have been better off never knowing."

"You're probably right about that." Maruchek clasped his hands together and leaned his elbows on his knees. "And I'm sorry that it had to come to this. I would have left you alone if there had been a choice."

"Would you?"

He spread his hands apart. "Had you heard from me before now?"

"No."

"And if circumstances hadn't warranted, it would have remained that way. But I couldn't ignore the threat to your life."

Morgan scowled. "I don't buy it."

Maruchek's somewhat regretful and patient expression shifted toward impatient and angry. "Why would I lie to you?" he asked sharply.

"Why wouldn't you? You lie about everything else. You lied about Digger."

"Digger?"

Morgan's temper flashed. *You don't even know his name?* She stood abruptly. "John Drygzinski. My best friend. The man who died in my fucking vac suit. You said the suit failed. That was a blatant lie."

Maruchek's expression darkened. "I am very sorry about your friend, Morgan, but I have a company to protect."

Morgan felt something snap inside her and the words tumbled out in a furious rush. "I don't give a flying *fuck* about your corporate profits! People are dying out there. My best friend. My mom. How many others? And what are you doing about it? Lying? Covering it up? You think we don't know what your priorities are, Mr. Maruchek? Power, money and politics, maybe, but not us workers who are getting our asses kicked out there every day and barely scraping by." She glared at him, her hands shaking, knowing by the fury in his expression that she'd probably crossed a line. But anger overrode fear. She didn't back down. "Don't bother feeding me your corporate line."

For a long moment they glared at each other. Maruchek was the first to master his anger. "Sit down," he said.

Morgan didn't move.

Maruchek spoke slowly and certainly. "You think I don't care. You are wrong, Morgan. I do care. If I were to speak openly about the terrorists, if the public knew the extent of the damage being done, we would have panic. Is that what you want?"

Morgan swallowed, feeling like a kid being lectured.

"The terrorists are well organized and well funded. A few of the smaller groups are simply anticorporate in general. But most are funded by a single underground group and those are targeting Mann-Maru specifically. My security and the System authorities are doing all they can to get to the bottom of that group and eliminate the threat. We've stopped several attacks. But not all of them."

"So, you know who's doing it?"

Maruchek's expression turned dark and cold. "We have good leads on the mid-level operatives, but not the complete overall picture. We're getting closer to proving who's funding them. But understand this: everything I do, and everything I say publicly, is meant both to protect my employees and to protect the company that employs them."

Morgan studied his face. Should she believe him or not? Certainly, he believed in what he told her. Sincerity showed in his eyes. She stuffed her hands in her pockets. Maybe he was just a good actor. He'd had enough practice over the years. On the other hand, he hadn't lied about being her biological father. Vinn Rahn— her dad—had verified his story. *Maruchek's my birth father. I don't want to distrust my own father. Even if he is a blood-sucking corporate bastard. Jesus. How's that for ironic?*

Maruchek watched her intently, apparently waiting for her to come to some kind of inner decision. She could tell he was trying to be patient, trying to control his emotions, and she wondered, for a moment, why he didn't just lash out at her, why he was so obviously trying not to? *He wants you to trust him. Do you do what he wants?* She warred with her inner voices. *Nobody tells me what to do and I refuse to be manipulated. But he hasn't killed me, called security, or told me to shut the hell up. What does he want from me? What do I want?*

She sighed and slowly returned to her chair. She perched on the edge of the seat. *What do I want?* She considered. At the moment, she really wanted answers. Maybe that was a good place to continue their little discussion. She cocked her head and asked, "Can you tell me why someone wants me killed? You said you had enemies. Shaine told me she's supposed to kill a man named Charun. What's really going on?"

Maruchek leaned back. "Would you like the long version or the short version?"

"Short version to start with."

"Okay, fair enough. More coffee?"

She shook her head.

"Do you know who Tyr Charun is?"

Morgan hesitated, remembering what Shaine had told her the night before, but decided she wanted to hear Maruchek's version. She trusted Shaine's information. She had yet to trust the man sitting in front of her. "No idea," she said evenly.

Maruchek seemed to consider his words and told the facts as though giving a lecture, with little emotion. "Tyr Charun is a businessman. His company, InterSys Enterprises, owns and runs dozens of subsidiaries, most of which are in the mining industry, as are my own. He and I have been rivals for many years. It was a relatively friendly rivalry early on. We knew each other in college, were in the same class. And then we both met Arella Danvers— your mother. Eventually I won her heart and we were married. Tyr never forgave me for what he perceived as stealing his girlfriend, nor did he forgive Arella for making her choice. He never got over her. I can't explain his obsession with Arella.

"Truly, I can't explain very much about the man's behavior over the years. Initially, it was competition between us. Once, I think it could even have been considered friendly, but over the years that changed. For more than two decades, I believe he's been trying to destroy me and my company. I believe he is part of the group behind the pirate attacks that killed your mother, Elise, as well as the recent rash of 'accidents' plaguing my companies, one of which involved you and your crew. Now he knows about you. He will be relentless in his attempts to kill you. You remind him too much of Arella for him to let you go."

Morgan struggled to understand. "If you know he's behind it, why not go to the authorities? Why does Shaine have to kill this guy? Can't you just have him put in jail?"

Maruchek raised a brow. "Unfortunately, we don't have enough evidence. Everything we have is either circumstantial or supposition. We cannot find an actual, direct tie between Charun and the terrorists. He has made no direct threats to you we could cite." He set his coffee down on the table at the side of his chair. "No, Morgan, these things are better dealt with our way."

Morgan looked away. She found herself twisting her mother's

ring on her finger. The habit helped her think. As expected, Tarm Maruchek seemed to believe he was above the law. She supposed maybe, in some ways, he was. She recognized the hardness in Maruchek's expression. Of course he'd take care of the matter internally—he didn't want the publicity of a trial. He wanted to deal with it and make it go away.

She raised her head. "But why drag Shaine into this? She doesn't deserve to be used. She's just trying to live her life."

Maruchek met her accusing gaze. "Because I trust her to get the job done."

Morgan got up, paced across the uneven slate, and stood watching the waterfall splash into the koi pond. Tiny waves played against the grasses and lily pads swaying at the edges of the pool. The water's quiet movement fascinated and soothed her, allowing a chance to think.

Using Shaine was simply a means to an end. She thought about the tormented look in Shaine's eyes when she'd said she was going to kill the guy. Her heart ached. Shaine didn't want to be their assassin, had insisted on trying to put that life behind her.

So how did she reconcile the gentle woman from last night's lovemaking with the coldhearted killer who worked for Maruchek's organization? Was she just being naïve?

Shaine planned to kill a man. She'd been a lethal Special Operations commando in Earth Guard. What did that say about Shaine and what she was capable of doing? Did it matter?

Maruchek's voice drifted quietly across the patio. "I take care of my people, Morgan. My family. My friends. My employees. I know you don't trust me. But I promise I will not lie to you."

Morgan didn't bother replying. She didn't know what to say. The whole situation felt like a tangled web of lies and games and power plays she didn't fully understand, and she didn't know if she wanted to. So what if Maruchek didn't lie to her? How would she know if he did? It mattered to her a hundred times more if Shaine lied.

She trailed her fingers absently through the cool water, trying to think everything through. Shaine hadn't hidden the fact she'd been a lethal killer in Earth Guard and intimated she'd done the same for Rogan and Maruchek. Shaine could have easily lied about her past if she'd wanted to.

Morgan closed her eyes, searching her heart. She trusted Shaine, despite knowing maybe she shouldn't. There was no reason behind the trust—only instinct.

She compared her trust in Shaine to what she'd felt with Gina. Although she'd repeated over and over to herself and to her friends that she trusted Gina, there had always been part of her heart that knew, down deep, the trust was a lie. Her inner knowledge had beaten her up with despair at the end. She'd been tormented by an inner voice screaming, "I told you so" when Gina laughed at her and walked away. The same deep-seated voice now insisted Shaine could be trusted, and this time, she actually listened.

She let go a long breath she hadn't realized she'd been holding. She was tired of thinking. Fuck. She hadn't even eaten breakfast yet and she was giving herself a headache.

"Come and sit with me, Morgan."

She turned. Maruchek had shifted in his chair, observing her with a veiled gaze. She couldn't quite read his expression, but detected no malice.

He spread his hands in an offer of peace. "Please," he said quietly. "Come and sit. You can ask me anything you want. Perhaps you can tell me about your life? I know I haven't been a father to you, but I do care. I would like to get to know the woman who is my daughter."

Morgan returned to the chair across from Maruchek. Something in his tone told her he meant what he said. She eased down into the chair, reached for the mug she'd set on the ground, and took a sip. The coffee was still warm. She cradled the mug in her fingers and gazed down into the creamy brown liquid, wondering where she could even start.

"Your mother was a wonderful woman," Maruchek said. "Kind and gentle, but strong. She never walked away from a fight, but she never started one, either." He smiled thoughtfully. "I've often wondered if you'd grown up to be like her."

She glanced at him, realizing he was asking a question as much as making a statement. She took a breath. "I don't know that I'm any of those things."

Maruchek only smiled. "I believe you are more than you think."

Morgan shrugged, uncomfortable with the conversation, not wanting to give too much of herself away, not sure what to say, but not wanting to put him off, either.

Maruchek seemed to want to talk, though. He took the lead again, this time a bit more direct. He commented, "My assistant, Lissa, told me she'd spoken to you last night."

"She stopped by, yeah. Gave me her card." Morgan paused and finally added, "I got the impression she and Shaine don't get along well." Okay, that was an understatement, but she was curious, and he seemed open to answering questions. She probably should have just asked Shaine, but it hadn't occurred to her at the time. They'd been distracted with other things.

Maruchek's smile widened. He leaned back in his chair. "No, there's no love lost between those two," he admitted. "Before she worked for me directly, Lissa was one of Rogan's high-profile agents. Wendt joined Rogan's security team and rather quickly became senior to Lissa. There's been bad blood between them since."

Morgan nodded thoughtfully. Well, that explained that, at least to a certain degree. She figured there was likely a lot more to the story than he was giving her, but she would ask Shaine about it when they had more time.

Maruchek continued, "Wendt is good at what she does. Knowing she was watching over you was a relief to me."

Morgan's breath caught in her throat. "Was Shaine joining my crew a setup?" Her voice broke on the words.

Maruchek looked startled. "What? Oh. No. That was a coincidence. A rather fortunate one, but no, Wendt being assigned to your crew was a fluke, though it certainly worked to our advantage."

Relief washed over her. She figured if she'd been standing, her knees would have given out. She took a shaky breath and tried to school her expression to neutral.

Maruchek asked, "Do you and Wendt get along all right?"

Morgan knew her face was flushed. "Yeah, sure. We're fine," she said quickly, covering her reaction by sipping her coffee.

Maruchek seemed to try very hard not to smile. Morgan scowled at him. The smile he tried to hide showed in his eyes. "I'd gotten the impression that was the case," he commented before artfully changing the subject. "More coffee?"

"No, thanks." She looked down. *Bastard, he knows. They probably had a freaking spy camera set up in the guest suite. Christ.*

Maruchek got up to refill his cup.

A shortish, robust figure dressed in a pressed white kitchen uniform arrived on the patio with a covered platter balanced in his hands. "Your breakfast, Mr. Maruchek."

Maruchek smiled. "Thank you, Ray. You can set it on the table."

"Yes, sir." The man set the covered tray down and disappeared without another word.

Maruchek lifted the dome. "There's plenty here. Please, take a plate."

Morgan hesitated. Her stomach clenched with nerves and she wasn't hungry. Still, she hadn't eaten since last night, so maybe a taste of something would be okay.

She stood and joined Maruchek at the table. He'd already piled his plate with fruit and cheese and a large croissant. She studied the tray. The warm, sweet scent of fresh bread wafted to her nose. The bowl of freshly cut fruit glistened alluringly. Her empty stomach grumbled. Okay, maybe food wasn't such a bad idea. She filled her plate, grabbed a set of silverware wrapped in a linen napkin, and returned to her chair.

Taking a bite of the croissant, she chewed slowly, hoping the bread would calm her queasy stomach.

She and Maruchek talked while they ate. Maruchek kept the conversation to pleasant generalities, talking a bit about sports, asking her if she'd ever gone to a soccer game at Luna City. After a bit, he apologized, saying he needed to attend to some business. He got to his feet.

Morgan followed suit.

"I've enjoyed talking with you this morning," he said.

Morgan managed an awkward smile in return. "It was nice."

"I have a holobook you might want to see. I'll have it sent up to your suite, if you like."

"Sure."

He nodded.

She and Maruchek stood uncomfortably for a moment. She sincerely hoped he wasn't going to try to hug her.

After a second, Maruchek simply smiled. "Please remember you're welcome to spend as much time as you'd like here in the gardens. If you need any assistance getting back to your suite, you can ask anyone you see, or call Lissa's number on the card she gave you."

Morgan nodded.

Maruchek said, "Have a good day then, daughter," and with a quick bow of his head, turned and headed down the flagstone path.

She watched him walk away. He had a strong stride, and the wide shoulders and narrow waist of an athlete. His physique had clearly filled in some over the years, but despite the graying at his temples and the lines at the edges of his eyes, he still seemed very young and vital. So very different than Vinn Rahn, she thought sadly.

Her dad seemed so much older, but she suspected the two men weren't that different in actual age. She pictured the line-etched planes of her dad's face and the way his eyes had faded. He used a cane now, his gait stiff and careful after so many years working in the asteroid mines. She remembered the occasional injuries he'd come home with—pulled muscles and backaches from working the heavy equipment in the processing plants, or just from spending too many hours in zero-g without a break, having neither the time or the energy to exercise in full gravity to rebuild bone and muscle lost to floating.

Morgan shook her head as despondency washed over her. The years had been a lot rougher on Vinn Rahn. It wasn't fair. But life rarely was.

Feeling a bit at loose ends, she wandered the gardens a while before turning back toward her suite. She wasn't certain she knew exactly where she was going, but she didn't want to ask for help, especially from Lissa. Better to just work the route out for herself. If it took awhile, that was fine, because what she needed right now was time to think and to process.

CHAPTER SEVENTEEN

As Maruchek promised, a thick book of holophotos waited for her when Morgan returned to the suite, left on the coffee table in the living room. She felt a bit unnerved at seeing it, knowing the only people able to access the suite were Shaine and herself, Maruchek and Rogan. She hoped the visitor had been Maruchek because the thought of Rogan in her space weirded her out, and the thought of having missed Shaine made her sad.

She found a sheet of letterhead with a short note written in neat, flowing longhand placed inside the front cover of the book.

"Morgan, I hope that you will enjoy the holos. The book is yours to keep. —TM."

Maruchek, then. She sat with the book for the next couple of hours, paging through the images, repeatedly going back to the ones of Arella Maruchek, fascinated by the woman who looked so much like her. Still, she couldn't shake the sensation that she was nosing into someone else's private memories. This wasn't her family. Not really. She looked at holos of strangers. If it wasn't for the eerily familiar face of her birth mother, she didn't think she would have been able to make any connection at all to the people on the pages.

While Morgan flipped through the holo book, Shaine called to ask how breakfast with Maruchek went. Morgan was glad to hear from her. Shaine didn't know when she'd be done with mission planning and made Morgan promise not to wait for dinner or wait up that night. Through the entire conversation, she felt like Shaine sounded rushed and distracted.

After the call, Morgan returned to the book for a while, but her curiosity waned and she set it aside. She cast around for something else to do, found a movie on the net, and stared blankly at the film awhile before turning it off. She thought about going back out to the gardens—at least she'd be moving—but didn't feel quite comfortable going there alone. For the hundredth time, she wished Shaine would return, and for the hundredth time she berated herself for being so damned needy.

Finally, she flopped on the sofa and scanned through the news channels on the entertainment center. The hours passed slowly.

By seven o'clock, Shaine still hadn't returned. Morgan gave up waiting and ordered a sandwich for a late dinner. She ended up only eating half. Too wound up to finish the meal, she abandoned her half-finished beer on the coffee table too.

Morgan prowled around the suite, mentally exhausted, but physically too wired to sleep. She stared out the windows, feeling restless and trapped.

The night skyline winked with flashes of light and neon color, the city alive with movement. Vehicles drew avenues of streaking light between the sky-scraping buildings. Airplane, space shuttle and helicopter running lights dotted the blackness over the city. She searched for stars, but only a few were bright enough to show through the ambient light. The moon was a pale, thin arc, partially veiled behind wispy clouds. She traced the outline on the windowpane, finding it odd to reconcile the sliver of faded yellow as her home.

The antique chron on the wall finally chimed eleven thirty p.m.

She turned from the window and padded into the bedroom, grabbed her comp pad out of her gym bag, and brought it back with her to the sofa. A couple of days had passed since she'd written in her journal and she had at least three books loaded in her reading list. At the very least, she figured she could waste some time playing mindless tile games.

She settled sideways into the corner of the sofa, leaning against the overstuffed arm with her legs stretched out the length of the seat. Powering up the pad, she closed her eyes and leaned her head back for a few moments. Her brain reeled. She wasn't doing very well with coherent thoughts. One image after another and muddled fragments of logic ran circles around each other—snapshots out of time from the holo book, memories of her past, thoughts of Shaine and her impending mission, flashes of the attack in the street, of the explosion that caused Digger's death and the gruesome sight of his blood-splattered faceplate. So much happening in just a few days. She hoped some time on her pad would push it away awhile.

Her friend Charri's avatar popped up on the small monitor almost instantly when the pad finished powering up. Her voice exploded over the tiny speakers, "Morgan Rahn, where the fuck have you been?"

Morgan jumped, instinctively hitting the mute button. Charri's pink and magenta jungle cat avatar glared up from the screen. *Aw, fuck*, she groaned internally. With all the security around Maruchek's compound, it hadn't even occurred to her she'd have an automatic net uplink here. She tapped the avatar messaging controls to go to text mode. Before she could decide what to type, Charri's continuing tirade popped up in a text window.

Morgan? Morgan! Her name in bold red blinked furiously at her, registering the emotion in Charri's voice as oversized lettering.

Morgan sighed. She could pretty much hear Charri yelling into her mic and knew the woman would be pissed she'd switched to text-only. She typed, *Hey, Char.*

Where the fuk r u? R u ok?? Talk 2 me Morgan!

I'm fine. I'm ok.

Put the f-ing mic on, Mor!

Can't.

WHERE R U??????

Morgan couldn't help grinning at the angry, frustrated expression on Charri's avatar. The typeface in the text window was getting bigger and bolder. But what could she say? *Hard 2 explain. But all ok.*

Even Strom doesn't know where u r! Ur going to get fired!

Char—calm down. It's ok. It's all good. I promise. Sure it was all good. Some obsessive bastard was trying to kill her because she looked like her birth mother, her family had lied to her all her life, her birth father owned half the freakin' solar system, and she was falling in love with an assassin. Yeah. All good. Really.

MORGAN! Charri's text blinked for attention. *MORGAN!! ur with her, rn't you? With Shaine???*

Morgan sighed. *Yeah.*

U know, if u were gonna ELOPE u could have TOLD ME!!!!!

Morgan almost laughed out loud. *I have not eloped.*

Then what the FUK R U DOING??????

2 hard 2 explain. Just trust me. I'm okay. I gotta go.

MORGAN!!!!

Char, I'm sorry. I can't talk about stuff right now…please, it's okay.

This is completely fukked, Mor.

Yeah, I know. I promise, I'll explain it all later, K?

K. Ur safe?

Morgan sighed. She could almost hear the resignation in Charri's words, knew her friend was worried about her, and knew there wasn't a damned thing she could do about it. Hell, she was worried about herself. She texted, *I'm safe. I gotta go. Talk 2 u later, k?*

K. B careful, Morgan, whatever ur doing.

I will.

She killed the pad's online connection before Charri could ask anymore questions. Her friend's avatar popped off the screen. "Fuck," she whispered to the empty room. "Fuck. Fuck. Fuck."

She didn't know if she'd see her friends again, let alone be able to tell them anything about what had happened. The only anchor she had in the whole screwed-up mess was a woman she hardly knew, whom she trusted implicitly without knowing why, and who made her feel more wonderful than she'd ever felt in her life.

She opened her journal app to write. Using her favorite lime-green stylus, she scratched in the date and sat for fifteen minutes trying to come up with something reasonably coherent to write.

Finally, she just closed the app, too wiped out to try to put her addled thoughts into words. *May as well just play a few rounds of tile games.* Maybe some mindless entertainment would quiet her brain enough to let her sleep.

CHAPTER EIGHTEEN

Shaine slipped into the guest suite, pausing to pull off her boots as the door snicked shut. She sighed, noting the lack of light and the silence. Only a dim lamp glowed in the corner of the living room. Morgan must've gone to sleep. She glanced at the chron on her wrist. One thirty a.m. Christ. No wonder she felt like crap.

As she moved through the gloom of the entry and into the living room, she realized the shadow in the corner of the sofa was actually Morgan's dark hair. The woman's head was pillowed on the soft cushions. She approached silently, a smile twitching her lips.

Morgan slept curled in the corner of the sofa, clutching her pad against her stomach with one hand. Shaine slid around to crouch at Morgan's side. Her fingers traced lightly along the soft skin of Morgan's uninjured cheek. *Damn, you're beautiful.*

Morgan's eyes fluttered open.

"Hey," Shaine whispered.

Morgan focused blearily. "Hey," she mumbled. "Wondered when you'd get back."

"Me too." Shaine eased the pad out of Morgan's grip, set it on the coffee table and took Morgan's hand in hers. "Come on, let's get you to bed, huh?"

Morgan sat up and rubbed a hand over her eyes. "You had a long day."

Shaine shrugged. "Yeah. You doing all right?"

"Fine, I guess. I don't know. It's all just—weird."

Shaine ran a comforting hand up and down Morgan's arm, not knowing quite what to say. "Yeah."

"I ran into Charri on the net tonight."

Shaine raised a brow. *Online? When did Rogan open their net access to external personal avatars?*

"She was freaking out, not knowing where I was. How the fuck do I explain all this?"

"What did you tell her?" Shaine's words came out sharper than she intended.

Morgan gave her a cautious look. "Nothing. I told her I was fine, and not to worry, that everything was okay. But it's not, is it?"

Shaine forced a smile she didn't feel. "It'll be fine, Morgan," she assured her.

Morgan didn't appear appeased.

She sighed and brushed the bangs out of Morgan's eyes, idly letting her fingers trail through the short, silky hair. Suddenly too exhausted to deal any longer, she held out a hand to Morgan. "Come on, I'm beat. Let's go to bed."

Morgan took her outstretched hand and followed her tiredly to the bedroom. Shaine stripped out of her clothes and helped Morgan with hers. Pulling down the covers, she waited until Morgan got settled, then slid in beside her. Morgan snuggled against her, laying her head on Shaine's chest. Shaine smiled and covered them with the thick comforter then wrapped her arms around Morgan. She kissed the dark hair, feeling Morgan's body relax with a sigh.

"Good night," she whispered.

Morgan murmured into her chest, already asleep.

Sometime later, the harsh, incessant beeping of a portable communicator eventually worked its way into Shaine's consciousness. She blinked into the darkness. Groaning, she realized the com was on Morgan's side of the bed even as Morgan flailed out a hand from under the covers to grab the irritating thing.

Morgan fumbled with the communicator, finally keying it on, and mumbled into the receiver, "H'lo?"

In the quiet, Shaine heard an agitated voice coming from the other end of the line. "Wendt? Wendt, get down here, we gotta talk!"

With her eyes still mostly closed, Morgan handed over the transceiver. "'S for you."

Shaine took the device from Morgan's boneless grip.

The voice on the other end yelled, "Wendt? Hello?"

Shaine groaned and rolled on her back. "Ellerand?"

"Yeah, yeah. Wendt, we gotta talk. You gotta get down here, now."

"Now?"

"Now. Just get here." The line clicked dead.

Shaine sighed heavily.

Morgan rolled over to face her and drifted a hand across her middle. "Something wrong?" she asked sleepily.

Shaine shivered at the light touch. She caught Morgan's hand and squeezed. "Ellerand gets excited," she said softly, rubbing her thumb across the soft skin on the back of Morgan's hand. "I'm sure it's nothing, but I'd better go find out what's going on." She leaned down and laid a gentle kiss on Morgan's mouth. "Don't worry. Go back to sleep. I won't be gone long." She held Morgan's gaze until the woman relaxed into the pillows. A quick kiss on Morgan's forehead, and she slid out of bed with a sigh.

She pulled on pants and a tunic, padded out to the living room and shoved her bare feet into the boots she'd left by the door. She let herself out of the suite and hurried through the building, back down to Security where Ellerand waited impatiently.

Ellerand spun around on the chair in front of his desk when she walked into his office. "About time, Wendt."

She gave him a dark look. "It's four o'clock in the fucking morning."

"Not like you were busy," he returned with a smirk. He laughed and got up, moved past her to the door and tapped a couple of codes into the security pad.

"Fucking voyeur."

"She's real pretty, by the way. Lissa must be pissed as hell."

Shaine rolled her eyes. "You locking us in?"

Ellerand snorted. "Private conversation. Program kills any bugs, jams any transceivers, overrides security codes. Nobody can get in. Not even Rogan. 'Cuz you're gonna love this."

Shaine followed him to his desk and pulled up a rolling stool. "This better be good, Kyle."

Ellerand dropped into his chair. "Oh, it's good." He leaned toward the monitors, swept a finger across one, then another, and gave Shaine an expectant look.

"Blueprints. So? We've already been over these."

"What do you see?"

"Just spit it out."

He zoomed in one of the screens. "What's that look like to you?"

She shrugged. "Some kind of electrical junction point."

"Close. Now look over here." He zoomed in on the image showing on a second screen. "What's this look like to you?"

Shaine reached to the screen, dialed in closer and studied the picture. "It's a fucking *phase* detonator," she breathed, her eyes widening.

"The whole place is wired to blow, Wendt."

"Rogan doesn't know about this."

Ellerand shook his head. "Just you and me. This is an updated version of the blueprints. I haven't passed it to him. It's uploaded to your pad."

Shaine rolled the stool back from the monitors. "This is supposed to be quick in, do the job, and quick out. Not a demolition."

Ellerand snorted. "Rogan's not expecting you to come back alive."

"Rogan never expects me to come back alive," she countered evenly. "And he's always wrong. We've talked about this before, Kyle." She frowned, thinking. "Why does Charun have the place wired?" she asked.

Ellerand shrugged. "He's either crazy paranoid, or he actually has something to hide. In any case, if all hell breaks loose, you can hit the big red button and get the fuck out. It eliminates the evidence and at least buys you a chance. It's better than the odds Rogan's giving you."

She sighed. That was true. But she wouldn't use that option unless she had no other choices. "Where's the big red button?"

Ellerand grinned and zoomed out of the blueprint. "In Charun's bedroom."

"Great. Any idea how much time I have if I hit the button?"

He shrugged. "No idea. But Charun's a planner. He's gonna give himself a way out. My guess is he's got an escape vehicle tucked away close by. Nothing showing in the blueprints, though."

"Yeah."

Ellerand tapped at the keyboard. The two monitors blanked out. "Now nobody else is gonna know," he said evenly.

"And Rogan can't tell me not to trash the place if he doesn't know about the self-destruct. I can always blame it on Charun." Shaine stood. "Thanks, Kyle."

Ellerand shrugged, giving her a bittersweet expression. "If anyone can do the job, it's you, Shaine. That's why I called you in now, without Rogan and Barill around. This'll give you a fighting chance if it all goes to hell."

She said nothing. *To save Morgan's life, I'll fucking move mountains.*

He gave her a serious look. "Get outta here, Wendt. I'll see ya in the morning."

She smiled tiredly and slipped away. Exhaustion washed over her as the door slid shut. She paused to lean against the thick frame, pulling herself together. *Just get back to the suite. Don't think, just walk.* She pushed off the wall.

It seemed to take forever to reach the suite. Feeling a distinct sense of déjà vu, she kicked off her boots when she got in the door and padded barefoot across cold tile and warm carpet. She half-expected to find Morgan sleeping on the sofa, but the living room was dark and silent. She walked through to pause at the bedroom door. A dim shaft of light cut across the bed from the partly open bathroom door.

Morgan had cocooned herself in the comforter, curled into an almost fetal position, nearly hidden in the soft folds. Dark hair spilled over the white pillowcase. Shaine found something almost painfully vulnerable about the image. *God, Morgan, I can't lose you. We haven't even had a chance to try.*

She kept running Ellerand's discovery of the self-destruct through her brain. It was an unexpected twist, and it made her uneasy. What was Charun hiding? Or was he, as Ellerand suggested, just a crazy paranoid bastard? Either way, she didn't like it. It added a complication that she didn't need, and a compulsion to understand what was behind it. But that wasn't her mission. Quick in, quick kill, quick out. That was the plan she needed to focus on.

Eight years in Special Ops had trained her not to think extraneous thoughts. Just do the job. Follow the orders. Find a way. Complete the mission. No outside concerns, no emotional involvement. Even in Rogan's security group, she'd been able to distance herself enough to just get the job done. This time, though—damn. There was no distance here.

Just watching Morgan sleep made her ache. Need, desire, attachment? God. Whatever it was, she could not fuck up this assignment—or this relationship.

She stripped out of her pants and top. Easing onto the bed, she wriggled her way under the covers and spooned against the warmth of Morgan's skin. Tucking a hand under her pillow, she draped her other arm around Morgan's waist.

Morgan mumbled and shifted closer against her.

Shaine closed her eyes and waited for sleep.

CHAPTER NINETEEN

Shaine leaned over a worktable scattered with maps, papers, and comp pads. Kyle Ellerand stood at her side, looking up some detail on his pad. Rogan and Cord Barill faced them on the other side of the table.

Rogan tapped something into his pad. After a couple of seconds, he glanced up. "We're good to go." His gaze touched Shaine and Cord Barill. "In three hours at the roof launchpad."

Barill nodded. "Yes, sir."

Shaine merely blinked expressionlessly.

Rogan acknowledged Barill, glared at Shaine, and turned and stalked away, taking the pad with him.

Shaine glanced at Ellerand. "I need your screens a minute."

"Sure."

She followed him back to the long counter serving as his desk.

"What'cha need?" he asked.

"To find Morgan."

"No problem. Told you, I got her covered." He tapped on the keyboard. An array of windows came up on the nearest monitor, which he surreptitiously turned away from other eyes.

Shaine scanned the security camera feeds—more than she'd expected. She was tempted to ask which cameras were official and which ones Ellerand had set up outside the system.

Ellerand's fingers sprinted over the keys. The windows shifted rapidly until one centered and highlighted a view inside the conservatory. "There," he said.

Shaine couldn't stop her quick intake of breath or her smile.

On a lush grassy patch tucked behind a row of thick, flowering thornbushes, Morgan lay on her stomach, propped on an elbow, scribbling with a stylus on her comp pad. She wore faded black cargo pants and a long-sleeved gray tunic. Dark bangs hid her eyes and shadowed her face.

"You okay, Wendt?"

She shook herself and shoved her hands in her pockets. "Yeah, I'm good."

Ellerand smirked at her. A tap on the keyboard, and the window went black. "Gee," he said, "looks like the camera went out."

Shaine laughed. Her face flushed. "Talk to you later." Grinning, she hurried out of the security room.

She found Morgan at the back of the garden, as far off the path as possible. She slipped silently through the break in the bushes that Morgan must have gone through, stood and watched her lover for a long minute. Morgan still lay on her stomach in the grass, her slim frame stretched out comfortably with her feet crossed.

Shaine licked her lips thoughtfully and eased forward.

Morgan's head snapped around, dark eyes wary for an instant before her expression relaxed in recognition. "Hey, Shaine."

"Hi." Shaine dropped onto the grass beside Morgan, who set her pad aside and rolled over to face her.

"You have some down time?"

Shaine took a breath, hesitated, and finally nodded. When Morgan cocked her head at the indecision, she said, "I'm leaving in a couple of hours."

A long second of silence hung between them. Morgan processed the statement. Her expression shifted to concern.

Shaine ran a finger lightly along the healing scar on Morgan's cheek. "I'll be back soon."

Morgan turned her head and kissed Shaine's fingers. "Please be careful."

"I will." Shaine tried to hide the shiver running through her at Morgan's touch. She didn't want Morgan to worry. She wanted Morgan to smile.

She shifted closer, gently pushed Morgan back onto the grass and leaned over her, smoothing her bangs back, tracing along her jaw and the soft lips that parted at her touch. Emotion and need rolled through her, blinded her. She covered Morgan's mouth with hers in a deep kiss. Her body stretched alongside Morgan's. She ran her hand along Morgan's side.

Morgan shuddered, wrapping arms tightly around her, deepening the kiss with an aggression Shaine found surprising.

A long time passed before they separated for air. Shaine's heart pounded in her chest. Need pulsed low in her abdomen. She shifted, pulling Morgan's head down on her shoulder, holding her close.

Morgan sighed against her.

Shaine reveled in the warm breath on her neck. She wanted so badly to make love to Morgan, but there wasn't time. She realized the tightness in her throat was because she wanted—needed—Morgan so badly. *God, get a hold of yourself. You are coming back. You will have this chance again.*

Morgan snuggled closer.

Shaine closed her eyes and tried to even out her breathing. She didn't want to admit it, but she was scared, on the edge of her careful control. This was the first time going into a mission that she'd ever felt like she had anything to lose.

She must've stiffened, because Morgan leaned away from her and cupped her cheek. "It'll be okay, Shaine. It will."

Shaine turned her face to kiss Morgan's palm and gazed into the depths of Morgan's gray eyes. *I want to believe that.* "Just let me hold you," she whispered.

Morgan relaxed into her embrace.

Shaine buried her face in Morgan's hair to breathe in her scent. Slowly, she felt her heart rate slow to normal. The fear receded. Morgan's weight against her was a comforting anchor—warm and inviting.

Morgan's fingers slid under the fabric of her shirt, tracing gentle patterns on her skin. The repetition was hypnotic, calming.

Shaine let the touch relax the tension in her shoulders until she felt almost normal.

Morgan whispered, "Can I ask where you'll be?"

Shaine sighed, shook her head, and murmured into Morgan's hair. "The less you know, the better."

"It's going to be weird here without you."

"I won't be gone long."

Morgan rolled away to lie on her back, folding an arm behind her head and finding Shaine's hand. She laced their fingers together.

Shaine smiled at the feel of Morgan's fingers twined with hers.

Morgan stared up into the domed glass ceiling, squinting at the light, and asked, "What happens when you get back?"

Shaine squeezed Morgan's hand. "I haven't honestly thought that far ahead," she admitted. "What do you want to happen?"

Morgan looked at her. "I think I'd like to go back to Moon Base," she said slowly. "I just want my life back."

Shaine felt a stab of panic. She managed a hoarse whisper, "Will I be a part of that?"

"God, yes. I mean—if you want to be." Worry flitted across Morgan's features and darkened her eyes.

Shaine sighed in relief. "Morgan, baby, you'd have a hell of a time getting rid of me."

Morgan grinned, leaned over and dropped a light kiss on Shaine's mouth. "Good." She smiled and eased down to use Shaine's arm as a pillow, sighed and closed her eyes.

Shaine studied Morgan's profile, the small nose, the delicate planes of her face. The word "elfin" floated through her head. She smiled to herself. After a bit, she said, "While I'm gone, you'll be careful, right?" She almost added a caution about Lissa Hedding, but stopped before the warning tumbled out. Morgan didn't need more suspicions and worries. Lissa might be an informer, but the woman had never been an assassin, never had the nerve for that line of work. She blew out a slow breath and forced herself to relax. "Remember what I said about having my pistol with you?"

Morgan nodded without opening her eyes. "It's in my pocket," she said. "And I'll be careful. Can't imagine there's going to be a whole lot going on here, anyway. I'll probably be bored out of my mind."

Shaine smiled. "Download a pile of movies and camp out for a couple days," she suggested. She shut her eyes, enjoying the moment with her lover.

"I guess." Morgan sighed. "Hey, Shaine?"

"Yeah?"

Suddenly Shaine felt Morgan's weight on top of her and warm breath against her lips.

"I don't want to talk anymore," Morgan whispered.

Shaine opened her eyes.

Morgan took her breath away, kissing her hard and deep.

Shaine surrendered to desire. She didn't want to talk anymore, either.

CHAPTER TWENTY

Shaine stopped off at Kyle Ellerand's office on her way to the roof launchpad. As usual, Ellerand sat at the back of the room, intent on his keyboards and monitors. Code scrolled quickly across one of the monitors while two others showed a series of red and green nodes across a network diagram, flashing almost in time to the rhythm of his fingers on the keys. He looked up as she strode into the room and hit a key to pause the code screen.

"Got anything new?" she asked.

He shook his head. "No. No changes." He reached across the workspace to hand her a comp pad. "Everything you need's on here."

"Thanks, Kyle."

He nodded. His face solemn, he said, "Be careful, yeah?"

"I will."

"I'll keep an eye on Morgan for you."

Shaine took a long breath, closing her eyes for a second when it hit her again that she wasn't going to be there to protect Morgan from harm. *God, what am I fucking doing?* She managed a thin smile.

"Thanks." The alarm on her wrist chron bleeped. "Gotta run. Later, Kyle." Relieved not to have more time to think, she escaped the cramped space before her emotions got the better of her.

By the time she reached the roof, Barill already sat in the pilot's chair of the heli-jet. The side mounted jet engines rumbled in idle. The rotor blades rotated slowly. Half jet and half helicopter, the craft could do a vertical takeoff and landing, and use its engines for forward cruising. Fast and maneuverable, it was her preferred method of transportation.

Shifting her gear pack more securely onto her back, Shaine crossed the launchpad and pulled herself up the three-rung ladder into the heli-jet. She hauled up the ladder behind her and locked it down into the floor, then pulled the heavy cargo hatch shut, spinning the manual seal. After stowing her backpack in a rear storage locker, she took a second to check the weatherproof crate packed with her survival gear and strapped into place.

She climbed up front and dropped into the co-pilot's seat, settling the headset over her ears and pulling the four-point harness across her body.

Barill glanced at her. "Ready?"

"Yeah." She glanced across the instrument board. "You did pre-flight?"

"I did." Barill tapped the com. "Control. This is Flyer One. Are we clear?"

"All clear, Flyer One. Anytime you're ready."

"Roger that. We're gone."

Fifteen seconds later, she and Barill were airborne, angling rapidly into the sky over New York City. Shaine loved the rapid ascent to cruising altitude near forty thousand feet, especially in clear skies like today, and she settled in for a long flight. She glanced at the controls, but was more than content to let Barill do the piloting. She could fly in a pinch, but her training had been intended only for emergencies.

She watched the land far below and ran through the plan she and Ellerand had devised. It wasn't much of a plan, really. Barill would fly her into Biskra. From there she'd catch a weather station chopper headed into the Sahara. The chopper would drop her at the specified coordinates and she would finish her journey to Charun's desert compound on foot. She and Kyle had figured out a route into the building through the air ventilation system, marked on the blueprints loaded in her pad. What happened when she got in and how she would get out—well, that would all just depend.

Hours later, they flew into Biskra under the cover of night. Barill landed the heli-jet in a quasi-military compound with Weather Service markings on its landing pad. As the heli-jet touched down, Shaine saw a figure jogging toward them from one of the low surrounding buildings, a uniformed body silhouetted against a shaft of light from the open door.

Barill idled the engines and gave Shaine a thumbs-up. "You're clear. Good hunting, Wendt."

She returned the thumbs-up and pulled off the headset, clipping it to the control board. She moved into the main cargo area, retrieved her backpack, and released her gear box from its place on the floor. Out of the corner of her eye, she noted the side hatch auto-releasing. Her ears popped when the air pressure changed. A swirl of gritty sand and dust scraped her face when the hatch swung open.

The man from the building leaned in. "Are you Wendt?" he yelled over the engine noise.

She nodded.

"Lieutenant Reyes, Global Weather Systems," he introduced himself.

Shaine acknowledged him and shoved the rectangular container toward the hatch. Reyes grabbed the handle on his end. Slinging her backpack over her shoulders, she dropped down to the ground and took hold of the other handle. With his help, she carried the box to the edge of the landing pad, dropped it off, and jogged back to the open hatch. She slammed the heavy door shut and slapped the side of the chopper a couple of times before ducking away. When she cleared rotor range, the heli-jet lifted off with a roar.

Shaine turned away from the blast of sand and returned to where Reyes waited. The chop of the rotors rapidly faded into the distance.

Reyes hitched up his half of the equipment box and palmed the door open. She grabbed the other end and followed him into the control building to set the container down in front of a short reception counter. Behind the counter, three rows of inter-linked desks trisected the room. Widescreen monitors and projected 3D holomaps took up the top of each desk. About a dozen uniformed men and women manned the computers. A couple of workers looked up curiously before turning back to their duties.

Reyes waved a hand, indicating the room. "Welcome to Desert Weather Central." He grinned. "Pretty low-key for the most part. Come on into my office and we can talk."

Shaine followed him through the three rows of workstations to a glass-walled inner office at the back. The door was open.

Reyes slid behind the desk and dropped into a creaking plasti-form chair.

Shaine took the chair in front of the desk and sat down, scanning the room. All the techs appeared focused on their screens rather than on her or Reyes, but she knew appearances could be deceiving. There were no shades drawn over the clear walls and her conversation with Reyes would be out in the open. She wasn't comfortable with the scenario. She shifted her body to face away from most of the room and turned her attention to the dark, muscular man.

Reyes leaned back in his chair, folding his hands over his middle. "Mr. Rogan says you need a lift to the deep desert. Doesn't sound like much fun. Nothing out there but sand and fleas."

She met his obvious probing with a flat stare. "Actually, you'd be surprised how much fun it can be."

He raised a brow at her sarcasm. "Is Rogan always so uptight?"

She asked, "You've worked with Rogan before?"

"A few times. I drop someone off in the desert, middle of nowhere, someone else picks em up. Or doesn't, for all I know. My superiors have a deal worked out with his people. I just do what I'm told."

Shaine nodded. She assumed Rogan was spying on Charun, using multiple drop points with evacuation provided by his own people. Unzipping the side pocket on her cargo pants, she retrieved a small data chip, which she handed across the desk to Reyes. "Drop coordinates."

Reyes took the chip and plugged it into his system. After a handful of seconds, he glanced at her. "Swing around and take a look."

Shaine got up and moved around the desk. The monitor built into the desktop displayed a topographical map overlaid with weather radar.

"This is where we are now," Reyes said. "This is the drop point. There's a big sandstorm blowing up. It'll reach us in a couple of hours and it looks like it'll last at least a day. The outer edges of the storm will hit your drop point within the next forty minutes or so."

Shaine studied the map and the storm data scrolling up the side of the screen. For the best cover, she'd want to time her arrival at Charun's compound at the height of the storm, so late morning was best. She glanced at her chron, considering the distances and the increasing wind speeds she'd be fighting. "I want to get to the drop point at oh-five-hundred hours."

Reyes nodded. "Sure. Then we leave here at oh four fifteen. Gives you a couple of hours before we take off."

"Fine."

"What the hell are you doing in the middle of the desert, anyway?"

She gave him an annoyed glare, wondering if he really thought she was stupid enough to answer his question.

Reyes shrugged when he got no response. "You can work on instruments only, right? Because you're not going to be able to see a damned thing in that storm, even in the daylight."

Shaine managed not to roll her eyes. "I have it covered," she said. "Is there a locker room where I can get suited up and maybe crash for an hour?"

Reyes said, "There's a locker room off the side hall."

Shaine glanced over her shoulder. "I could use a hand with the equipment case, lieutenant."

"Yes, ma'am. Not a problem." He stood.

Shaine hid a grin and continued out of the office.

Reyes left her alone in the cramped locker room with her equipment case. She flipped open the box packed with a desert survival suit and her weapons. She went through the contents, double-checking everything. She glanced again at her the wrist chron and decided she had time to relax and get focused.

She stretched out on the long plastic bench, folding her arms over her stomach and closing her eyes, listening to the quiet hum of air-cyclers. She sought a quiet space in her head. A picture of Morgan formed in her mind's eye with the memory of how good it had felt to hold her and be held. She let the comfort and warmth seep through her consciousness.

Her mind wandered to Morgan lying in the grass beside her, staring at her with those deep gray eyes. She could feel Morgan's warm skin under her fingertips, feel Morgan shiver under her touch, smell the clean scent of her hair, and taste the pulse point of Morgan's neck beating wildly under her tongue. Calm slipped away.

She shook off the vision and the need and scraped her fingers hard through her hair. *Focus. Focus. Jesus, Shaine. Get your fucking libido in check.* She sat up, swinging her legs to the floor. *You know what you need to do. You know how to do it. Just get in there and get the job done.*

Three hours later, Shaine balanced in the cargo space behind the heli-jet's cockpit, suited up and ready to make her drop. Glancing out the front windshield, she saw nothing through the darkness.

Still a couple of hours before the sun comes up, she thought. Not that it would matter much in the middle of a sandstorm.

Without the headset, the drone of the rotors and engines nearly drowned out the howling wind and the sizzle of sand whipping against the fuselage. Earlier, Reyes had told her he would keep the heli-jet hovering about two meters above the ground, but the way the wind buffeted the craft around, she figured anywhere from a half meter to probably upward of three or four.

The heli-jet lurched up and did a freefall back down. She grabbed a handhold for support. She shut the faceplate of the desert survival suit with a sharp slap and adjusted the pack on her back. Reyes gave her a thumbs-up and a grin. She acknowledged him with a quick nod and hit the hatch release. The door grated open. A blast of sand streamed into the small compartment. Fighting the gusts, she swung down until her feet rested on the heli-jet's landing skid. Taking a breath, she jumped clear.

It was a longer drop than she'd hoped.

Her boots connected on solid ground with a jarring impact. She let her knees flex, tucked and tumbled down a sharp incline. Rolling to a stop, she took a few seconds to lie on her back, doing a quick inventory to make sure she was in one piece.

Sand pelted her helmet's faceplate. The blackness enveloping her was nearly complete. She hauled herself to her feet, finding her balance in the shifting wind, and pulled her comp pad from one of her suit's sealed side pockets to get her position and direction.

Shifting her pack more comfortably on her shoulders, she started forward, head down against the buffeting wind. Unable to see more than vague shadows, she shuffled her boots lightly over the sand to keep her footing and followed the directional heading provided by the blue-lighted comp pad screen. Fighting winds that pushed her backward and sideways more than ahead, she resigned herself to a long hike.

CHAPTER TWENTY-ONE

Morgan relaxed in bed against a pile of pillows with her comp pad on her knees. She'd wanted to catch up on some reading, but found herself spending most of her time staring through the open bedroom door to the living room windows and out at the flickering lights of the New York City skyline. After going over the same page five times, she still had no idea what she'd read.

She sighed, contemplating her current reality, which felt so surreal. She missed the familiarity of her own bed in her own tiny apartment, surrounded by the domed safety of Moon Base. Not an exciting existence, and admittedly, there wasn't much of a future in it. She would never be rich or famous. She would never be noticed outside her group of friends. She didn't care. She was content with her life.

These last two days, she'd felt like she was drowning—cut off from her safety lines. So many things she thought she knew were twisted into half-truths and outright lies. The certainty of tomorrow had become an uneasy knowledge that nothing was going to be quite the same again and she couldn't yet fathom what the changes might mean.

Even Shaine fell into the category of the unknown. Regardless, she clung to the somewhat slippery support Shaine represented. She saw the irony of leaning on the strength of a woman she probably shouldn't trust, given Shaine's dubious background with Maruchek's company. Her head warned her off while her instincts trusted implicitly. *Instinct or hormones?* she wondered dryly. Either way, she couldn't deny the attraction.

Her thoughts drifted to the afternoon she'd spent in the garden with Shaine. She had found it so achingly difficult to watch Shaine walk away from the hidden clearing where they'd laid in the grass touching, kissing and holding each other. Shaine had seemed to need the comfort of contact as much as her.

She set aside the pad and grabbed Shaine's pillow from the other side of the bed, hugging it and burying her face in the cool fabric. She breathed in traces of the light, musky scent of Shaine's shampoo and imagined the strength of Shaine's arms around her.

God, Shaine, you haven't been gone a day and I miss you. What is going on with me? Was I ever this needy before? With Gina, my feelings were more fear and anxiety and waiting for the relationship to blow up around me. This thing with Shaine is so very different. I'm not scared, except to lose her. Even not knowing what the future holds isn't as terrifying as the thought of Shaine not being with me. I've always been okay being on my own. Now, I just don't know. She squeezed the oversized pillow tighter.

Over the course of the evening, she considered bringing up a net connection and contacting Charri, but tossed the idea aside. There wasn't much she could say without either lying outright, or completely avoiding all the important details. And it was possible talking to Charri would somehow put her friend in danger. She thought, too, about calling her dad on Moon Base, but put the notion aside for the same reasons. In any case, she didn't think she had the emotional strength to deal with trying to explain everything that had happened.

She wished for the millionth time Shaine was with her. Shaine would understand. She didn't know why she believed that, but she knew it was true.

She took a last deep breath into the pillowcase and set it purposely aside, forcefully shoving down her raging emotions and grabbing the pad again. Hoping to distract her brain from thinking anymore, she brought up a tile game. With any luck, at some point she'd just fall asleep.

She had drifted into semi-conscious dreams when a soft click in the outer room snapped her eyes wide open. Her muscles stiffened. She peered into the darkness, her mind suddenly alert. "Hello?"

An indistinct shadow moved toward her.

Her heart slammed against her ribs. She slid a hand under her pillow. Her fingers closed around the cold stock of Shaine's pistol. She brought the weapon around in front of her, hidden under the covers, and sat up, repeating her greeting. "Hello?"

The shadow morphed as it came toward the dim light from the bedside lamp, shifting into the vaguely familiar shape of a tall woman purposefully crossing the living room. "Ms. Rahn?" Lissa's lithe form moved fully into the light at the bedroom doorway. She carried a thick holo album similar to the one Morgan already had. She held out the album. "I'm sorry to intrude, but your father asked me to bring this to you."

Shaine's words from the previous night echoed in her head: *The only people who can come through that door without you physically unlocking it from the inside are you, me, Maruchek and Rogan.* A cold shiver ran down her spine. "Just leave it on the coffee table," she said, impressed her voice sounded so confident. "You startled me—I was almost asleep."

Lissa smiled apologetically. "I'm sorry, I didn't mean to."

"Yeah, well, it's been a busy couple of days." Morgan paused, but Lissa didn't seem to get the subtle hint. She added, "Um, if you can let yourself out, I'm really tired."

"Oh, yes, of course." Lissa nodded. She didn't move to leave. "If you're sure you don't need anything else?" she asked.

"Just for you to leave," Morgan returned.

A dark expression flashed across Lissa's features. Her hand twitched under the photo album. A dull glint flashed in the dim light.

Time slowed painfully between pounding heartbeats.

The thin streak of a laser bolt hissed past Morgan's head, leaving behind a whiff of burnt hair. Her finger tightened on the pistol's trigger.

Lissa stumbled and fell backward with a startled look on her face. Her gun went off again, firing wide into the wall.

Morgan fired twice more at empty air, unable to stop the reaction.

Time resumed its normal course.

Morgan's heart pounded deafeningly in her ears. For a long moment she held herself completely still, trying to remember how to breathe. Slowly, she folded away the comforter with its three new singed holes. She eased her legs over the side of the bed and stood on shaking legs. Her trembling hands held Shaine's pistol in front of her. She was vaguely aware she'd seen people adopt the same posture in the holovids.

She stepped around the bed, half expecting Lissa to surge up firing, but nothing happened. The tall woman lay in the doorway, a charred hole burnt through her jacket and blouse into her chest, eyes open wide in shock. The hole was bigger than Morgan would have expected.

Lissa's breath came in shallow, pained gasps. For a brief second, the glassy stare focused on her, then Lissa slipped away after a ragged sounding wheeze.

Morgan dropped bonelessly onto the edge of the bed. The pistol slipped out of her fingers and clattered on the floor. She stared at the dead woman in the doorway. Lissa's fingers were loosely wrapped around a palm-sized laser pistol.

"You probably won't hit anything," Shaine had told her.

Well, fuck. Now what?

Call Maruchek. He'd given her his private com code.

She got up and fumbled for the com unit on the nightstand. After a couple of tries, she managed to punch in Maruchek's code. The call only buzzed once.

His voice sounded tinny over the small speaker. "Maruchek."

She stared blankly at the communicator for a long moment.

Maruchek's voice became somewhat impatient. "Hello?"

She swallowed, cleared her throat. "This—um, it's Morgan."

"Morgan?" His tone instantly changed from impatient to concerned. "Morgan, what's wrong?"

"Um…there's a body…well, Lissa—I just shot her."

"What?"

She heard motion in the background, as though Maruchek had jumped up and was suddenly moving around. "Morgan, are you all right?"

The world slid away for a moment, her focus narrowing to the com in her shaking hand. "I killed her," she mumbled, shocked at the words coming out of her mouth.

"You're not hurt?"

"No. I—"

"Morgan, just stay put, I'm on the way."

The connection clicked dead, leaving her to stare at the small rectangular unit. Her gaze returned to the body in the doorway and the charred holes in the bedding. Her knees gave way. She slid down against the side of the bed until she sat on the floor staring at her hands, her whole body trembling.

Morgan didn't know how long it took for Maruchek, Rogan and a number of others to burst into the suite. She heard Maruchek calling for her, but she had no voice to answer. She was barely able to look up and focus when he dropped to his knees in front of her.

Other voices gave orders. All the lights came on, glaring and making her blink.

Maruchek gathered her into his arms, hugging her, murmuring over and over, "Morgan, I'm so sorry. I'm so sorry."

Unresisting, she let him hold her, thankful for the safety of his presence, while part of her wondered why she should feel safe with a man who was a virtual stranger.

A voice snapped sharply, "Tarm, she's okay. She's in shock."

Maruchek's arms loosened around her.

She looked up. "I'm not hurt," she rasped.

Maruchek smoothed her hair. "Probably not, but we need to get you out of here." He eased to his feet, bringing her up with him. "Can you walk?"

Morgan nodded. "I...yeah, I think so." She wavered, her knees still rubbery, but he put his arm around her waist and guided her to the bedroom door.

She didn't want to, but she had to look down to step over Lissa's body. She shuddered and fought back a wave of nausea. *I did that.*

Maruchek murmured, "Morgan, come," and urged her forward with a gentle nudge.

She let herself be led away from death.

Not long afterward, Morgan curled into a corner of a love seat on the far side of Maruchek's office, her knees pulled up to her chest. The lights were dim in her corner of the big office. She was glad to have at least the illusion of hiding in the shadows.

She still wore the short-sleeved, oversized tunic and boxers she'd worn to bed. The medic had given her a soft, maize-colored blanket, which she'd wrapped tightly around her shoulders. The young doctor had pronounced her physically fit and merely "shaken up" by the experience. Of course, he had only been told she'd had "a bit of a scare." At the moment, she felt rather like she'd been run over by a freight train.

On the other side of the office, Maruchek and Rogan faced off. Anger and frustration flew between them. Their voices grated through her aching head. They'd been at it for a half hour, intermittently interrupted by stilted com calls from Rogan's security personnel.

Maruchek paced behind his desk. A glowering Rogan leaned against the side of the same desk, his his arms crossed over his chest.

"I cannot believe you had a hole that big in your security!" Maruchek roared.

Rogan glared defiantly. "I ran personnel checks three days ago and the bitch came up clean! I don't know who got to her, but I will find out."

"My daughter could have been killed! I will not lose another member of my family, Duncan!"

Rogan's head snapped around. "How do you know Hedding was even there to kill her? They both had weapons!" He motioned sharply toward Morgan. "And where did she get a fucking gun?"

There was a long, pregnant silence. Both men turned to look at her.

After a moment, she realized they were waiting for her to answer. She turned to Maruchek. "It's Shaine's. She told me to keep it with me."

"Did she tell you to shoot Hedding, too?" Rogan demanded.

Morgan sat up straighter. "No. Shaine just told me to be careful. She changed the lock on the suite so only she and I, and you two, could get in. I think that's why I reacted. Lissa shouldn't have been able to let herself in."

Maruchek crossed the room to sit beside her. "Can you tell us exactly what happened?"

Morgan looked at him. She flicked a glance at the still glowering Rogan, who remained leaning on the desk. She struggled to sort out her thoughts and put all the fractured images into a single whole. Finally, she took a breath and let it out slowly. "I was in bed reading, I'd just about fallen asleep. I heard something and Lissa was standing at the door to my bedroom. She had a holo album, like the one you'd left for me. And she said you wanted her to give it to me." She paused and looked a question at her birth father.

Maruchek said, "I didn't send her. And there was only one album." He rested a hand, briefly and lightly, on her arm. "Please, go on."

"I'm not sure, after that. We said a few things and then—" She shook her head. "There was a flash. I think she fired at me. I pulled the trigger and she fell—" She shuddered, picturing Lissa blinking in surprise when she realized she'd been shot and crumpling to the floor. Just as clearly, she remembered Lissa's empty eyes staring sightlessly at her when Maruchek guided her out of the bedroom.

Maruchek gave her shoulders a comforting squeeze. "You saw her gun?" he asked.

"Yes—no—I don't know. I think she fired and I fired almost at the same time."

"You did the right thing, Morgan," Maruchek said.

Morgan glanced at him and refocused on the floor. Whether right or not, Lissa was dead and she'd done it. What if Lissa hadn't intended to kill her after all? She closed her eyes and felt sick again, wondering if Shaine ever felt this way. Did taking a life haunt her, too? Was this why Shaine wanted to get away from Mann-Maru Security? How many times did Shaine have to make a similar decision? Kill or be killed. Kill or maybe be killed. How did Shaine deal with it? Because she didn't think she was going to be capable of processing Lissa's death for a long time.

"She would have killed you," Maruchek said. "You did what you had to do. You defended yourself."

Rogan said, "We need to get her out of here, Tarm."

Maruchek stood and turned to face his security chief. "I agree. The question is: what's secure at this point? I don't want a repeat of this incident."

Rogan started toward the door. "I need to make a couple of calls. I think we should head over to 2333, to Garren's facility. Brodderick Fenn will have the whole place locked down and there are EG cruisers in the area."

Maruchek asked, "You're sure that's a good idea?"

"If you have a better one, let me know. I'll be back shortly." Rogan stalked out the door.

Morgan watched him leave. She closed her eyes, exhausted.

CHAPTER TWENTY-TWO

Shaine slogged through the sand, fighting the gusting winds that increased as the temperature rose. Sharp particles strafed her suited body, clattering against her helmet and the flex-armor neck and shoulder plating. Every couple of minutes, she glanced down at the GPS on her comp pad to make sure she trekked in the right direction.

The day brightened into a brown-red twilight of sand and dust.

Despite the storm, she remained on her scheduled ETA to Charun's compound. She smiled grimly. The mostly underground warren wasn't truly hidden, but its secluded existence in the middle of nowhere ensured Charun's center for research and security stayed relatively unnoticed by the outside world.

She didn't know the details of Charun's internal corporate hierarchy, nor did she much care. Based on what Rogan's spies and investigators had put together over the years, the mining research and development was more a cover than anything else. Sure, they did some R&D, but Rogan believed the desert compound was the base for Charun's more covert corporate security force and the so-called "pirates" who'd been plaguing out-system mining facilities for years.

Neither the justice system nor Maruchek's private investigators had managed to pin that particular accusation on Charun, though not for lack of trying. Based on the reports Ellerand had provided her, the only evidence gathered was either circumstantial or inadmissible in court. Charun covered his tracks and his money trails incredibly well. Even so, she figured it was only a matter of time. If this mission actually succeeded, his time was up.

She was careful not to push hard too early, though now that it was daylight, she could move faster than she had when she couldn't see a thing. She sipped sparingly from the tube connected to water pouches in the suit's sides. A compact unit on her back pumped air into her helmet. Even filtered, the air left a dry, gritty feeling in her mouth and nose.

As the morning temperature rose, the storm intensified and visibility went from a couple of meters to pretty much nothing. The slap of wind and sand against her faceplate became white noise she tuned out. The repetition of putting one foot in front of the other became an internal rhythm to which her body moved, allowing her mind to wander.

Memories of old missions flitted through her thoughts in piecemeal images. In contrast to the dryness of the desert, she remembered vividly the feel and stench of damp, sweltering heat and the buzz of insects as she crawled through a jungle swamp. She remembered picking her way through the dark, musty ruins of an ancient subway system under New York City to catch a group of terrorists at a secret meeting site. Always, she'd relied on painstaking and careful movement forward, remaining focused on the destination. The journey created a slow buildup of tension, a tightening of the spring that would be ready to snap when the time came.

One big difference between then and now: her current mission lacked a plan. Her objective was to take out Tyr Charun, but the details remained a blank slate. There was no appointed meeting place and no specific time for a public activity leaving Charun in the open. She had no idea where he might be at any given time, just that he was somewhere in his secured compound.

In the military, the only time she'd flown by the seat of her pants had been when the mission went FUBAR. Working for Rogan, she'd always been meticulous—planning out her missions to the most minute details. The current mission meant life or death for Morgan, and yet she had no strategy past how she was going to break in.

She hated not having a plan.

She glanced at the GPS, adjusted her direction and checked the time. At this rate, she would reach Charun's compound just past oh-ten-thirty hours, about the time the storm would be at its strongest, giving her the most protection from detection. If there were any working cameras, they were less likely to pick her up with all the blowing sand. Her personal body temperature would blend into the background if there were thermal scanners in use.

She plodded forward.

CHAPTER TWENTY-THREE

The sound of an argument rose from the transport's cockpit, echoing back into the main cabin. Morgan recognized Rogan's low rumble.

"Do you really think I take this situation lightly?" Rogan asked.

"My concern is that arrogance and complacency have put us in this position."

"Don't insult me, Tarm."

"Then don't fail me again." The last was spoken flatly, evenly, and with unmitigated authority.

Morgan half-opened her eyes when Rogan stalked furiously through the cabin, slamming the aft hatch behind him. He didn't look at her as he passed. She was glad. She'd had more than enough of his accusing glare in the last few hours. His constant animosity wore on her raw nerves. He seemed to blame her for the situation, which pissed her off. Yes, she was to blame for Lissa's death. The thought made her nauseous. But it wasn't her fault that Lissa broke into her room with a gun.

She didn't remember clearly who shot first and clung to the belief that her reaction wasn't a mistake. She wouldn't have used the pistol if she hadn't been threatened. If she'd misjudged the situation…she wasn't sure she could live with the guilt if that were true. *It's not murder if Lissa shot first. I'm not a murderer, am I? I didn't mean to kill her.*

She squeezed her eyes shut, forcing the thoughts away. *I can't deal with this right now.* Too much was happening, too fast. Digger's death, a new family, people trying to kill her. *I just need to get through the next couple of days.*

Morgan glanced around the main cabin's dull gray interior. She had unclipped the four-point restraint harness, but didn't have the energy to leave the relative comfort of the reclining acceleration seat.

This shuttle was faster and more maneuverable than the one she and Shaine had ridden in earlier and bare bones in its creature comforts. The cramped main cabin contained four reclining acceleration chairs. A computer workstation and secondary communications setup were built into the opposite bulkhead. A food dispenser unit took up the rear wall beside a semicircular booth and the hatch leading to the rear sections of the ship.

Morgan scrunched down in the chair, huddled into her jacket with her hands jammed into the pockets, wishing she had a blanket against the chill of the dry, recycled air. She knew by the smoothing out of the ride and the settled hum of the engines that the shuttle had broken free of Earth's atmosphere and entered open space. She'd overheard enough snatches of conversation over the past couple of hours to know she, Maruchek and Rogan were headed to one of the mining facilities in the Belt. She wasn't sure what leaving Earth was supposed to accomplish.

Since Rogan had gone aft, the muted voices from the cockpit sounded like business as usual. She closed her eyes again, allowing the droning of the ship's drives to lull her closer to sleep.

Sometime later she heard light footfalls coming toward her from the cockpit and a pause as Tarm Maruchek's voice was directed up front. "Mr. Loh, I need to you to contact Facility 2333. Get Garren on a secure line and transfer the call back to the captain's cabin. I need to speak with him privately before we arrive."

"Yes, sir."

Maruchek's footsteps stopped.

Morgan sensed his presence at her side. She opened her eyes.

"How are you doing?" he asked.

"Still kicking," she returned.

Maruchek studied her face. "You're strong, like your mother." He smiled and squeezed her shoulder.

She received the gesture without reacting. She eyed the man she was beginning to accept as her birth father. "What happens when we get to where we're going?"

"We'll stay at Garren's mining facility until Rogan has the situation at the main compound in hand."

"We'll be safer in the Belt than on Earth?"

"Yes." He paused. "You've heard about the attacks that damaged one of our mining facilities?" He waited for her nod and continued. "Since then, the facility has been in secured lockdown. There is a heightened Earth Guard presence in the area. Rogan believes, and I agree, that your presence there will go unnoticed, at least until my compound on Earth has been secured and we've rooted out any additional threats."

Morgan chewed on his answer. She didn't feel reassured. She recalled what she'd seen about the attack. The installation had taken mostly superficial damage, but she still felt uneasy. She'd lived in similar places and didn't consider a mining facility anywhere near secure.

"Don't worry, Morgan. It's all going to work out."

She looked up at Tarm Maruchek. She knew he was trying to help, but his attempts weren't working. She closed her eyes. Her head hurt and her thoughts whipped around in a crazy muddle. She heard a rustle of movement and Tarm's retreating footsteps, then the metallic click of the rear compartment hatch opening and closing. She tried to clear her head, but images continued to flash relentlessly behind her eyes. She thought of Lissa's lifeless body lying in the doorway and relived the shock of the gun going off in her hand.

Lissa Hedding tried to kill me. This is the third time in three days I've been targeted. For the first time, reality really sank in. She felt a surge of anxiety. What would be next? When? And what about

Shaine? Where was she now? Was she okay? If Shaine killed Charun, would the threat be over? Or would someone else just step in? If the secret of her birthright got out, would she ever be safe again?

Her thoughts spun out of control. *I can't live my life like this!* She wanted to scream. *Stop it! Just stop!* She forced herself to imagine the warmth and safety of Shaine's arms around her, struggling to find the comforting feeling of waking in Shaine's embrace. She clung desperately to any hint of solace in those memories. Eventually, she succumbed to exhaustion and the drone of the engines and lost herself in sleep.

* * *

Morgan tumbled through the blackness of space. Desperately, she slapped at the controls on the rocket-pack's handlebars. The ignition switches were unresponsive under her gloved thumbs. She caught dizzying glimpses of the mining facility falling away as her body twisted into the black. She wanted to scream, but couldn't get any air. Warning alarms screeched in her ears. Panic blossomed excruciatingly in her chest.

A fluorescent orange vacsuit tumbled into her path. Blackened, burnt gashes were seared across material ripped open by laser fire. Blood red ice crystals covered a woman's gently smiling face behind the shattered helmet.

"Mom!"

Another vacsuit floated past her, this one white with a blue stripe down the arms and legs. She didn't want to look but couldn't stop. Suddenly the fractured helmet was in front of her eyes and Digger stared accusingly at her.

"No!"

Morgan woke with a start, gasping for breath, clamping down on what she knew would have been a scream. Her fingers twisted around the edges of a thin, dark-blue travel blanket. She blinked, struggling to comprehend where she was and where the blanket had come from. *Transport shuttle. I'm on a shuttle with Maruchek.*

A motion caught her eye. Rogan turned in his seat at the computer console. He said shortly, "We're within half an hour of the facility."

Morgan nodded automatically and had to process the information for a couple of seconds before it made any sense. Facility. She, Maruchek and Rogan were headed for a mining facility in the Belt that was supposed to be safe. No wonder she was having nightmares. She rubbed the sleep out of her eyes, then pushed the blanket to the side of the acceleration chair. She shifted the chair from reclined to seated and got to her feet, rolling her head to loosen her neck muscles.

Remembering the small bathroom just aft of the rear hatch, she slipped inside and locked the door behind her. The cramped space contained a tiny sink, a sonic shower and a toilet. She met her tired gaze in the mirror above the sink. Against skin paler than normal, her eyes seemed too big for her face and were darkened by lack of sleep.

You look like crap, Rahn. Her long bangs hung limply into her eyes. She brushed them away with a swipe of her hand, did her business and wandered back out into the main cabin.

Rogan leaned over the computer console, muttering to himself.

She walked past him to the cockpit, hoping to find out what to expect when they arrived at the mining facility.

Maruchek looked over his shoulder when she paused at the cockpit's hatch. The second officer said something to Maruchek, who replied, then turned his head and gave Morgan a smile. "Are you feeling better?"

She nodded. "Rogan said we're almost there."

"Yes." Maruchek straightened and nodded at the two folding jump chairs against the wall beside her. He took one.

Morgan took the other, aware of his steady gaze on her. "What happens when we get to the mining facility?" she asked.

"First, I want you to meet your brother, Garren. He runs the operation there."

Morgan nodded and propped her elbows on her knees. Her gaze remained focused on the floor. She fiddled with her mother's ring. *My brother.* The words sounded odd when she considered them. *I have a brother. I've always been alone.* She'd seen pictures in the holoalbum of a young man with dark hair and a serious expression and eyes like his father. Other than hair color, there was little resemblance between her and Garren. He was much taller, broadly built and angular, while she, like her birth mother, had a whip-thin, almost child-like frame.

She wondered if Maruchek had told Garren about her and assumed he had. She felt a second of panic, of things spiraling out of control—too much change, too fast. Her heart rate jumped. She took a long breath and forced herself to relax. She asked quietly, "Any word from Shaine?"

"No, nothing yet. I'm sure soon, though."

She hoped he was right. Shaine had been so casual about the whole assassination thing. In and out, quick and dirty, she'd said. No problem.

But Morgan had seen the worry in the depths of Shaine's deep green eyes. She was glad she didn't know any details of Shaine's mission. Knowledge would only have given her more dangerous scenarios to imagine.

CHAPTER TWENTY-FOUR

By the time Shaine's destination showed on the GPS, her muscles ached from walking against the wind and she figured she'd lost a fair amount of hearing from the the sand's incessant pelting against her plastic helmet. What remained of her tepid water supply tasted like sand. Dusty grit itched and irritated her skin under the tight-fitting suit.

She ignored the annoyances and focused forward. It didn't matter if she was uncomfortable. Irritations had to be tolerated in the same way she'd accepted the entire situation. *I'm doing this for Morgan. And I'm doing it for me, because it would hurt so damned much to lose her. I don't give a fuck about Maruchek and Rogan. But Morgan needs to stay alive, and if this is the only way, then so be it.* Determined, she held a vision of Morgan's playful smile in her mind's eye, using the image to keep the discomfort and unease at bay.

Finally, the blocky concrete bulk of Charun's compound loomed through the storm—a darker shadow against the haze of blowing sand and dust. As she approached the massive building, most of which was actually underground, she pulled up a set of apps on her pad and started running scans. The readings wouldn't be a hundred percent trustworthy because of the sandstorm, but it was still better than nothing. She thought it unlikely guards would be posted during a storm, but Tyr Charun had a reputation for paranoia and she had no intention of getting caught flat-footed.

After a minute and a half, nothing pinged the scanner—no thermal readings that might be human, no movement other than the constant background motion of the sand. She shifted into the relative shelter of the building's wall and brought up Ellerand's blueprints. She overlaid her GPS position on the diagram. The entry point she planned on using was only about five meters to her left. She hugged the wall, moved to the spot she'd marked and looked up. In the twilight, the outline of the top of the wall was only a slightly darker shadow.

She unclipped a winch-and-cable gun from her belt. Sighting to the top of the wall, she raised the gun and fired. She clicked on the winch, but the grapnel didn't catch and the line fell down the wall. Forcing herself to be patient, she wound the line back in. She aimed higher and back further, and set the grapnel's internal charge so it would automatically lodge into whatever it hit. She didn't want to waste any more time, and the small charge wasn't likely to be noticed over the storm's noise.

She fired and felt the slight vibration of the charge through the cable. When she thumbed the winch, the grapnel caught and the line tightened. *Wonderful.* She wrapped the safety straps around her wrists, triggered the winch, and started walking slowly up the two-story wall. She scrambled over the meter-high lip at the top and dropped on the sand-coated rooftop to lie flat on her back. She retrieved her pad again and flipped on the scanner.

Nothing. Good.

She released the grapnel, reset its charge, and reeled in the rest of the line before resecuring the winch gun to her utility belt.

A tap on the pad screen flipped the display to the blueprints and called up an overlay of the break-in route along with the GPS of her current position. She studied the route a second and peered through the reddish twilight, visually locating landmarks.

She got to her feet and crossed the roof toward the shadow of the air vent. The intake pipe was a meter and a half in diameter and rose about two meters above the roof. It had several narrow rungs up the side. She climbed up to see a finely meshed screen covering the top. Looking inside, she noted a fan blade, now stilled, just below the mesh. She pulled a laser cutter from her utility belt.

Sand gusted around her. Shaine struggled to anchor herself while she worked. The short-beam laser bit through the quarter-inch mesh as she cut around the edge. She bent back the mesh, flicked on her helmet light and pulled herself up and over. She wriggled through the flap, holding her breath as she dropped past the fan blades.

Balancing on her toes on the thin climbing rungs, she used a low-energy fuser to solder the mesh back into place. She replaced the tool and started feeling her way down into the blackness of the air vent. Wind rushed past her, directed and concentrated by the pipe.

A couple of meters down, her foot slipped on a broken rung. She hung awkwardly a moment before she caught the bar again.

While she climbed, she went over the blueprint's layout in her mind. The initial section of the intake pipe ran down about fifteen meters, at which point there would be another mesh barrier as well as an electrostatic filter to keep out micro-dust particles.

The further into the vent Shaine moved, the less the wind was an issue, though dust still swirled around her. She reached the second mesh barrier, stopped a rung up from it and peered down. *Okay, this is awkward.* There were no hand- or footholds other than the narrow rungs she balanced on. *I need both hands here.*

She set one foot sideways on the rung and stretched her other leg out, placing her booted foot flat against the opposite wall of the pipe and lodging herself into place. She took the winch gun from its holster and released the cable, pulling a length of cord and tying it around her waist. She measured out an additional length and opened the grapnel hook, locking it manually around a rung at chest height. Using the rungs as handholds, she flipped upside down, hanging from the cord tied around her waist. She smiled as she got into position, pleased she didn't drop through.

This mesh barrier was much finer than the one outside and drifted over with a centimeter of sand. While she watched, a rectangular crack in the vent wall slid open just above the mesh. She heard a dull hum and the loose sand was sucked into the opening. The opening snapped shut. She blinked. *Huh. Vacuum. Cool.*

A static field buzzed a handbreadth below the mesh, a plane of hissing electricity meant to hold back the ever-present dust. Shaine scanned the wall for a control panel or at the very least, a power conduit. As expected, she located the power conduit and control box on the other side of the barrier. She considered her options and quickly decided she'd just have to gut it out. She was gloved and suited, so it couldn't be any worse than the Taser hits she'd taken in training.

She unclipped the cutter from her belt and made quick work of slicing through the mesh and folding it back. The electrostatic barrier crackled and popped loudly as sand fell through. Sparks snapped in front of her faceplate.

She opened the zippered pocket on her suit's forearm, retrieving a thin rectangle as long as her thumb with retractable connectors extending from either end, and two LED lights on its surface. Each connector had an auto-clip with micro-lasers that would burrow in and make contact with the power lead. The small controller shunted power through the device, bypassing whatever control she was trying to avoid.

Shaine made sure she had a good grip on the power shunt, took a breath, and shoved her gloved hand through the electrostatic barrier. Her jaw clenched as stinging shocks skittered up her fingers and into her arm. Her hand jerked involuntarily, but she managed to keep hold of the device. Gritting her teeth, she clipped one end on the exposed conduit just below the power switch. The first indicator showed green—connected. She attached the other end. The second indicator turned green and the barrier disappeared.

Her right arm tingled wildly. She took a couple of long breaths to steady her racing heart and pulled herself upright on the rungs. It took a few seconds to disconnect from the makeshift harness and stow her equipment.

She clambered down the rungs past the static barrier, pulled the wire mesh into place and soldered it, then disconnected the shunt. The barrier hissed into existence when power was restored.

Shaine climbed down the last set of rungs to where the intake pipe connected to a rectangular horizontal vent. She pulled off her helmet. The air remained hot and dusty, but it felt good to be out of the helmet's stifling confines. After removing the faceplate and the flexible neck and shoulder armor, the rest of the helmet collapsed nearly flat. She fitted the pieces together and secured the package under the backpack straps across her chest.

Ducking into the shoulder-width space and worming into the vent, she was relieved to find the space high enough that she could crawl on hands and knees rather than shimmying through on her elbows. She clipped a flexible penlight on the neck of her suit. The dull beam pooled on the dusty metal surface, barely making a dent in the darkness. Her ears rang from the noise of the sandstorm. She concentrated, trying to listen past the annoying hum. The only sound she heard was the soft slide of her suit against the metal.

She crawled until she came to another "T" junction. Checking quickly against the blueprints on the pad, she took the vent to the right, which would bring her to a down vent, hopefully with rungs. She needed to reach the compound's main levels four stories underground.

Her thoughts drifted while she crawled. She wondered what Morgan might be doing, and if Morgan might be thinking of her, as she was thinking of Morgan.

She smiled to herself. At least Morgan was safe, hidden away in Maruchek's corporate headquarters. She might not get out of this in one piece, but at least by accomplishing the mission, she would make sure Morgan would be all right. And if she did manage to get through this mission, well, she'd cross that road when she got there. She didn't want to think that far into the future. Right now she needed to function moment to moment.

CHAPTER TWENTY-FIVE

The shuttle's retro-thrusters whined loudly as the craft slowed to land at Mining Facility 2333. The small transport swooped into the docking bay and came to an abrupt stop. Morgan grimaced when the restraints cut into her shoulders, wondering if the pilot was showing off for the boss. A few seconds later, she heard the metallic clank of the boarding ramp folding down.

Taking a deep breath and blowing it out slowly, she unclipped the four-point restraints and braced mentally for whatever might be waiting. She swung off the recliner and reached her arms up over her head, gratefully stretching cramped muscles.

Maruchek walked into the cabin. "Morgan, I'd like you to come with me."

Rogan appeared behind him and put a hand on Maruchek's arm, turning him away from her. The men briefly spoke in low murmurs, then Rogan turned to the hatch. He palmed the release, barely waiting for the door to slide aside before he hurried out.

Maruchek smiled and gestured to the hatch.

Morgan followed him into the docking bay. She glanced around as they walked quickly through the expanse. Besides the shuttle they'd come in, she noticed two fighters sporting Mann-Maru colors on the far side of the hanger: big three-man fighters with their cockpits open. She admired the angular ships. She'd seen them up close and personal once or twice at the docks. They were sleek and well-armed, but not nearly as mobile as some of the smaller one- and two-man fighters the EG used.

Walking a half-pace behind Maruchek, she left the docking bay and entered a main hallway leading to a bank of elevators. They rode up several floors to the administrative level of the facility. A couple of quick turns brought them to a nondescript doorway in a secondary corridor.

Maruchek touched the call-pad at the side of the door, which slid open. He waved Morgan ahead of him.

She stepped through and eased aside to let him move past her into the small office. A sizable desk took up the center of the room. The workspace was ringed with monitors and covered with semi-organized piles of papers and comp pads.

The young man behind the desk jumped to his feet and came around. Dark, almost blue-black hair hung past his shoulders. He wore working cargo pants and a casual tunic with the company logo on the breast. He grinned widely as he clasped Maruchek's outstretched hand. "Father, it's good to see you."

Maruchek returned the smile, clapping the younger man on the arm. "You as well, son. Sounds like things are well in hand here."

"Yes, sir. With all the damage, it'll be a while before we're back in full production mode, but we're secure and cleanup is well in hand."

Maruchek nodded. "Good job." He looked over his shoulder at her silently observing him from just inside the doorway. "Morgan, come here," he said softly. "Garren, this is your sister, Morgan."

She straightened and took the few steps necessary to stand at Maruchek's side.

Garren regarded her warily. She forced herself to hold still under his scrutiny. His dark gaze flicked from her to his father and back. After a long moment, he swallowed and shook his head in wonder. "I can't believe I never saw it. I read the reports and looked at the photos, and I never saw the likeness."

Maruchek smiled. "You weren't expecting to, so you didn't."

Garren looked at Morgan with a sheepish smile. "I'm sorry," he said, "that was rude of me. It just—you look so much like her. It caught me by surprise." He held out a hand. "I'm Garren."

Morgan took his hand, finding his grip strong and sure. "Morgan Rahn. It's good to meet you."

He grinned at her. "Always wondered what it would have been like to have a little sister," he admitted.

Relieved there wouldn't be a scene or uncomfortable silence, she smiled back. "Probably not all it's cracked up to be," she said. "But thank you."

A short while later, Morgan leaned back in a stiff plastic chair, her head resting against the wall, her legs stretched out and crossed in front of her. One arm rested on the table at her side. Her hand curled around a mug of steaming coffee. She was more than content to remain unobtrusively on the side, observing while her brother and his—their—father talked business.

Garren sat in a heavy leather chair behind his desk. Maruchek perched on the edge of a chair beside him. She decided Garren looked very much like the images she'd seen, though in real life he seemed much more passionate than the holos suggested. He carelessly brushed his dark hair out of his eyes, never losing focus on what his father told him. His serious concentration reminded her of Maruchek.

Still, there was something about Garren making him seem younger than his years. Morgan found it hard to believe he was actually almost four years older than her. She didn't feel like a younger sister. Watching him, she felt old. She'd been working her ass off for years, dealing with whatever crap the universe threw at her as best she could, while he seemed like a wet-behind-the-ears young executive who'd lived in some kind of skewed, privileged reality that had nothing to do with her own.

Then again, who was she to say? They'd both grown up without their mothers. And she knew better than to assume growing up being Garren was any less painful than growing up being her. She figured they'd both had their fair share of trials and tribulations. She shrugged inwardly. It didn't matter, really. *I wonder if I'll ever see him again after all this is over, or if we'll ever get to know each other.*

A buzzing alert cut into the relative quiet. Garren leaned across his desk to tap the com console. "Garren."

"Is your father with you?" Morgan recognized Rogan's rumbling voice.

"Yes."

"Come down to Security. We have an issue."

"On our way." Garren tapped off the com. "Wonder what this is about."

Maruchek was already moving toward the door. Garren started to follow and stopped to look over at her. "Come on," he said.

Morgan didn't hesitate in following. She, Maruchek and Garren hurried to the elevator tubes and down to the Security Center at the lowest level of the complex.

Brodderick Fenn, head of security at the mining facility, and Duncan Rogan stood behind a scanner console, leaning over the shoulders of a nervous-looking attendant, who adjusted a series of controls at the side of his board. Maruchek and Garren moved to stand beside their security chiefs. Morgan hung back, wondering what had happened, but knowing she was better off staying out of the way.

Rogan said, "About a dozen small ships heading in our direction, fast. ETA twenty minutes. They came in from out-system, hidden by the Belt. Too much interference for long-range scans to have picked up."

Garren asked, "Pirates?"

Fenn reached past the attendant to scroll through a window on the console. The screen refreshed. "Too small to be haulers. Any EG ships would have transceiver IDs and would have identified themselves by now."

"Launch intercept," Garren said.

Fenn nodded. "Already started. Fighters are in the air in thirty seconds."

"Good. What about Earth Guard?"

"Fighter wing is on the way. Commander Sho gave an ETA of twenty minutes."

"And all our people are being moved to shelter?"

"Yes." Fenn glanced at another monitor. "Pearson is down there checking people off."

Rogan broke in, "We need to leave."

"Garren, go with them," Fenn said. "I'll stay back."

"No. I'm staying," Garren said. "Father, take Morgan and go."

Rogan turned and grabbed Garren by the arm, giving him a shove toward the door. "Don't be a stupid ass," he snarled. "Tarm, take them. I'll meet you at the ship in two minutes."

Garren glowered at Rogan.

Morgan threw an arm around his waist, pulling him with her to the door. "Come on."

Muttering a string of oaths under his breath, Garren trotted with her and Maruchek back to the elevators on their way to the docking bay.

CHAPTER TWENTY-SIX

Tarm Maruchek led Morgan and Garren up the boarding ramp and into the shuttle.

The pilot waited near the cockpit door. "Go strap in," he said. "We're taking off as soon as Rogan gets here."

Morgan claimed one of the four acceleration chairs, pulled the restraints across her chest and settled in. Garren and Maruchek followed suit.

Rogan arrived seconds later, pausing at the entrance to hit the boarding ramp controls and seal the hatch behind him. "Reed, let's go!" he ordered. He headed into the cockpit as the shuttle lurched forward.

The engines revved. Morgan felt the vibration rumbling through her chest. Her grip tightened on the chair's arms. Pirates were coming. Old memories haunted her. Her heart rate picked up.

The shuttle exploded out of the docking bay with a deafening roar. Morgan sank into the foam of the acceleration lounge. Her skin pulled against her cheekbones as the ship hurtled into space.

The shuttle banked hard to port and nearly straight down. She clamped her jaw shut to keep her stomach from coming up out of her throat.

After a few seconds, their speed leveled out. Morgan looked toward the cockpit, listening to the rapid exchange of voices, but unable to discern much more than unintelligible, anxious, staccato voices. Beside her, Garren shifted in his seat.

Seated on her other side, Maruchek clipped a transceiver to his ear. She assumed he was listening to whatever went on in the cockpit and probably to what Brodderick Fenn's people were reporting as well. She wondered why Garren didn't have his own transceiver.

The ship banked sharply again.

Garren looked past her to Maruchek, frustration in his expression. "What's happening?"

"We're running," Maruchek said shortly.

"To where?"

Maruchek gave Garren an impatient look. "Away from those ships." He paused to listen to the transceiver and added, "Back to Earth, for lack of anywhere else to go at the moment."

"Will we get clear?" Morgan asked.

Maruchek met her gaze with a frank look. "If we get lucky. They're faster than we are—more maneuverable—and better armed."

Morgan's stomach twisted. She white-knuckled the arms of the chair and hoped if the shuttle got hit, the end would be quick. She didn't want to take a long time to die. She didn't want to die at all, but better fast than slow.

Garren growled under his breath. "I'm going up front."

"Sit down. You can't do anything up there," Maruchek said. "Let them handle it."

Garren glared, but sat back, his fists clenching.

The ship rolled—threading through the Belt, Morgan presumed, trying to keep asteroids between them and their pursuers as the pilot headed in-system. Not that she'd had any experience with this sort of pursuit, she thought. When pirates had attacked the mining facility where her parents worked, she and the other children and nonworking family members had been hustled into the shelter at the bottom of the facility.

The shelter had been made of solid melded concrete and rock and provided enough air and emergency power to wait out a rescue if responders came quickly enough. Morgan remembered how slowly time had passed while she and the others waited. She'd sat in a corner wrapped in her favorite quilt, staring at her hands, too terrified to hope and too young to truly know what she feared. In her dreams, she still heard the rumble of explosions from above, still heard children around her crying as the emergency lighting blinked fitfully.

When the all clear had finally sounded and the air lock released, she had searched the crowd while anxious parents swarmed into the room. She remembered seeing her dad and the lost, empty expression on his face when he crossed the room and pulled her into his arms. He hadn't said anything. But she'd known. She'd clung to him, tears running down her face. Everything had changed—her world ripped out from under her—and there hadn't been anything she could have done about it.

A voice echoed from the cockpit, shattering her thoughts. "Here they come!"

An expectant, cold dread settled in the pit of her stomach. She swallowed bile and closed her eyes.

"Coming across the starboard bow!"

Sharp, insistent beeping pierced the air.

"They've got a lock!"

The shuttle shifted abruptly, surging nearly straight up and to port.

Restraints dug into her shoulders and chest.

"Shunt aux power to the mains!"

The ship wrenched violently to starboard.

Garren swore.

Morgan clamped her jaw shut.

An explosion rocked the rear of the ship and the lights flickered. The shuttle swerved again, slewing hard to port.

"I'm losing—!"

Another explosion reverberated from somewhere aft. Red emergency lighting popped on. Warning beeps and whistles blared from the cockpit. The engines shuddered and choked off. A moment of hushed silence fell. The smells of hot metal and burnt plastic wafted through the cabin.

The second officer, Loh, ran into the cabin. "We're hit," he announced as he loped toward the rear engine compartments.

"Damage?" Maruchek snapped.

"They got the primary thruster controllers and blew out the rear supply compartment," Loh said. He disappeared through the back hatch.

Controllers? Morgan considered. She could fix them.

Rogan poked his head out from the cockpit. "The pirates have left us for the moment and turned back to the facility. They probably figured they vac'ed us. They blew a hole in one of the supply holds and we lost some debris out the back. All the inner seals are holding, though, so we're okay. EG fighters just arrived at the facility. Fenn says the pirates took out their primary power plant. One of our fighters bought it, but we got two of theirs. If we don't get up and running, you can bet the bastards'll be back for us on their way out."

Morgan unhooked her restraints and slid out of the acceleration chair.

Rogan gave her a dark look. "Where do you think you're going?"

She glanced toward the aft hatch. "See if I can help," she said shortly, following Loh's route to the rear compartment.

She eased through the access hallway. A couple meters in, she found Loh kneeling on the floor, his torso half-buried in a maintenance portal in the wall. She heard him curse. He backed out, startled when he realized he wasn't alone.

She gave him an apologetic look. "I'm a mechanic. I may be able to help."

"Not sure there's much you can do. Can't reach the damage from inside."

"You guys got a vac suit in here? Tool set? Spare parts?"

Loh stared at her.

Garren came up behind her. He had a similarly incredulous expression.

"Well, do you?" Morgan prodded.

Loh gave her a doubtful look. "Yeah. In back. By the emergency air lock."

She brushed past him.

"Where are you going?" Garren asked.

"Guess I'm gonna suit up. There's a good possibility I can fix the problem and I don't feel like dying today." She ducked through a second hatch into a compartment no more than three meters long and two and a half wide, lit by two glowing red bulbs in the ceiling. Lockers lined the inside wall. She noted an emergency exit hatch on the outside wall, just big enough for a suited person to squeeze through.

She turned to the lockers and started opening them, her gaze flicking over the contents. The first two she shut quickly. From the third, she retrieved a tool belt and pouch. From the fourth, she picked out a handful of optic fiber patches of various lengths and some connectors. She turned and handed the parts in her hands to Loh, who'd followed her into the small chamber. "Hang onto this stuff."

She opened the oversized end locker containing a vacuum suit. The emergency suit was much more basic than the specialized mechanic's suit she was accustomed to and certainly wouldn't be sized to fit her, either. But she could deal with that. She looked past Loh to Garren. "Can you give me a hand with this? I need some help getting suited up."

"You're going out, then?" From the open hatch, Maruchek's sharp gaze took in the scene.

Morgan said, "If it's a lead that got severed, I can fix that."

"You don't have much time before they head back for us. Twenty-five, maybe thirty minutes at the most. Earth Guard is engaged with the pirates at the facility. They'll try to hold them there and take them out to buy us some time. The pirates will probably come this way when they've had enough. It's their easiest escape route. It could be a race to see who gets to us first."

She nodded. Her window would be long enough. "I'll be on the emergency channel." She pulled the suit out of the locker. Instead of the form-fitting suit-liners she and her crew wore, the maintenance suit had a loose-fitting inner layer providing a few basic diagnostic functions while allowing the wearer to remain fully clothed. "Garren, can you hold this up?"

Garren came forward and took hold of the suit's stiff trunk.

She put her back to him and stepped into the too-long legs. She cast a glance over her shoulder. "Arms next. Left, then right."

"Okay."

She reached behind her and felt the weight of the thick, insulated sleeves slide over her arms and settle against her shoulders. She shrugged the suit into place, stretched her arms, and let the sleeves hang down past her hands. She sighed, hoping once the gloves were attached she could tighten up the wrist closures so the length would be easier to deal with.

She attempted to get the outer zipper and seals connected, but the suit was stiffer than hers and the extra long arms made it awkward and hard to reach. "I need some help with these closures."

"Sure." Garren came around to the front. "Zip it, then seal the outer closures?"

"Yeah. Thanks."

He did as requested and stood back. "What next?"

"Boots. They're in the bottom of the locker."

Garren retrieved the boots, setting them down in front of her.

She balanced against the lockers with one hand while she stepped into first one boot, and then the other. They were big. Really big. But there was nothing to be done about it. She leaned over, connecting the suit's legs to the boots' seals. Garren helped clamp them shut.

"Helmet next," she said.

"Okay." He lifted the helmet over her head.

She shifted the heavy rim a bit before the helmet dropped into place. The faceplate was clear rather than mirrored, so she knew Garren could see her. "I need you to help me seal this properly. I can't reach the back clamps."

"How do I know if it's right?"

"When it's locked properly, I'll get a green light on the diagnostic here." She held up her right arm to show a small flat monitor with a series of power and life support readouts. "And the life support system will start cycling." She fingered the clamp on the left and shut it, feeling the solid snick of the seal closing. She did the one on the right while Garren closed the two in back.

The almost soundless whir of the air cyclers flushed a stale breeze over her face. She glanced down at the readout on her wrist. All good. She keyed the outer helmet speaker so they could hear her and shifted so she could see Loh. "I need the tool belt and pouch."

He handed them to her. She clipped the belt's ends to the outside of the vac suit, adjusting the fit more tightly across her middle. She took the spare parts, put them into the pouch and sealed it. "There should be a pair of gloves, then I'm ready."

Garren handed over the gloves.

She pulled them on and tightened the wrist buckles as far as they would go. Without waiting for her to ask, he helped her seal the gloves to the suit sleeves, then stepped back. She turned toward the air lock. "How much time?" she asked.

Maruchek spoke lowly into his ear-transceiver and looked at her. "Twenty-five minutes, tops. They're on the move."

She nodded. "Clear the compartment so I can go out."

Garren stepped in front of her. "You sure you know what you're doing?" he asked.

She gave him a grin. "Can't be that different than in space dock, can it?"

His expression remained doubtful, but he clapped her arm supportively. "Good luck, Morgan." He followed the others out.

She waited until the inner door sealed before turning to the air lock and starting the cycle. She figured it would take a minute before the air lock opened to space.

There were two sets of safety lines secured to the wall just to the side of the hatch. She grabbed one of the line's end clips and pulled it toward her, securing the clip on a safety loop at her right hip. The line would spool out as she moved away from the air lock and spool back in when she returned. She also grabbed the second line and secured it too.

A crackle of static sounded in her ears. "Morgan, can you hear me?" Maruchek asked.

She nodded automatically. "Roger that. Loud and clear." She glanced at the air lock readout. "Lock's cycling now. I'm leaving it open, so don't let them override it."

"Acknowledged. Morgan, be careful."

"I will."

The air lock unsealed and slid open. Morgan shuffled to the edge, looking out for a second. Shadows of asteroids floated in the field around the shuttle. Bright pinpoints of stars glared against the black of open space. She assumed the mining facility and the pirates were somewhere behind her, out of her present line of sight.

She located handholds on the sides of the air lock hatch and wrapped her gloved fingers around the one to her right, stepping out and automatically swinging her feet forward so the soles of her boots connected to the hull with a solid metallic clunk. She straightened and clicked on her helmet mic. "Hey, any idea where we got hit?" she asked.

After a pause, a voice she thought was the pilot's said, "Aft of the air lock about three meters and around to the bottom hull."

"Roger that. Should be there in a minute." She moved around the hull, her boots chunking tight to the metal, forcing her to work hard to pull each foot free since the boots were too big and the magnetic releases weren't set to her stride.

Looking away from the hull she could see the mining facility—a tight pattern of lights and the shadows of buildings on the biggest asteroid near them. Rapidly moving lights and flashes surrounded the rock. Probably the pirate and EG ships fighting it out. She swallowed. *Don't look. Don't look. Do your job.*

She turned away and concentrated on the hull under her boots. Black scorch marks scarred the white metal. She followed the burn pattern. A jagged slash cut lengthwise through the hull, maybe two and a half meters long and a couple of handwidths wide. She whistled under her breath, ignited the headlight on her helmet, and leaned over to investigate the damage.

A surface break, she thought, since they hadn't lost atmosphere. That alone made her believe the damage was something she could work with. She wished she had her own equipment bag and all her specialized diagnostic tools.

She went down on one knee at the edge of the charred opening to study the bare twist of wires and optical leads. She edged further down and reached into the mess, carefully pulling out a jagged piece of metal.

Ah. Okay. She could see the primary leads now. Still intact here. She dug in her pouch for the one useful piece of test equipment she'd found. All it would tell her was whether or not she was getting a signal from the cockpit controls, but that was really all she needed to know. She leaned forward so she could touch the tester to each of the leads, watching the readout on the flat end of the tester.

"Reed, can you give me some power to the thrusters?" she asked.

"Aye. You've got it."

"Leave the power where you have it, so I can trace to the break."

"Roger that, Morgan."

She eased her way along the gash, careful to keep one boot connected to the hull, kneeling on the other knee and tracking the leads aft with the diagnostic tool.

Maruchek broke into the helmet speakers. "Morgan, pirates are on their way back to us. ETA fifteen minutes. EG is right behind them."

She felt her stomach twist. "Right."

Sweat beaded on her forehead and along her neck. She edged the diagnostic tool further down one lead and the next, and had to stop to pull away more of the bent, half-melted metal and insulation. The tool vibrated in her hand, the indicator going from green to red. "Got one."

She studied the break and dug in her pouch, removing a patch. She hoped she had enough of them to fix all the breaks. She connected the end to the good side of the lead and used the diagnostic to find the next clean spot and connected the other end to the break. "Reed, check the center port thruster."

"Powering up." A pause. "Looks like about fifty percent."

"Okay, back it off. There must be another bad spot."

"You're running out of time. ETA twelve minutes."

"Right." She moved forward, running the diagnostic tool along the leads, looking for the breaks. She took another full step. The gash in the hull was widest here, showing charred insulation and metal, fused and broken optic leads. She'd need to double up the patches to get around the damage.

She wanted to work quickly, but knew rushing would only make the problem worse. *Calm down. You can do this.* She took a breath, resisting the urge to look out into space for the fighters coming toward her. She pulled two more patches from the pouch and clamped them end to end, using the fuser to connect them. She spent a few seconds clearing debris around the seared wires, letting it float away in front of her. She cut a clean end on the lead, clamped on the patch and fused it. Using the diagnostic tool, she searched out a place on the other side that was still intact, snipped off the bad end, and fused the patch to it.

"Reed, I just made a fix, not sure which thruster, let me know if you're getting any response." She held her breath.

"Got about seventy-five percent on the primary starboard. I can work with that. Down to about eight minutes. EG fighters are slowing them down some."

"Roger that."

She bent down to repeat the process and again requested a response. This time, his answer wasn't helpful. "Nothing. Port side's still dead. Five minutes, Morgan."

She resisted the imposible urge to run her hands through her hair. There had to be another break further back. She slid past the main breakage.

There.

She could see where the metal of the hull was bent inward into the gash, severing the lead. The hull was too thick to pull away, though, and not charred enough to break off. She wished she had a good heavy cutter, but there hadn't been one in the equipment lockers.

Well, if I cut a clean end here, maybe I can just go around it. She eyed the distance the patches would have to cover. Did she have enough to span the break? She dug in the pouch. *One, two. Damn, I thought—oh. Okay. Three. But will it be long enough?*

"They're almost on us, Morgan!" The voice in her helmet sounded more agitated.

"I'm working on it!"

She clamped and fused the three remaining patches together and bent over the gash in the hull. She clipped away just enough of the broken lead to get a clean end and got one side of the replacement patch attached before edging over to the other end of the break.

A flicker of light off to her left caught her eye. She glanced up to see three pirate fighters closing the distance in a V formation—sleek, flat, elongated triangles with slightly raised, bulbous cockpits. Fear twisted in her chest. She clenched her fists to keep her hands from shaking, knowing how exposed she was on the hull. Would she end up dying like her mom? Like Digger? Would she be just another body in a vented vac suit? She shuddered.

"Morgan, hurry!" Garren's voice this time.

She shook her head and pulled the patch across the bent fragment of hull, breathing a sigh of relief when it crossed the breach. Quickly, she clipped a clean end on the lead and clamped the patch against it.

She was blinded by a sudden flash of light. Instinct sent her sprawling awkwardly to the hull, managing to keep the toe of one boot connected and grabbing an edge of the gash for a handhold. Her helmet smacked hard and bounced against the hull with a sharp clank.

A long, sleek shadow whipped over her. Another flash. Despite the impossibility in vacuum, she swore she felt the heat when a second shadow blasted past.

"Morgan!" Maruchek sounded panicked.

She took a second to breathe. "I'm okay." Her ears rang from the sound of her helmet hitting the hull.

"Get in here!"

She was surprised to realize she still held the fuser in her gloved fist. "Almost done."

She sat upright, getting one foot solid on the hull and doing a quick check of her vac suit and glancing at the wrist diagnostics to make sure all the lights remained green. Swallowing hard, her heart pounding wildly, she leaned forward to connect the other end of the patch to the damaged lead. If her repair worked, they had a chance, and if it didn't, they were dead. Sweat dripped into her eyes. She blinked furiously at the sting of salt. *Damn it!*

"Morgan!"

"Shut up! Let me do this!" Her hands shaking, she managed to fuse the connection. "Reed, try it!" She felt the hull shift and the vibration of the engines powering up.

"We're good!" Reed replied.

Maruchek broke in. "Morgan, get in here!"

Reed shouted, "EG wing incoming!"

"Go! I'm on my way in!" She struggled to her feet and started a clumping walk across the hull. She moved as quickly as she could in the too-large suit and the too-big boots. She felt the pull of the safety lines at her waist and the roll of the ship under her feet.

"Morgan, get down!"

She dropped into a hunched ball on one knee. A shadow whipped over her head, then a couple more in quick succession. An explosion lit the blackness barely three body-lengths past the edge of the hull. Debris whipped over her, pelting against her helmet and suit.

Fuck!

Rapid beeping rose to a scream inside her helmet with a matching red pulse on the diagnostic on her wrist. She stood, stumbling desperately across the remaining few meters and practically diving through the open air lock. She slapped the emergency seal when she passed the threshold. The air lock slammed shut, slicing her free from the safety lines that hadn't reeled in all the way.

The shuttle lurched forward and up. She slammed into the back wall of lockers, her ears ringing with the impact. Stars danced in front of her eyes when her nose hit the faceplate. Red emergency lighting dimmed and flickered furtively. She managed to get to her knees.

Voices and beeps screeched in her ears. "Morgan! Say something!"

She blinked away the shock. "Yeah, yeah," she mumbled, trying to figure out if she was still in one piece. She felt light-headed from the adrenaline and had difficulty thinking through the shrill scream of the helmet alarm.

She glanced down at her arm. One of the life-support controls pulsed red, two more flashing deep yellow. *Oh. Fuck. Running out of air. Must've ruptured a line.* Little gray spots floated in front of her eyes.

Her gaze darted to the air lock readouts at the side of the door. Had it cycled through? Was the compartment sealed? Pressurized? The light above the hatch blinked. Yellow, yellow, yellow... Her vision blurred. She blinked hard, trying to stay focused. *Come on, come on, go green, you stupid fuck!* Finally the indicator flashed green and the red lighting flickered to blue.

Desperately, she fumbled with the helmet. The seals released with a hiss of cool air over her face. She pushed the helmet backward over her head, forcibly releasing the rear seals and letting the helmet drop to the floor as she slumped against the wall, gulping for breath until the floor dropped away and the ship twisted hard to the right.

Morgan rolled with the movement, hitting the outside wall with a grunt. The loose helmet bounced and smacked her in the head. More colorful stars splashed in front of her eyes. Cursing, she grabbed at the helmet while trying to brace herself against the wall.

The ship settled. The inner hatch swung open, metal clanging on metal. Garren stumbled through. "Morgan! Are you okay?"

She hauled herself upright. "Yeah, fine, if I don't bash into anymore damned walls."

Garren grinned. "You were great! Earth Guard just chased 'em off—man, that was close!" He offered her a hand up, which she accepted.

Odd that she found it natural to think of Garren as her brother. She felt weirded out by the sense of familiarity. "Will you help me get out of this suit?" she asked.

"Sure. Man, that was nuts."

A shudder ran through her. "Don't remind me."

"You do this stuff often?"

She rolled her eyes. "I don't do this stuff at all, if you mean fixing a ship in open space in a firefight. I work at the Moon Base docks. Closest I get to excitement is the bars after hours."

"Could've fooled me. What do you want help with first?"

She yanked off the gloves. "Can you unlatch my boots?"

The shuttle banked and shifted a couple more times before she managed to get out of the vac suit and return it to the equipment locker. She made a mental note to let Reed know he'd have to get the suit checked out and recertified. For sure, the life-support system needed repairs, and probably the helmet and helmet seals the way she'd forced the helmet off. She stowed the rest of the gear and followed Garren to the cockpit.

The pilot, Reed, anxiously tapped buttons and watched readouts. Loh had the controls in the co-pilot's seat, and Rogan was in the third seat manning the long- and short-range scanners.

Maruchek stood behind the pilot's chair. He turned when Garren and Morgan entered the cockpit. He smiled. "Good job."

Reed glanced back over his shoulder with a grin. "You rocked it, kid!"

Morgan beamed, although she flushed at the attention. "No problem."

Reed returned to his controls. "Ya got us out of a pickle. We're in the clear now. The EG scared the rest of the pirates off."

"The fixes are holding?" she asked.

"Yeah." He made an adjustment on his control panel. "Starboard thruster's finicky, but she'll hold together until we get back to Earth."

Garren suggested, "Why not go back to my facility?"

Rogan said, "The home compound is secure and I don't want to risk another attack."

Morgan stared out the front viewport for a long second, searching the stars in the blackness, trying to locate the light indicating Earth or the Moon. "Any word from Shaine?"

Rogan turned, his dark gaze meeting hers. "No," he said.

Morgan didn't look away. "Maybe," she said slowly, "we should go see if there's anything we can do to help her."

Rogan tossed her an irritated scowl. "Wendt can take care of herself. We're listening for her call beacon. We'll go in when we get it."

"And if we don't hear it?"

"Then there's nobody to get." He turned back to the monitors he'd been studying.

Morgan glared at him. "Bastard," she hissed under her breath and walked out of the cockpit.

CHAPTER TWENTY-SEVEN

It took Shaine two and a half hours to worm her way through the vent system to the Security headquarters. She shimmied toward the open louvers at the end of the shaft, careful to stay back far enough that her shadow wouldn't be evident to anyone who happened to look at the vent on the inside wall of the room.

She peered through the shuttered opening and nearly whistled aloud. She'd been expecting a control room similar to Rogan's. Instead, she saw a darkened room with a 3D holo map taking up a four-meter square at the center. The holo map, which was in motion, showed the Asteroid Belt. Pinpoints of red and blue and green lights dotted the map. A couple of men in Security uniforms moved within the holo field, using what appeared to be small remotes to bring up scrolling 3D data for individual asteroids.

A handful of monitoring stations surrounded the holo map, manned by serious-looking men and women wearing headsets. One of them said something Shaine couldn't make out and the holo display shifted, zooming in on a specific area.

Shaine sucked in a breath. The asteroid coming into focus supported a mining facility. She grabbed for the mini-binocs on her belt. *What the hell?* She saw green and blue dots moving around the asteroid. With the binocs, she could also read the scrolling data. *That's Facility 2333. That's Garren's station.*

A voice piped over loudspeakers in the control room. "Attack commencing."

Sweet fuck. We were right. This is the pirate command base. If I take out the whole compound with that detonator Ellerand found, I can put the pirates out of business, too. At least for a while. But why are they attacking the same station again?

What about Charun? She scanned the area she could see, but didn't recognize him among the other personnel. The surest way to find him was to head to his quarters and wait for him to show up, if he wasn't already there. Still, it might be useful to remain here a while and try to gather more information.

She glanced at her wrist chron. She was doing all right, time wise. She didn't have a hard deadline, though the sooner she was out, the better. Morgan was safe in Maruchek's compound, so there was no reason for her to rush needlessly.

She decided to hang around another five minutes and see if she could overhear anything useful. She set down the binocs and shifted to access the small equipment pouch on her utility belt. She dug for one of the "toys" she'd brought along and removed a tiny case containing a microphone the size of a pinhead at the end of a hair-thin wire attached to an in-ear receiver/recorder. She wasn't much interested in the automatic recording aspect, just listening real-time to the microphone—much better for distinguishing voices and suppressing background noise than her own ears.

She eased forward, setting the mic close to the vent grill and letting the wire spool out so she could stay deep in the vent. She settled as comfortably as she could in the close confines and tapped the earpiece to turn it on, closing her eyes as the voices in the room amplified in her head.

In the background, she heard doors open and shut, the hum of equipment and the random rattle of keyboards. She concentrated on distinguishing individual voices from the general group, focusing on two or three voices that seemed more authoritative than the others.

"—sandstorm's still blowing...more hours...send maintenance out, make sure..."

"Probably just cleanup...systems down..."

"—word from New York?"

"Activated our mole...Maruchek girl."

Morgan! Shaine stiffened and held her breath, wishing she could get more than a few words at a time.

"—reported in. Stupid bitch...dead...the girl was with them..."

The voice over the P.A. announced, "Facility breached. Mann-Maru fighter down. Earth Guard incoming."

Shaine's pulse pounded in her ears. What the hell? What had she just heard? Did they have a mole inside Maruchek's organization? Who was dead? The mole? *God, please don't let it be Morgan!* For a moment, all she could hear was the scream inside her head, accusing, furious and self-destructive. *You're too late! You fucked up! You couldn't save her and she's already dead!* She resisted the need to pound her fist on the floor. *Okay, shut up! Think! Get a hold of yourself and think!*

What had she overheard and what did she really know? Taking a long breath, she blew it out slowly. There seemed to be two things going on. It appeared obvious that Charun's fake pirates were attacking a mining facility. She rewound the conversation and listened again. One guy mentioned a mole, but it wasn't clear where. He also seemed to indicate someone was dead, but it wasn't clear who. The mole, possibly? They knew about Morgan. But was she okay?

Shaine sighed, frustrated. Staying here wasn't going to answer her questions, and if Morgan was in danger, she needed to move. She reeled in the tiny mic and returned the recorder to her pouch, grabbed her pad and pulled up the blueprints to review the route to Charun's quarters. The vent system would get her close to Charun's suite at the lowest level, but not inside. The last bit she'd need to do in the open.

She studied the path she intended to take and finally put the pad back in her pouch.

There wasn't enough room for her to turn around, so she snaked backward through the vent—an awkward way to go, but at least it wasn't far to the junction where she could turn in the right direction.

After negotiating the passage she'd chosen, Shaine wriggled out of a vent in the ceiling and dropped lightly to the floor of a deserted hallway. She took a second to get her bearings before she slipped silently down the corridor. She would have preferred a less obvious route, but there was only one way to reach Charun's suite.

She stopped at the first junction and listened for a few heartbeats. Nothing. She poked her head around the corner. Empty.

On the upside, traffic seemed nonexistent on this level of the compound, five stories underground. She held her pad in one hand with Ellerand's favorite jamming program running. The program would momentarily disrupt any video monitors in the hallway. Her free hand moved automatically to the laser pistol at her side, touching the weapon's grip, but leaving it holstered. She continued down the hallway toward Charun's quarters.

She noticed a handful of unmarked doors along the way. None showed much use. The keypads and palm scanners at the sides of the doors were unmarred. She turned down several smaller hallways before arriving at the final corridor, which ended with an ornately carved, wood inlaid door with a dark-stained frame. *Well, guess this is the place.*

She pointed the comp pad scanner at the entrance and got a negative reading. Of course, that only meant there was nobody within about three meters of her position. *Damn. I hate being this blind.* She pocketed the pad. Removing a lock pick from her pouch, she pressed it against the palm scanner beside the door. She tapped a couple of keys on the device and drew her laser pistol from its holster when the door silently slid open.

Shaine slipped through, pocketing the lock pick as she passed into a short vestibule. The silence around her felt empty. The entryway opened into a formal living room, lit only by dim recessed lighting above the far wall. She padded forward on plush carpeting, practically bouncing on the springy nap. A set of double doors on the side of the living room opened to an expansive office, also lit by recessed lighting.

She peered into the gloom, the pistol held in front of her. She sensed she was alone.

The monstrosity of a desk at the center of the office had to be nearly three meters long and almost as wide, she thought, and sparsely decorated with a couple of small sculptures, a comp pad, and a com console. An executive chair was positioned behind the desk, dark leather with leopard spots. Bookshelves built into the walls held a handful of books and a wide variety of risqué statuary carefully illuminated in backlit flamboyance.

Shaine rolled her eyes at the erotic sculptures, wondering if Charun fancied himself as well-endowed as some of the statues. *Sick bastard.*

She glanced around the office, searching out a place to hide while she waited for Charun to arrive. She crossed to a sliding door and opened it, peering into a storage space with what looked like a diagnostic maintenance interface built into one wall, some nearly empty shelves along the back, and just enough room for her to squeeze inside and shut the door.

How clichéd, hiding in a closet. She chuckled and leaned carefully against the shelves behind her, glad they didn't give way. Settling in to wait, she forced herself to relax, allowing her mind to sync with the quiet around her, learning the sounds—the humming rhythm of the air cyclers and the building's vague creaking.

Her mind shifted to think about Morgan, wondering how she was doing and if she was all right. She kept running the pieces of conversation she'd overheard through her head, frustrated. If Morgan was in danger, she wasn't there to do something about it. She shifted on her feet and bit down on a sigh. *I hate this. I hate waiting.*

She closed her eyes, concentrating on the sounds around her, blocking out the darkness and the questions. With her eyes closed, she found the waiting easier to bear.

Time in the closet passed agonizingly slowly. Two hours. Three. She quit stealing looks at the chron on her wrist. Not only did opening her eyes leave her with spots in her vision, it didn't make her feel any better. Charun hadn't shown up. Nobody had. She briefly wondered if Ellerand had been mistaken and nobody even used these quarters. But the room looked at least marginally lived in.

She waited. Minutes passed. An hour. Another.

Finally, she heard the soft grating of the door opening and a muffled but familiar and irritating voice in mid-sentence. "—care about the details, Arrens. Are they dead?"

Shaine stilled.

Arrens' reply came in a much deeper register, the sound moving past the closet, further into the room. "The captain said the lot of 'em were in the shuttle when they hit it—Maruchek, the Maruchek girl, and that bastard Rogan. I haven't gotten the final report yet, but you know how reliable Thomas is. He said they breached the hull, saw debris spewing out."

"I'd say it's time for a drink, then!"

Charun's high-pitched laugh enveloped Shaine in a suffocating blanket. *Morgan!* she screamed silently, biting her lip hard to hold in the agonizing sound. Her chest contracted painfully, cutting off her breath. Her eyes squeezed shut, leaving her in star-blasted blackness. Through the haze of loss, she felt her anger building. She reached desperately for the rage, wrapping it around her, immersing herself in hot fury, igniting the pain.

When she opened her eyes, she had buried the agony, leaving only the hard-core commando and the clarity of cold, deadly surety. *You are a fucking dead man, Charun.* She felt a slow, humorless grin twist her lips.

She shifted her position from slouched against the wall to poised on the balls of her feet. She heard a vague rustle of movement to her right, dulled by the carpet, and the squeaking sounds of someone settling against leather. *Charun at his desk.*

She eased the laser pistol from its holster and curled her fingers around the grip, clicking off the safety. She felt along the wall for the control pad to open the door.

Arrens said, "It's about damned time we took Maruchek out. I've been telling you to do that for years, Tyr."

"Don't get smart with me," Charun snapped, "or I'll get rid of you, too."

A shuffle of movement, more clinking of glass.

Shaine slowly let out a breath, envisioning the room in her head, placing the desk, the sound of the clinking and the second voice more toward the rear. She touched the indented metal on the wall, wincing at the barely audible click of the latch.

The closet door slid open.

She burst into the room and fired once. The dark-suited man—Arrens—standing at the bar slumped to the floor with a hole in his head. The bottle in his hand clunked heavily onto the edge of the granite countertop and tipped on top of him, dribbling liquid on his chest.

Shaine leveled her pistol at Tyr Charun's head and pulled the trigger, putting a neat hole between his wide, surprised eyes. His body slumped sideways in the chair. She stared at him for a long moment.

The righteous fury disappeared, leaving nothing but cold emptiness. *Morgan is dead.*

Slowly, she stepped away from the desk. *Morgan is dead.*

She looked at the pistol in her hands. What was the point? Ending her life would be so easy. So quick. She'd screwed up. She was supposed to save Morgan. She was too late. So what was the point? *I can't live through this again.* Just like when all the others died and she couldn't save them. *Morgan, I'm sorry.*

In the back of her mind, she heard her platoon sergeant screaming in her ear. She remembered him leaning over her as she lay in sick bay. She remembered thinking his crewcut had grown out.

"Suck it up, Wendt!"

She had been immobilized, half her leg gone, broken ribs and arms, unable to discern between the pain of losing her friends and the physical pain of her injuries. She'd wanted to die.

Sarge dared her to live. "You gonna just give up like a fuckin' loser? What are you? A fuckin' grunt or a commando? You're alive for a reason, girl. Don't go throwing it away!"

She took a breath, and then another. Someone had to tell Morgan's dad, and her friends, what had happened to her. That was her job now. Her reason to keep going. She forced herself to take another step toward the door. With one last look at Charun's dead body, she turned away. She could destroy this place, destroy the pirates' base...her thoughts were interrupted by beeping.

She spun around, pistol aimed at the body. *What the hell?* She moved closer, stepping around the desk. The beeping got louder and seemed to be coming from the dead man's torso. The room lights flickered out and shifted to red emergency lighting. The beeping stopped.

Suddenly, a claxon sounded from the hallway, a disembodied female voice came from a hidden speaker. "Attention. Attention all personnel. The death-kill switch for the auto-destruct sequence has been activated. Auto-destruct will commence in T-minus twenty minutes. You have twenty minutes to clear the building."

Shaine blinked rapidly as realization dawned. "You fucker," she muttered. "You arrogant little bastard. You had the damned auto-destruct wired to your own bio-feedback monitor."

Straightening her shoulders, she headed for the door.

CHAPTER TWENTY-EIGHT

Red emergency lights bathed the hallway. The warning siren rattled in Shaine's ears. She headed quickly toward the compound's center. When she approached the first junction in the corridor from Charun's suite, a squad of guards carrying assault rifles ran around the corner.

Shaine fired four times before the guards had a chance to blink. Four bodies hit the floor. She holstered her pistol and grabbed an assault rifle out of a dead man's hands as she passed.

Checking the corner, she moved to the next hallway. The corridor remained empty, but she heard yelling and clattering footsteps as she approached the compound's central hub and the main stream of traffic. She strode purposefully into the main hallway, knowing if she believed she belonged, most people would just ignore her.

Smaller corridors crossed at regular intervals. Growing numbers of personnel paraded in an anxious flow toward the primary elevator banks. She jogged up behind a group of technicians in lab coats, hoping her black survival suit might blend in with facility operations and Security uniforms.

"Hope they figure how to turn that off," a lab-coated man said.

"What's going on, anyway?" asked another.

"Who knows? Probably a drill. Or someone set off a false alarm."

"They said go up, so I'm going up."

Armed guards raced into the hallway from a side entrance, nearly plowing into the group.

"Move, people!" one of the guards bellowed. "Evacuate! Now!"

The technicians slowed to look at the guards. Two security men shoved them down the hallway.

"Go!" The guard noticed Shaine. He shared a silent glance with another guard.

A person she assumed was the squad leader barked, "Who the fuck are you?"

She bluffed, "Wendt, external maintenance." She started to move past them.

He grabbed her arm.

She twisted away, kicking out and slamming him against the far wall, using the butt end of her rifle to take out a second man before she turned and ran. Long, sprinting strides propelled her down the hall and around another corner.

She followed the red-lighted signage to the main elevators to the surface. More people crowded into the hallway from opening doors and side corridors, putting themselves conveniently between her and the guards caught in traffic behind her. She urged the civilians toward the exit as she ran. "Go! Go! Get out of the building!"

The claxon continued its deafening screech. "You now have fifteen minutes to evacuate the premises." The announcement only caused more yelling, jostling and panicking.

Another group of guards joined the mêlée. "Move, move, move!"

Shaine kept up with the crowd, almost to the elevators.

Someone screamed, "Oh, my God! He's dead! Charun's been shot!"

A guard noticed her when she slipped past him in the middle of a larger group. "Hey!" He made a grab for her.

Two other guards shouldered toward them.

Shaine fired her rifle from the waist, dropping him as she darted ahead. Shots and screams sounded behind her. She felt the heat of a laser hiss past her ear.

The hallway opened into a circular lobby ringed with elevators up to the surface. She raced into the open area, closely followed by a growing group of guards. Personnel shoved desperately into the elevators, yelling and ordering each other around.

Noting an emergency stairwell to the side of the elevators, she made for the door, shoving a couple of people through and then plowing past them. She started up the stairs two at a time. The door slammed open again when she rounded the first flight. Laser blasts exploded into the wall behind her.

Go, go, go… Five flights to the surface. She sucked in air and pushed herself faster, dodging around a growing number of people entering the stairwell from other levels, tangling up the guards, keeping them from firing. Still a flight ahead of the pursuit, she was glad the guards had given up trying to shoot her.

"You now have ten minutes to clear the compound. Ten minutes."

The stairwell ended at a final landing. Shaine took the last three stairs in a single bound.

The people in front of her joined the chaotic panic in the main entrance hall. Dusty air swirled through the open doors. People streamed out into the continuing sandstorm.

The stairwell door opened just to the right of a security desk manned by three very nervous-looking men. When she ran past, one of the men vaulted over the desk, brandishing a pistol and heading toward her. "Hey! Stop! She's a spy!"

Shaine made for the exit, pushing through the crowd. Hands grabbed at her. She twisted away. Someone grabbed her backpack and jerked her backward. Without thinking, she unclipped the strap lock and slid out, losing the pack and the collapsed helmet tucked into the straps.

Wind whipped around her when she cleared the doors. She squinted through the flying dust and sand, unable to see more than two or three meters in front of her. She dodged the workers dashing away from the building.

Laser blasts whizzed past. She heard shouting behind her.

White-hot pain suddenly stabbed through the back of her right thigh. She stumbled to her knees. Someone kicked her in the ribs when they tripped over her fallen body. She scrambled up, falling again when her leg collapsed under her in a shock of pain.

People pounded past her. A stray boot planted her face in the rough sand. Gritting her teeth, she struggled to her feet and stumbled forward in a limping run. Someone shoved her roughly aside and she lost her footing and fell again. A boot connected with her head and her vision went black with the explosion of pain. She tried to push to her feet, but the world tunneled gray and she collapsed onto the sand.

She could hear, but everything was muffled and distant, as though she were underwater—the wind, the yelling and the footsteps running past her. She knew she needed to get up and run, too, but when she lifted her head and opened her eyes, everything spun crazily and she nearly threw up. She closed her eyes and let her head fall back to the sand.

When she opened her eyes again, she wasn't sure if it was a minute later, or five. A few workers ran past her, but she could no longer see the crowd of panicked evacuees. She pushed to her knees and looked behind her. Through the blowing sand, she could make out the compound, which remained intact with the doors open, but people no longer streamed out.

Blinking, she looked at the chron on her wrist. Did the self-destruct fail? She hadn't been down more than three or four minutes, but it appeared most everyone had evacuated. No one else was coming out. She got to her feet.

Suddenly, she felt the low thundering of buried explosions rumbling under the sand. The ground shook. A second later, a deafening shock wave slammed into her, picking her up like a rag doll and flinging her into the storm among shards of debris. She tumbled in midair, smashing into something solid that drove the breath from her lungs.

She caught a fleeting glimpse of charred gray plastic and concrete flying at her before her world went black.

CHAPTER TWENTY-NINE

Consciousness returned with sharp, breath-stealing agony. As the waves of pain subsided, Shaine tried to remember what she'd been doing. Short scenes flashed behind her eyes—the sandstorm, the sickening sensation of being thrown through the air, Charun's dead body in the leopard skin executive chair. *Oh, Morgan.*

A different kind of pain squeezed her chest and twisted her stomach. *Morgan, I'm sorry.* For a long time she lay still, just breathing and remembering.

She blinked dry, gritty eyes. The night sky came into focus, scattered with pinpricks of stars and the glare of the white-yellow moon. *Okay, so I've been out a while.* A day? Longer? It had been daylight when she left the compound. At least the storm had passed.

Her head pounded. A coating of sand covered her whole body. She realized she lay against something solid. Gingerly, she turned her head to see a broken off, jagged chunk of concrete half-buried in the sand. Had the debris been there before the explosion, or had she come that close to being crushed? She vaguely remembered impacting something in the air.

She shifted her muscles, sorting out the damage. Searing pain sliced through her right shoulder blade. Her vision tunneled. She forced herself to breathe through the agony. After the initial spasm passed, a steady, sharp throbbing continued. Another experimental twitch of the muscle caused the knife-like stabbing to return. Something was lodged in the back of her shoulder blade. She sighed. Not much she could do about it, even if she could manage to reach it.

She stretched her legs. Pain lanced through her right thigh. Gritting her teeth on a groan, she remembered being hit by a laser shot. She lifted her left hand to her head, exploring her scalp with careful fingers. She noted a nice lump behind her ear and a bigger lump on the back of her head. Her hair was matted, sand coated and sticky around a gash that felt like it might be scabbing over. So she probably had a concussion on top of everything else.

Need to get up. Need to get moving. She gathered her strength and started to sit up. She didn't get very far before dizziness and pain swamped her and she fell on her back. She bit off a scream when whatever was stuck in her shoulder cut deeper and grated sickeningly on bone. Somehow she managed not to pass out, forcing herself to breathe. *It's just pain,* she told herself. *Been there, done that.*

After a bit, she eased her body upright more slowly, taking a few seconds to look around. She was able to see more than she expected in the moon's bright illumination.

She lay at the far edge of the debris field. All that remained of Charun's compound was a three-hundred-meter crater in the sand. She saw the shadows of two heli-jets with Charun's silver company logo on their tails perched beside the crater. Several people wandered around the edge. Between her and the crater, she made out scattered chunks of concrete, metal, plastic and a few bodies. She saw no movement. She wondered where the others who'd escaped before her had gone. Maybe they'd been picked up. Maybe they'd gotten lost in the storm.

How did I manage to be a live body? If they did a sweep, they must've assumed I was dead. I sure as hell won't stay alive if they happen to notice me. For the moment, discovery seemed unlikely, since she was several hundred meters away. Eventually, the group would start searching for survivors. She wondered how many people got out before the compound blew. Certainly there were many who'd been with her when she'd left, and before she passed out. She sighed. She needed to get away from the area.

She looked down at her injured leg. There was a neatly singed exit hole in the thick fabric of her survival suit. The laser blast had gone right through the side of her leg. She could twist just enough to see the entry hole. No wonder her thigh hurt like a bitch.

Lower down, her suit was ripped open from her knee down. *Aw, fuck.* Debris had ripped into her prosthetic leg and torn away a fist-sized chunk. She saw an open gash of wrecked bio-mechanics and damaged synth-flesh. She could actually see through to the inner titanium core. Broken wires and synthetic nerves hung limply from the electronics that controlled movement. She was glad the nerve clusters had been damaged so she couldn't feel anything below her knee.

She dug for the comp pad in the pouch at her waist, relieved to find it still functioning. She needed to get to the homing beacon she'd planted and initiate a call for pickup.

The GPS software tracked her current position and the position of the homing beacon, just shy of twenty kilometers away. It would be a long slog, she thought, remembering she didn't have her backpack anymore. No water and no energy bars. Damn. Not good. She had a small cache of liquid remaining in the suit's internal water pouch, which would have to do. At least starting out at night, she would stay cool a while.

She managed to get to her feet using the concrete behind her to haul herself upright with her good arm, groaning when the jostling shot knives of pain into her shoulder blade. Carefully, she shifted her weight onto her injured leg and took a careful step. Her thigh hurt like hell. She couldn't feel the surface underfoot, but she remained standing. She couldn't feel or move the bio-mech ankle joint, but at least the tight fit of her boot acted as a brace to keep her foot flat. *One step at a time.*

She took her direction from the pad and limped slowly through the heavy sand, hoping the darkness would hide her motion from the investigators still poking around by the crater.

* * *

The noon sun hung above her like an incandescent heat lamp, pouring fire onto her head, sapping the little remaining moisture and energy from her battered body. Shaine stumbled over another sand ridge on another dune. Her injured leg collapsed under her. She tumbled down the slope, her body rolling to the bottom. Unable to stop the moan escaping her cracked lips, she lay curled on her side, her eyes squeezed shut, waiting for the pain to pass.

Stabbing agony radiated through her shoulder and down her arm. She felt blood seeping across her back under the tight-fitting survival suit. At some point, a fall had broken off some of the debris lodged in her shoulder, but the remaining fragment continued to tear her skin and muscle and scrape against her shoulder blade.

She dragged herself to her knees and staggered to her feet. She trudged forward, fighting exhaustion. She needed to sleep, but didn't dare stop moving. She wondered over and over why the hell she bothered pushing herself. Morgan was dead. What was the point of enduring such agony?

The aching emptiness felt like her soul bleeding away. But she couldn't give up. *Someone has to tell Morgan's dad what happened.*

Shaine lifted the comp pad with shaking hands, rechecking her direction. She was so close. The homing beacon was here, somewhere. According to the GPS, she was practically on top of it. After a couple more meters, the pad beeped loudly.

She dropped to her knees in the sand and started digging. Her vision blurred and tunneled. She blinked. Barely able to think coherently, she scrabbled awkwardly, her strength almost inadequate to move the gravelly sand. Finally, a half meter down, she saw the flat blackness of the container holding the homing beacon, a small shelter, water, energy bars and a first-aid kit. Just finding her cache gave her enough energy to dig it free.

She dragged the plastic box out of the hole and managed to pop open the case. She initiated the homing beacon's retrieval call and removed the ultralight shelter and shook it out. The stays sprung into place, creating a person-length tube. At the top end, she'd have almost enough head room to sit up.

She knelt in the sand, staring blankly and zoning out for a few seconds before she blinked and forced herself to grab the package of supplies from the container and drag it with her. She crawled into the shelter, managed to twist around and zip the seal shut. She willed herself to stay conscious long enough to suck down the contents of a water pouch before she stretched out and collapsed facedown, letting exhaustion close over her.

CHAPTER THIRTY

Morgan leaned back in the reclining acceleration chair, her fingers laced behind her head, her legs stretched out with her ankles crossed.

Garren had followed her to the main cabin and stood studying the options on the food processor. He chose a button. The machine produced a beverage container. He looked over his shoulder. "You want something to drink?"

"Naw, I'm good, thanks." She closed her eyes. The exhilaration of her jaunt out the air lock had worn off, leaving her emotionally drained and physically exhausted. No word yet from Shaine. Nagging worry pulled at her guts.

Garren dropped into the seat to her right. "I hate this," he muttered. "Rogan said he hasn't gotten a final report from Brodderick, so I don't know what the damage is at the site, how many injured or dead. Damn it. I should be there instead of being dragged away like a child."

Morgan turned her head to look at him. "You could have refused to leave," she said.

Garren snorted. "You ever try to tell my father or Rogan no?"

She shrugged.

He sighed, sprawling in his seat with a depressed, frustrated expression.

Morgan let her eyes close again. *I'd have refused to go. Shaine would have too.*

She tried to remember ever being afraid to say no to her dad. How many times had she and Vinn Rahn gotten into it when she was a wild teenager? Usually the argument ended in her bull-headedly going ahead even though Vinn was as pissed as hell. He let her make her own mistakes, though, telling her she was stubborn like her mother. Maybe she was. Either way, she didn't let anyone tell her what to do.

"Morgan."

She opened her eyes.

Tarm Maruchek leaned into the cabin. "We picked up the signal from Shaine's call beacon."

She couldn't stop her grin. "Someone's going to go and pick her up, then?"

Maruchek smiled. "I thought we would do it since we're more or less on the way."

She found it hard not to jump up and down and dance in her seat. She managed to limit her excitement to a nod and a widening of her grin. "Thanks."

A little later, Morgan leaned forward, her fingers locked on the back of the pilot's seat while Reed guided the shuttle down through Earth's atmosphere.

He leveled off just above the cloud layer. "ETA about ten minutes," he said. "Everything's holding together."

She smiled, glad she had been able to do something to help.

The co-pilot, Loh, flipped a couple of switches to his left. "Damn, Reed, this is the most excitement we've had in a long time."

"Yeah. My wife's gonna go nuts when she hears this stuff. My kid, on the other hand, is gonna think it's great."

The shuttle sliced through the wispy clouds.

Loh nodded at a small monitor on his right. "I've got long-range satellite visual on the homing beacon. No motion detected in the vicinity."

Reed throttled forward, banking slightly.

Morgan stared at the living map of land and sea.

Reed tapped a monitor to his right and the surface below appeared on screen, marked with a small red dot near the center. He pointed. "That's where we're headed."

Morgan asked, "The middle of the desert?"

"Yeah."

"What the hell was Shaine doing in the middle of a desert?"

"Killing people," Rogan answered flatly from his seat at the com station. "And if she actually made it out alive, then she did her job."

Morgan turned a glare on him. "You're a bastard, Rogan."

"I know how to use my resources."

She clenched her jaw. Her knuckles turned white from her grip on the seat in front of her. She wanted to pound Rogan's stupid ass into the ground. Shaine wasn't a "resource." And Rogan didn't have the right to use her. The man didn't even have the balls to do his own dirty work.

The shuttle swooped in over the desert.

Reed throttled back as the shuttle dropped lower. He watched his instruments. The desert whipped past beneath the ship, almost too fast for Morgan to focus on. The shuttle slowed abruptly and dropped. Reed set the ship on its landing gear with a slight flourish.

Morgan let her knees flex with the bounce, turned, and made her way out of the cockpit, brushing past Rogan.

Garren had barely opened the hatch before she dashed outside, not waiting for the ramp to lower. She jumped to the sand and ran to the small, sand-dusted shelter, dropping to her knees when she reached the zip-sealed opening. Her heart pounded in her ears. "Shaine?" Anxiously, she worked the zipper, shoving the thin material out of the way.

Shaine lay half curled on her side, unmoving. One hand clutched an empty water pouch. Dark stains covered the back of her survival suit from a jagged, bloody tear behind her shoulder.

"Shaine!" Morgan scrambled into the small shelter, practically crawling over Shaine's body. The tall woman's skin was hot to the touch, dry and feverish. Her chest barely moved.

Morgan leaned close enough to feel short, shallow breaths puff through Shaine's cracked lips, felt along Shaine's neck to find a pulse beating fast and light.

She backed out of the shelter and turned toward the shuttle. Garren and the two crewmen hurried across the sand. "Bring a med kit and a gurney!" she shouted to them. "Hurry!"

She ducked back into the shelter on hands and knees. "Baby, come on, wake up," she murmured, gently stroking Shaine's face. She found another water pouch within reach and popped it open, wetting her fingers and running the dampness over Shaine's cracked lips. "Please wake up," she whispered. "I need you."

She wanted so badly to gather Shaine into her arms and hold her, but was afraid to move her, not knowing her injuries. She hoped to hell the two pilots knew at least some basic medical first aid. Guilt mixed with fear and worry while she waited impatiently for the others. Tears rolled down her cheeks. *This is my fault. You're here and hurt because of me. I'm so sorry, Shaine. I'm so, so sorry.*

CHAPTER THIRTY-ONE

Awareness made itself known through increasing levels of discomfort. Shaine's head throbbed in time to her heartbeat. Sharp, deep pain drove through her right shoulder blade when she shifted. A constant throb pulsed in her thigh. She had a vague memory of getting her survival tent set up, but no memory of getting inside or blacking out.

Cool air wafted against her face, making her wonder if night had fallen. The desert day had been stiflingly hot and breathless.

She sensed light behind her closed eyelids. She blinked slowly, squinting against the harsh glare sending blinding pain across her temples. She waited out the discomfort. After a few moments, she focused on the white metal ceiling barely a meter above her. *Bulkhead. I must've been picked up.* She turned her head and almost blacked out from the dizziness. She stilled, concentrating on breathing, slowly opened her eyes again, and very carefully rolled her head to take stock of the situation.

She lay in a bunk in a very small cabin. By the snugness of the sheet around her body, she could tell she had been safety-netted in place. She noticed a slight weight on her arm and a spot of warmth.

She looked down. Under the netting, a hand rested on her forearm. She followed the hand to someone else's arm, then to a dark tangle of hair resting on it.

Her breath caught.

The dark head snapped up from the edge of the bed. Wide gray eyes behind tousled bangs met her gaze.

Morgan! Shaine's mouth moved to form the syllables, but all that came out was a weak breath. *But you're dead. Maybe I'm dead too—or hallucinating.* She closed her eyes, trying to relieve the band of pain tightening around her head. A different kind of pain contracted around her heart. *Please, don't tease me like this!*

Gentle fingers traced her jaw, helping her focus. "Shaine?"

She stared at the apparition in front of her. "You're dead," she whispered hoarsely.

Morgan shook her head slowly. "No, I'm right here. And so are you."

Shaine sighed. A small smile turned up her lips as her eyes fluttered closed again.

* * *

The following morning, Shaine leaned against the pillows of a hospital bed in the med facility in the Mann-Maru corporate compound. She had only been in the med unit since last night, having arrived in the shuttle with Morgan and the others at dusk. Now the chronometer on the wall said the time was barely past dawn. The bed was absurdly comfortable. Diagnostic and monitoring equipment lined the walls, humming and beeping quietly. To her right, Morgan sprawled half asleep in an oversized recliner positioned close to the bed. Behind the recliner, windows overlooked the New York City skyline.

She shifted, easing herself more upright against the pillows.

An IV fed fluids and antibiotics into her system, but on the whole, she didn't feel half bad. Her leg and shoulder hurt like a bitch, but the other aches and pains had faded. The badly damaged bio-mech prosthetic had been surgically removed. The trauma surgeon told her that he'd repaired the connection site below her knee to prepare for a new prosthetic. She didn't know when she'd be able to have that done. The doctor who checked in on her said she was badly dehydrated, suffering mild heat exhaustion and a concussion.

From her point of view, none of it mattered except Morgan wasn't dead. She didn't know yet what had actually happened and hadn't been awake long enough to ask. For the moment, it was enough to know she hadn't lost her. Maybe she hadn't failed in her mission after all. She rolled her head toward Morgan. "Hey, you can take a nap, you know, or go get some real sleep."

Morgan smiled placidly. "I'm fine. You need anything?"

Shaine managed a grin. "No, but thanks. I'm probably more comfortable than you." She lifted a hand. "You could join me—there's room."

"Tempting as it is, I don't think I want to hurt you."

Shaine sighed dramatically. "Well, can't say I didn't offer."

Morgan smiled. Her gaze shifted to the window, following the flight of a heli-jet across the horizon.

Shaine let the comfortable silence settle between them, too tired to break into Morgan's thoughts. She was surprised Morgan hadn't asked about her mission in the desert. Rogan had barged in while she'd been in the trauma bay and got a very brief, semi-coherent version of what had happened in the compound before she lost consciousness again. He hadn't been happy about the complete destruction of Charun's compound, and was angry that the destruction left no proof of Charun's tie to the pirates.

Shaine didn't really care what he thought. The assignment was done. Charun was gone, the threat eliminated. She and Morgan were still alive. The rest didn't matter. Someone would put a spin on the story for the media. Someone always did. Maruchek had people who excelled at such things.

She reached out and caught Morgan's hand, grimacing when she jostled her shoulder, but needing the contact, wanting the reassuring warmth of Morgan's fingers tangled with hers. Feeling that way seemed odd, but she couldn't deny the rush of contentment when Morgan squeezed her fingers gently.

She had no idea what would happen next. She wasn't sure how long Maruchek and Rogan would try to keep her here, and she knew that having her prosthetic replaced would involve some time in the hospital and rehab. If it were up to her, she would pack up right now and go back to Moon Base to try and reclaim her hard-won life. She didn't know, either, what Morgan planned on doing. She couldn't see Morgan staying with Maruchek and leaving her dad and her friends, but stranger things had happened, and how was she to know? The bigger question, though, was if Morgan still wanted to be with her. *I don't want to lose you.*

After a while, Morgan spoke quietly into the silence. "I know you probably don't want to talk about it, but what happened out there, Shaine?"

Shaine turned her head to meet Morgan's gaze.

Morgan regarded her seriously. "If you don't want to talk about it, that's okay."

She took a breath. Did she want to talk? Did she want to confess to ending all those lives? Because although many had evacuated, she was certain there had been far more than just Charun killed when the compound blew. She hadn't personally set off the destruction, but she killed Charun and his death started the countdown. Besides, she'd intended to blow the place before he'd beaten her to it. In her mind, that made her as guilty as if she'd hit the button herself. She sighed. Better if Morgan knew what she was capable of.

"There really isn't much to tell," she said. "I got dropped off in the desert, walked through a sandstorm to Charun's compound and snuck in through the ventilation system. On my way to find Charun, I discovered the compound was a pirate command base and they were attacking one of the mines. I heard some stuff, maybe about you. Then Charun and one of his buddies bragged about killing you, so I kind of freaked out. I killed Charun. He was wearing a bio-monitor and his death initiated the self-destruct system on his compound. All that's left is a massive crater and a pile of bodies in the desert. I would've blown the place if it hadn't gone up automatically."

She heard the flat, emotionless tone of her voice and forced down a wave of guilt. She had to shut away her emotions over the deaths she'd caused. Sometimes she found gaining that distance harder than other times. Being a trained killer was like that.

"Not much to tell," Morgan repeated softly.

Shaine nodded. Part of her wished she could, somehow, justify what she'd done. "I was supposed to eliminate the threat to your life." Her words came out in a rough whisper. "Then it seemed I was too late and you were already dead." She swallowed and sucked in a breath. "After that, it was just another mission I wasn't sure if I wanted to live through."

"Damn, Shaine," Morgan murmured. She rose from the chair, crawled on the bed, and carefully embraced her, snuggling close.

Shaine leaned into the warmth, clinging to Morgan with her good hand.

Morgan kissed her lightly. "I'm so glad you came back," she whispered.

"Me too, baby, me too." Shaine closed her eyes and rested her head against Morgan's hair. *So close.*

For a long time, she and Morgan just held each other. Finally, she eased away. Her shoulder had started to scream from her position.

Morgan helped her lie back on the pillows and shifted so she rested facing her. Their bodies still touched. Morgan twined their fingers together. "You did what you had to do. Charun and the pirates had to be stopped."

"Morgan, innocent people died," Shaine whispered.

"You killed Charun. It's not your fault his death set off the auto-destruct."

"Morgan, I would have done it anyway."

Morgan swallowed visibly. "You would have done it to stop the pirates, not because you enjoy killing people."

"Does it matter?"

She met Morgan's gaze, and saw uncertainty there, but not disgust or hatred. Morgan didn't look away, only shook her head slowly. "You did what you needed to. Leave it at that, Shaine. Just leave it at that."

Shaine desperately wanted to do just that—let it go. She squeezed Morgan's hand and lay quietly with her eyes closed, struggling to rein in the tempest of emotions and guilt. After a while, she asked, "Why did they think they'd killed you? What happened?"

"Well, it all kind of started because Lissa tried to kill me the night you left and—"

"What?" Shaine jerked upright, her anger eclipsing the pain. "I'll fucking strangle that bitch!"

Morgan gently but firmly guided her to lie back on the pillows before settling next to her, the dark head pillowed on her good shoulder. "You can't," she said softly. "She's already dead. I shot her."

Shaine blinked, speechless.

"She came into the suite with a holo album she said was from Maruchek, but I'd already gotten it from him, and there was just—I don't know—something not right. Next thing I know there's laser blasts going past my head. I pulled the trigger and she was on the floor, dead."

Shaine traced her fingers gently along the woman's face. "God, Morgan, I'm sorry you had to do that. I'm sorry I wasn't there."

Morgan kissed her palm. "It's okay. Not your fault."

She nodded slowly, not quite believing, but accepting for now. "Then what?"

Morgan told her story, leaving Shaine gaping in wonder. "I can't believe you went out to fix the ship. Morgan, that's insane. Incredibly brave and heroic, but seriously insane."

"Seemed like the thing to do at the time."

Shaine shook her head. It sounded like something that she'd have said. Her heart ached with emotions—pride, admiration, love. *Maybe you really are brave enough not to run screaming from me. But are you brave enough to want to stay? After all you've been through, is there still a chance for us?*

Morgan ran gentle fingers along Shaine's jaw and cupped her cheek. "You're thinking too hard, baby." She kissed her on the lips.

Shaine leaned in to trace Morgan's lower lip with her tongue, feeling the passion spark between them as she gained entrance, exploring deeply, losing herself in the warmth and taste of Morgan's mouth. She felt dizzy with the rush of need and wanting and pulled back only because she needed to breathe. She leaned her forehead against Morgan's. *God, I hope you need me as much as I need you.*

Morgan sighed and cuddled against her, wrapping an arm

around her stomach. Shaine covered Morgan's arm with hers and closed her eyes, soaking up the closeness.

"Hey, Morgan?"

"Yeah?"

"What are you going to do now?"

"What do you mean?"

"Well, are you going to go back to Moon Base? Or stay here? Or—" She wanted to ask if she'd be part of Morgan's future, but wasn't sure if she should.

Morgan traced abstract patterns on her stomach. "I'll go back to Moon Base," she said decisively. "That's where my life is, where my dad is. I'll probably stay in contact with Maruchek and Garren, but I don't belong here." She met her gaze. "What about you?"

"I want to go back to Moon Base, try to pick up my life where I left off."

Morgan grinned. "Good. Then we can pick up our lives together, huh?"

Shaine studied Morgan's face, trying to read her intentions. "Me and you? Together?"

"Absolutely. If you're up for it?"

Shaine couldn't have stopped her grin if she tried. Relief flowed over her in waves. "Absolutely."

Bella Books, Inc.

Women. Books. Even Better Together.

P.O. Box 10543
Tallahassee, FL 32302

Phone: 800-729-4992
www.bellabooks.com